D1143140

Bear is Broken

Lachlan Smith

headline

Copyright © 2013 Lachlan Smith

The right of Lachlan Smith to be identified as the Author of
the Work has been asserted by him in accordance with
the Copyright, Designs and Patents Act 1988.

First published in Great Britain in 2013 by
HEADLINE PUBLISHING GROUP

1

Apart from any use permitted under UK copyright law,
this publication may only be reproduced, stored, or transmitted,
in any form, or by any means, with prior permission in writing
of the publishers or, in the case of reprographic production,
in accordance with the terms of licences issued by the
Copyright Licensing Agency.

All characters in this publication are fictitious and any resemblance
to real persons, living or dead, is purely coincidental.

Cataloguing in Publication Data is available from the British Library

ISBN 978 1 4722 0116 4

Typeset in Palatino by Avon Data Set Ltd,
Bidford-on-Avon, Warwickshire

Printed and bound in Great Britain by
Clays Ltd, St Ives plc

Headline's policy is to use papers that are natural, renewable and
recyclable products and made from wood grown in sustainable
forests. The logging and manufacturing processes are expected to
conform to the environmental regulations of the country of origin.

HEADLINE PUBLISHING GROUP
A division of Hachette Livre UK Ltd
338 Euston Road
London NW1 3BH

www.headline.co.uk
www.hachette.co.uk

COUNTY LOUTH
LIBRARY SERVICE
Acc. No. 5660225
Class No. AF
Invoice No. 400145715
Catalogued 24/1/13
Vendor. O'mahonys

For Sarah

Chapter One

This is how it happens. I am standing on the sidewalk with my brother, Teddy, while he listens to this morning's phone messages. We are outside Coruna, where Teddy always eats when he's in trial at 400 McAllister, the Civic Center courthouse, which has increasingly been forced to receive the overflow from San Francisco's criminal docket at 850 Bryant, down under the elevated freeway eight and a half blocks south of Market.

Message after message, client after client, he listens long enough to identify the caller, then deletes. It is 1999, and cellular telephones have only recently become universal accessories. Teddy is one of the few private criminal defense lawyers I know who gives out his cell number to clients. I'm not sure why, since he never answers the phone and always deletes the messages before he hears them.

It's the last week of November and warm as summer, the kind of day people think of when they imagine how it must be to live in California. I got my bar results last

Friday and took the attorney's oath Monday morning.

I thought Teddy might at least take me to dinner, give me some subtle but unmistakable sign that, in his eyes, I've become someone. In wishful daydreams I imagine him leading me to the empty office beside his own, unused since he and Jeanie split two years ago, and telling me, 'This is yours now, kid. Try to remember how ignorant you are and you might make a good lawyer. Now you're just a half-trained monkey in a suit, but with God's help someday you'll be a man.' My brother often talks like this, although he hasn't done anything so magnanimous as offer to bring me into his practice. Jeanie's office is still locked, her unwanted stuff still boxed up in there, the desk coated with dust, and I am still my brother's monkey boy, as he calls me, and it does not occur to him to trust me with any task more complicated than filing papers with the court clerk's office. My workspace is a precarious corner of Teddy's desk, with hardly room to balance a legal pad.

I catch the sound of a woman's quavering voice serving up unheard entreaty; then Teddy hits DELETE one last time and slides the phone into his pocket. The car is coming, though neither of us can know to look for it. It must have already turned off Market onto McAllister. Probably it's waiting in the throng of noontime traffic behind the red light at Leavenworth. My brother stabs out his cigarette in the sand bucket and turns to me with a sardonic look, as if to say, You're still here? I open the heavy door of the restaurant, wait for a group to come out, then nod to Teddy, and follow him in.

The hostess smiles at him, and he leans in close to whisper something into her ear, looking past her with a wolfish smile. I don't know what he says, but it causes her to blush, her hand going to the base of her jaw as she turns to lead us to our table, giving Teddy a smile and a hand on the shoulder as she does so. At two hundred fifty pounds, you would think my brother would have lost some of his attractiveness to women; you'd also think he would be slow on the tennis court, but on both counts you would be wrong. My brother reminds me of one of those glamorous movie stars starting to go to seed, a bloated Brando or Welles. A brilliance realized most fully in its decadent form.

He *is* brilliant – no one doubts that. Through win after win Teddy has become one of the most sought-after criminal defense lawyers in northern California.

He likes Coruna for precisely the reason many other lawyers avoid it: At lunchtime it's packed with city hall types, people who come to see and be seen. A juror or two invariably wanders in, and there's my brother sitting at his table in this upstanding establishment as calmly and seriously as if he hasn't any doubt of winning the case, as if he's already won, his briefcase unopened on the bench beside him. He hasn't explained this to me, but after four months of shadowing him and doing what he calls his monkey work, I'm beginning to understand.

The waitress comes, and Teddy orders what he always orders, the Caesar salad with double anchovies and a glass of cabernet. I get the club sandwich and fries. We were up half the night practicing his closing state-ment, and my head feels stuffed with cotton. Almost as soon as Teddy begins the argument he will abandon his prepared script, yet he's compulsive about certain things, treating preparation as a superstitious ritual, like the extra anchovies on his salad or our father's cuff links on his wrists.

The shooter must be out of the car now, crossing the street to the restaurant, the driver continuing around the block to the parking lot that adjoins the back patio. We hear nothing, see nothing. We wait for our food. Teddy looks up with a smile. You wouldn't know he got only four hours of sleep. He looks animated, fresh. He has evidently decided to be charming. The shooter must be coming through the door now, walking toward us between the tables in the crowded dining room. 'I ought to let you close this one,' Teddy says, tilting his head and giving me a pondering look. I know he must be kidding – he hasn't let me so much as question a foundational witness or even be alone in a room with one of his clients – but I feel a rush of warmth. It's only a scrap he has thrown me, but it gives me a fleeting giddiness to finally be recognized by my brother as a fellow lawyer, a

4

member of the California bar, someone who in theory could stand up and give this afternoon's closing argument in his place.

And now the stranger has come up behind me. Aiming over my shoulder, he shoots my brother in the head.

Chapter Two

My ear was still ringing, and the fabric of my suit was starting to stiffen. The smell was in my nostrils, and the taste was in my mouth, as if I'd been drinking from a rusty can. I hadn't even seen the guy, and the shot was so close that I didn't really hear it, like a punch to the head, but I hadn't been touched. All I saw was my brother. I didn't realize Teddy had been shot. I didn't know what had happened.

The police were there within minutes. I was sitting on the floor with my brother's head in my lap. Then someone was coaxing me up, pulling me by the arms, while two paramedics wearing latex gloves moved in to take my place.

I sat very still in the chair where the cops propped me, my eyes on the back of the paramedic kneeling beside my brother, working on him.

'He didn't even blink, he just kept walking,' I heard. 'Did you hear a car squeal its tires back there?' A woman was sobbing, but soon the police got the diners out of there. I gathered that the killer, a man in a Giants cap and sunglasses, wearing a heavy sweatshirt and baggy pants, had walked in, calmly pulled a nine-millimeter handgun, and shot my brother before Teddy or I had a chance to see the weapon. He then put away the gun and, walking slightly faster, proceeded through the restaurant and out the back door to the patio, where he hopped the low fence and jumped into a waiting car.

They kept trying to get me out of there, but I wouldn't budge. I would have fought them rather than be moved from where Teddy was. I'd walked in there with my brother, and it looked like I was going to walk out alone.

Teddy had raised me, more or less, getting me out of bed and off to school each morning from the Potrero Hill apartment where we'd lived with a series of housekeepers after our mother died and our father went to prison, while Teddy worked to establish his practice. He was twelve years older than I was and my only close relative unless you counted our father serving a life sentence across San Francisco Bay at San Quentin. We didn't.

They had Teddy on the stretcher and were lifting him, no easy task. It took four paramedics, one at each corner, plus a fifth to hold the oxygen mask, and a sixth with the IV bag. I tried to stand up but my legs wouldn't hold me. There was a pair of bricks in my chest where my lungs should have been. I wanted to go with him but I couldn't.

Two men in suits, one black and thin, the other husky and redheaded, with badges around their necks and guns at their waists, stood near the pool of blood on the floor pointing out details to each other. They wore thin blue latex gloves. As my lungs opened and I breathed the sweet air of life, the black detective prodded the white one and the white one came over to me, stripping off his gloves and offering me his right hand.

'You're the brother?'

'Where are they taking him?' I didn't know what I wanted from him, but the need was powerful.

'Think you'd be up to riding down to the station and giving one of the technicians there a composite?'

'A what?' I said, though I knew what he meant. 'I need to go wherever they're taking Teddy.'

'A composite drawing. From your description of the shooter.' He flipped open a notebook. 'Black, white, brown?'

'I didn't see him. He was behind me.'

'You didn't look to see who shot your brother?'

'I was looking at my brother.'

He flipped the notebook closed. 'So you didn't see anything?'

A thought passed through his eyes, like the sun breaking through clouds.

'Or you didn't want to see anything.' Nothing in his face had changed, but his eyes became venomous.

He didn't believe me. He thought I was stonewalling.

9

It was as if he assumed that Teddy or I had a dirty secret, that any defense attorney who got shot probably got what was coming to him. 'That was my brother they just carried out of here. You don't think I would tell you what I saw?'

I noticed the black detective shoot the white one a glance.

'All right, all right,' the one I was talking to said. 'You say you didn't see anything, then I agree, you didn't see anything.' He lifted a pair of linebacker's shoulders, then let them fall. 'There are plenty of people who did.'

'You got a name, Detective?'

He was of that pink complexion that registers the slightest change in blood-vessel dilation as a flush. If he was embarrassed at having treated me so brusquely, his face gave no sign. 'Anderson.' He handed me his card.

There seemed to be some confusion. Two men in blue jumpsuits with MEDICAL EXAMINER patches had wheeled in a gurney. Now they stood looking at the mess and the blood, clearly thinking, Where's the body? There's supposed to be a body here. For some reason they hadn't gotten the information they needed, that, alive or dead, Teddy was in the ambulance.

They exchanged glances and by wordless assent went to sit at one of the tables. Maybe they thought the body might be coming back, and they should wait for it. Not yet, I wanted to tell them, he's not dead yet. The table had been abandoned just after the food arrived, giving the former occupants time to take only a bite or two. Two orders of burgers and fries. One of the ME's men eyed the plate before him. After a moment I watched his hand dart down and seize a fry while the man's head swiveled lazily toward the window. The head seemed to have no inkling of what the hand was doing, even as the hand popped the french fry into its mouth. An instant later it struck again. This time, on its way to the mouth the hand managed to swipe the french fry in a pool of ketchup.

My stomach lurched. The room was wavering, sweat filming on my forehead.

The detective had to repeat his question: 'Your brother seem worried about anything recently? Like he knew someone had it in for him?'

'No,' I said.

'Any conversations that sounded strange to you? Unexplained meetings?'

'No,' I said, and realized this was wrong only after I said it. There *had* been something, but instinctively I held it back. Anderson wouldn't have given a damn for my reasons.

'You spend much time with your brother?'

'Every day for the last four months, since August, after I took the bar exam. I've been shadowing him.'

'Thinking of following in your brother's footsteps?'

'Hoping to.'

11

He made a noise in his throat and stepped back, studying me with his head tilted, disapproving of what he saw, and wanting me to know it. Most cops, along with a substantial crosssection of American society, do not differentiate between the criminal and the lawyer who defends him, and I could see that Anderson was of this stripe.

'So tell me, Counselor,' he said, and through my grief I felt the same confused rush of professional pride I'd felt in those seconds just before Teddy was shot, when he made that joke about me giving the closing argument. 'When we catch the scumbags who did this, what should we do with them?'

I just looked up at him from where I sat in my chair, covered in my brother's blood.

'Suppress the evidence? Maybe these bullet casings? Maybe the gun if we manage to find it? Maybe suppress the confession if we grab one of these guys and he talks before we finish reading him his Miranda rights? Maybe after that we should just let these animals plead to disturbing the peace?'

He was watching me closely.

'No, I didn't think so,' he went on. 'Just remember this the next time you're in court trying to embarrass some honest cop, make him look as bad as the shitbag you're trying to defend. Remember what it feels like to be a victim, pal.'

I sat looking at him in astonishment. He watched me

for a moment more, then gave a dismissive shake of his head. Turning away, he suddenly turned back. 'Let me see that card again.'

I was still holding the card, and I handed it to him. He scrawled on the back. 'This is my home number and my cell. The city has killed off the very idea of overtime, but I want you to call me when you decide you want to remember something. And I mean right away. It doesn't matter if it's nighttime or daytime or if the goddamn state is sliding off into the Pacific Ocean. Your brother defended the scum of the earth, and he ruined a lot of good cops, and I will personally piss on his grave as soon as they get him in the ground, which isn't fast enough for me, I shit you not. And just to shove it up his ass I'm going to find the people who did this, and I'm going to give the DA a case so tight even your brother couldn't get that tiny little dick of his inside it, and I'm going to make sure the people who did this go to prison. I don't care that your brother probably did something to deserve what he got, that he had it coming from eight different directions. Whatever shit he was into, you can be damn sure I'll be in it. This is my city, and no one's going to light up a restaurant a block and a half from city hall and get away with it.'

He finished writing on the back of the card, then flicked it at me. It hit my chest and slid down into my lap, where my hand caught and clutched at it. 'I'll need a list of your brother's clients. You can fax it to me at the number on the card.' He turned away, and all of a sudden his face was blank, placid. His partner, still standing over the crime scene, met my eyes with a rueful smile and gave me a long, slow shake of the head, as if to say, There he goes again.

'Officer, drive this man to San Francisco General Hospital,' Anderson said to one of the uniformed officers milling over near the bar.

The medical examiner's men were just finishing the hamburgers.

Chapter Three

Teddy would have taken heart from that little scene. I have never known a person to thrive on confrontation as he did. What makes that so especially remarkable is that I have no memory of my brother losing his temper or raising his voice in anger, not even when I was provoking him, giving him every reason to shout at me. I'm talking about those dark years when Teddy was establishing his legal reputation, and I was fifteen, sixteen, seventeen, living behind a wall of punk-rock music and cannabis and focusing my considerable store of anger, confusion, and resentment onto him.

The detective's feelings were no surprise. Teddy was the lawyer responsible for the now infamous acquittal of Ricky Santorez, who four years ago killed two San Francisco police officers as they served a search warrant on his Mission District home. The DA charged Santorez with murder, but Teddy argued that the cops had failed to follow departmental procedure and that Santorez did not know they were police officers when he picked up his illegal assault rifle and fired a fusillade at the men breaking down his door. One of the more notorious acquittals in the city since the Twinkie defense, the case sparked outrage. For several weeks after the verdict, the press and the city power structure made out my brother to be public enemy number one.

I followed the uniformed cop out into the early afternoon sunlight. In the car he didn't try to make conversation, either out of respect for me or knowledge of who my brother was.

It was as if they'd brought Teddy home. That's because after my mother's death we'd lived for several years not four blocks from the hospital. Returning to the neighborhood only strengthened the certainty in the pit of my stomach that he was going to die.

People turned to look at me as I walked into the emergency room. My clothes. Not to mention the way I was moving – too slowly for that busy place. The emergency room at San Francisco General is the collection point for the city's misery and violence, a place of blood and weeping. People looking more or less like me walked into that waiting room every day. Probably not many of them were wearing suits, though.

At noon on an autumn Wednesday the waiting room was not at its fullest. I went to the desk and asked after my brother. The nurse seemed to know who I was before I spoke. The clothes again. 'Teddy Maxwell?' she asked. 'I'll get a doctor out to talk to you.'

She lifted a phone, and I heard a page.

A young resident appeared after a few minutes, pulling down his mask with one hand while offering me the other. He introduced himself as Dr Singh and told me that they were resuscitating my brother, trying to get his blood pressure and oxygen up. If they stabilized him, he would undergo an emergency CAT scan, then surgery if the doctors thought it was warranted.

'Warranted?'

He hesitated. 'If they think your brother has any chance of recovery.' The good news, he went on, was that either Teddy had moved at the last instant or the shooter had terrible aim, because the path of the bullet had been glancing, and only Teddy's right frontal lobe appeared to have been damaged, leaving the rest of the brain intact. That was how it looked from the outside, anyway. Only after a CAT scan would they know for sure. 'Realistically, for patients with this type of injury, the survival rate is below ten percent. His chances depend on how responsive he appears in the next few days and on whether we're able to control the pressure in his brain.'

He stretched the paper mask back over his face and disappeared back through the doors.

I used my brand-new cell phone to call Jeanie, Teddy's ex-wife and former partner. I left messages on her cell, her home answering machine, and on her voice mail at the Contra Costa County Public Defender Office. This last had a message saying that she'd be out of the office until Monday. When I rang the front desk they had no idea where she was or how she could be reached. I called Teddy's office and left a message for Tanya, his secretary, who took long lunches and might conceivably not return, since she'd be expecting us to be in trial the rest of the afternoon.

There was no one else I could think to call. Few of my friends knew Teddy. I'd formed a habit early on of dividing my life into compartments, each hermetically sealed from the others – the effect of having a father in prison, I suppose. I could have called my cycling friends, or my law school friends, or the few friends I still kept in touch with from high school. People always come through when you need them – but then I would have had to admit needing someone.

Around two o'clock a hurried-looking doctor, not Singh but another resident, came to tell me that Teddy had just been taken into emergency surgery to remove a blood clot. At six the same guy returned to tell me that Teddy was out of surgery. I would be able to see him in a few hours, whenever he was moved from recovery into a regular room. He was on a respirator, with minimal brain activity, and I should prepare myself for the chance that he would be dead before morning. The doctor spoke with the clipped bluntness of someone who disliked the human aspects of his job.

Sitting alone, thumbing through the same grubby six-month-old magazines I'd already thumbed through once, I realized that my brother was going to die. My skin crawled. I was afraid, and I didn't even know of what – seeing him hooked up to machines, I guess, all his weakness so terribly obvious.

I stood and walked straight out through the front entrance and into a cab that had just let off an elderly woman. 'Civic Center,' I told the driver. Maybe some part of me thought that I could go back to Coruna, sit at our table, and finish our lunch.

The cab let me off on Market Street, and I nearly stepped in front of a Muni streetcar when a pedestrian grabbed my arm and yanked me back to the curb. I didn't hear what the person said to me, or how I replied, if I did. When I came back to myself, I was in the gaudy rococo elevator heading up to my brother's fifth-floor office down at Mission and Sixth.

It was only when I got to the office door that I remembered Teddy hadn't given me a key. I stood outside the door and laid my forehead against the cool pebbled glass. Why couldn't he just have made me a key? He must have been afraid that once I got in, I wouldn't leave, that I would contrive some way of making him let me stay on after I passed the bar. And to be perfectly honest, I suppose that was my intention.

I don't know how long I stood there, but when I opened my eyes again the light was different. It was dusk. The ding of the elevator brought me to my senses.

I just had time to square my shoulders before Tanya came toward me in her hip-hugging skirt, her body perched forward atop ultrahigh heels. As she walked she fumbled in her purse for her keys.

She nearly ran into me, then gave a start. She stood looking at me in frozen horror, then seized my arm so hard that I felt her nails almost meeting through the layers of flesh and clothing. She opened the door and pushed me into the office.

Tanya was five feet four inches tall, and amply padded. Her body and face were a testament to years of ill use. Her hair was bleached blonde, a puffy helmet that drooped over her eyes. Her shapeless body was contained by undersized skirts, blouses, and under-garments. At some point her nose had been broken and badly reset. It was hard to imagine that there had ever been anything tantalizing about her, but before her rehabilitation at Teddy's hands she'd made her living on the street. I had no doubt that even now a man could meet a quick end by surprising her at the wrong moment.

'I went over to the courthouse,' she said. 'They sent the jury home.'

'Teddy's in the hospital. He's not expected to make it. Someone shot him in the head at Coruna.'

'Well, I can see that,' she said, raising her voice in outrage and incomprehension.

I looked down, then smelled myself. My hands were

shaking too badly again to be of use to me. I got my jacket off okay but couldn't manage the shirt buttons. Tanya stood there watching me, her hands at her sides. The shirt was ruined. I grabbed it by the lapels and yanked downward, popping off the buttons, like Superman casting off his secret identity, but I was the same person underneath. Just Leo.

Her eyes went straight to the tattoo. They registered no emotion, no reaction, but they were fixed, almost entranced. Probably she didn't realize what she was seeing, but part of her saw, and later she'd remember. On my upper left arm I have a fist-sized rendering of the Batman symbol, the stylized bat inside the oval. This is the symbol Gotham City sends into the nighttime clouds by spotlight whenever the Dark Knight is needed. I got it when I was seventeen and beset by the conviction that my life couldn't keep going the way it had been going, that without change I might do something crazy, hurt myself or someone else.

When I got the tattoo I was in need of strength and protection, and somehow it worked. It still works. Whenever I'm feeling beleaguered or inadequate or wronged, I have only to think of that tattoo beneath my shirt, and I am suffused with peace and strength, as if my true powers are a secret I've been keeping from the world.

The tattoo changed nothing, of course; it was just the outward sign of changes I'd begun to make in myself. I

21

got it around the same time I bought my first racing bike and began riding on Saturday mornings instead of moping around the apartment or hanging out in Golden Gate Park and smoking dope, waiting for something bad to happen. Cycling wasn't a purpose in life, but it helped me blow off steam. And it got me out of my self-created prison. The summer after I graduated from high school I bought a used mountain bike and, with a friend, rode through California, Oregon, and Washington, then took the ferry to Alaska.

I had no other clothes at the office. This was my only suit. 'I need you to go out and buy me slacks and a shirt. Can you do that?'

Tanya didn't answer. She was still staring at my arm, and her gaze had turned derisive.

'Tanya.' I wanted to snap my fingers in her face. 'Please, there are things I need to be doing, things I need to take care of, people I need to talk to, and I have to be back at the hospital as soon as possible. Please,' I repeated. 'I'll give you my credit card. Just go to Men's Wearhouse.'

Her gaze slowly rose to my face as if she were seeing me for the first time, not understanding who I was or what I was doing here. Then she reached out and took the card.

I wrote out my measurements, and with a doubtful backward glance she left me standing there, feeling too soiled to sit, though it hadn't bothered me at the hospital, and too distraught to think of spreading a newspaper over a chair.

As I waited, I replayed the past few days. I wondered if I really had noticed something or if it was just hindsight playing tricks on my imagination. And if what I'd noticed was meaningful, I wondered if I should tell the cops about it.

What I was thinking of had occurred a week ago, during one of the recesses in the prosecution's portion of my brother's current trial, the one in which he was supposed to give his closing argument this afternoon. It was a domestic violence trial, an ugly case. Ellis Bradley was a middle-aged man whose wife, Lorlee, had accused him of raping her. Teddy had successfully defended Bradley ten years ago on a battery rap; there was almost a cozy atmosphere in the pen each morning as he and Teddy sat together going over the day's strategy like two old friends. I tried not to let it bother me that Teddy seemed easier and more natural with a client accused of a violent crime than he was with me, his own brother.

After Lorlee had finished describing what Ellis had done to her, the judge called a ten-minute recess. I'd gathered the heavy trial binders in my arms and followed Teddy to one of the small conference rooms just outside the courtroom.

As we came down the aisle, a small, muscular man stood up in the back row. This was Car, the private investigator Teddy used in all his most important cases.

Car's neck was covered with abstract tattoo work of tangled foliage, and he carried so little fat on his body that his face might have been sculpted by a flint knapper. He looked about nineteen, but in his eyes you could see many more miles than that. He had a knack for tearing apart the work of law enforcement, going back over ground the police had covered and spotting inconsistencies they'd glossed over, evidence they'd missed or disregarded, the seemingly harmless but potentially meaningful lies they'd told to cover the inevitable shortcuts in their investigations. When he succeeded, Car's reward was to play a starring role as Teddy's chief witness. When Car testified, Teddy usually won.

That day he was wearing his standard uniform of black jeans and high-tops and a brown hooded sweatshirt, his wallet attached to his belt by a chain. Over at 850 Bryant he fit right in. You wouldn't look twice. He might be a defendant waiting for a court appearance or a plainclothes cop waiting to testify. Here at Civic Center, where the typical fare was multimillion-dollar asbestos cases, where the hallways were floored in marble and the courtrooms were oak-paneled visions of civic taste, with not a scrawled gang symbol in sight, anyone not wearing at least a five-hundred-dollar suit looked out of place.

Car had fallen into step with Teddy, forcing me to drop back. He put his arm at the small of Teddy's back and leaned in close to whisper something that made my brother draw himself up and shoot Car a look. They went on out through the doors.

Dumping the trial binders in the conference room, I'd followed them. The hallway in a courthouse is a terrible place to have any kind of private conversation, and they were making for the stairwell. The windows to my left showed the gold dome of city hall, the parking lot, and kids' playground in back. My brother glanced back furtively as they went through the door. If he saw me, his face didn't show it.

I was stopped a foot from the door by an explosion of curses from Car. 'Well, you've got to fix it,' my brother said. My hand was on the handle but I didn't open it. I heard a series of angry, stomping footsteps coming up: my brother's. Then I heard Car's lighter steps going down a flight below, all but running, a final loudly spoken 'God damn!' and the echoing report of the fire door slamming against the wall at the bottom three flights down.

My brother was just on the other side of the door. I heard him breathing deeply, as if catching his wind after mild exertion. I waited for him to appear, but he didn't move. After a moment I turned away as if I'd forgotten something and walked back toward the courtroom.

I was sitting in the conference room when Teddy came in a moment later, looking calm and composed, as if he and Car had just been having a quick strategy consultation. He sat next to me, pulled a binder toward him, and began taking out documents he thought would be useful in his cross-examination of Lorlee. He was about to confront her with the fact that she'd supposedly told her best friend, Sharla, who happened to be sleeping with Ellis, that she'd fabricated the rape charges to get custody of the children.

When we went back into the courtroom it was the Wild West. Sharla, Teddy's only witness, fell apart under the DA's cross, coming across as a skank and a sneak and a liar, and Teddy accused Lorlee of lying when he recalled her for questioning, after Sharla testified about the phone conversations in which Lorlee admitted to fabricating the rape story. 'So you told nothing but the truth in your testimony here,' he said, then reminded Lorlee of her oath, asking if she understood that perjury was a crime. Then he went into her reasons to lie, the divorce she and Ellis were going through, her admitted desire to deny him custody of their children.

It was a pretty typical case, so I didn't think anymore about what happened or didn't happen in the stairwell until my brother was lying in the hospital with a hole in his head.

Chapter Four

The phone rang three times before my grief-addled brain registered the sound. I was going to let it ring, but then I picked up. 'Law office,' I said, because that was what Tanya always said when she answered. My voice sounded like the voices you sometimes hear between elevator floors.

There was a tremendous amount of noise in the background on the other end of the line, shouts and echoes reverberating off concrete. 'Who's that? Monkey Boy?'

It was Ellis Bradley calling from the lockup down at 850 Bryant.

I flushed. I hadn't ever heard Teddy use that nickname in front of him. 'Yeah, Mr Bradley, it's Leo.'

'Okay, I only got five minutes, so listen close. They brought me back over here after lunch, said no court this afternoon. So I'm sweating, wondering what's going on with my trial that all of a sudden there's no court and no lawyer to tell me why. When I get back in here I'm hearing lots of stories, the kind I don't want to believe. So you tell me straight. What happened to your brother?'

'A guy walked into the restaurant at lunchtime and shot him. Right in front of me. Shot him in the head. He's probably going to die.'

Ellis let out a long, wondering exhalation. 'I am sorry to hear that, Monkey Boy. Real sorry. Your brother's the best. Ask anyone in here. I can't take a leak in here without some dude asking for his number.'

'I thought they had it written on the wall in there.'

'Yeah, they keep erasing it, changing the numbers. The ones who know your brother, they want to cut out the competition.'

'It's a hard world,' I said, but Ellis didn't deserve my attitude. It was only natural for him to worry about his situation. The shooting meant he would have to find a new lawyer, who'd be forced to retry the case from the beginning. I doubted the evidence would come out as well for him the second time around. The DA wouldn't be caught by surprise by Sharla's testimony this time, that was for sure. Bradley had paid Teddy his cash retainer rather than try to make bail. I doubted he'd be able to afford to go to trial with the new lawyer, who would likely do little more than negotiate with the DA for the best plea bargain he could get. The DA would have him over a barrel.

We had to wait for some echoes to die away before either of us was able to hear the other. This was all too much to break to Ellis over the phone. I would have to sit down with him face-to-face and explain the situation, and his options. I would need to do this for all Teddy's clients who were in jail awaiting trial or sentencing or something else. I didn't feel in any shape to give legal advice, but someone would have to pick up the pieces of Teddy's practice.

'Look, Mr Bradley, I'm going to come see you tonight or tomorrow. We need to talk about what's going to happen with your case now that Teddy isn't going to be able to continue, and there's too much to cover over the phone. I want to assure you that I'm going to do what I can to help you find another lawyer. A good one.'

'I know you will, Leo. I'm sorry to trouble you at a time like this, with your brother lying in the hospital. You want to be with your people. But I'm in a bad situation here. I don't think I can go through this all over again.'

'I understand. We'll talk. I'll be seeing you soon.'

I ended the call, then dialed the hospital, and learned that Teddy was now in the recovery room. He wouldn't be allowed any visitors until the morning, starting at six. I left my cell phone number, then dialed Jeanie again, hoping that she'd heard the news, that I wouldn't have to be the one to break it to her. I was relieved when the call went to voice mail. I left a second message telling her that Teddy was out of surgery and clinging to life, that no one would be able to see him until morning, and that she could reach me at his office.

I hung up and went to stand in the window. *My people*, Ellis had said. The very idea was like a foreign concept. Who should I be with now, I wondered – Jeanie? The guys from my cycling club? Around my normal friends, the very idea of Teddy seemed unreal.

Even at the height of the dot-com boom, the neighborhood around Teddy's office was mostly free clinics, residence hotels, and liquor stores. This time of year the sun hit the west side of Sixth midmorning, the east side midafternoon, rousing the homeless from their doorways. In the evenings from Teddy's window we watched the hookers parade toward the feeding grounds at Tenth and Mission. Those are some of the unfortunates on whose shoulders Teddy built his practice in the early years, when much of his income came from court appointments on cases where the public defender's office had declared a conflict of interest.

The area is considered a dangerous neighborhood, but there's danger and then there's *danger*. You can come to feel a grudging affection for the drunks and addicts, the stink and the noise and the squalor. I know Teddy did. He made a life for himself among those people and their problems. The city you live in comes to feel like a projection of yourself, mirroring both your aspirations to splendor and your darkness. In the same way that Teddy felt more comfortable with clients than he did with ordinary people, even his own brother, I know that Teddy only really felt at home in those parts of the city avoided by others.

Not that he lived in such a place. He and Jeanie had been building a house in Contra Costa County, in the hippie enclave of Canyon, over the first range of East Bay hills. The divorce two years ago had interrupted construction. Teddy had left the house as it stood, half-finished and barely habitable. He worked late most nights and often missed the last BART train. He kept a room at one of the neighborhood residence hotels, the Seward – the manager was a former client who'd given him the room in lieu of a fee – and on nights when he didn't make the train, he'd sleep there, oblivious to the noise of the drunks, junkies, and prostitutes.

I heard the rattle of the elevator, then the clacking of Tanya's heels in the hall. She came in wiping her eyes, with a vinyl suit bag over her shoulder. She'd gone to Nordstrom instead of Men's Wearhouse, and she'd bought me a suit and two shirts instead of a shirt and slacks. 'They had a sale,' she said, handing me the credit card and receipt.

Even on sale the suit had cost seven hundred dollars.

'Teddy bought all his suits at Nordstrom,' she said.

There was nothing for me to do but change if I expected to go out in public. I borrowed one of Teddy's ties from the closet, then went back out front and asked Tanya to pin up the unhemmed pant legs.

'Men's Wearhouse,' she said with a sniff of disdain.

While she knelt beside me I asked her to get together

the list of Teddy's clients for Detective Anderson. Though I'd decided not to tell Anderson about that argument in the stairwell, at least not until I knew what it was about, I intended to do everything else in my power to help him find the shooter. It seemed to me that the client list was the logical place to start.

She was holding a pin in her mouth as I spoke. There was a frozen moment in which neither of us moved a muscle. Then with a sharp inward breath she took the pin and jabbed it hard into the top of my foot. I jumped back away from her, hopping on one foot to avoid stepping on the other unpinned leg.

'Are you out of your mind?' she asked, rising and taking a menacing step toward me.

I stepped backward again, my hands up. 'He wasn't running a candy store. They can't all be satisfied customers.'

She was still advancing, still holding the pin, her eyes making little darting movements to different parts of my body, her shoulders rigid, as if she might strike again at any moment. 'We're not giving the police any list,' she said in a low voice. 'We're not giving them anything from this office. Until Teddy recovers, I'm in charge of this law practice, and you'd better do as I say, or you'll get a lot worse than you already got. Monkey Boy.'

I flushed. 'Don't you think Teddy's killer is probably connected to a case?'

Her voice came from deep in her throat. 'Teddy's

clients loved him. No matter how their cases turned out, he always did right by them, and they knew it.' She had taken up a position between me and the tall oak filing cabinets, indicating her willingness to defend Teddy's secrets with violence.

'It's not just about the clients. What about witnesses, victims? Someone Teddy might have humiliated, somebody who thinks they didn't get justice.' There was a person like that in literally every case, a whole sorry trail of Lorlees littering my brother's career. My foot was throbbing but I didn't want to acknowledge it. Passing the bar exam had not prepared me to deal with a legal assistant who resorted to corporal discipline in matters of attorney-client ethics.

'Teddy always did right by his clients,' she repeated, 'and now you want to have the cops all up in their business, busting them for no reason. People who are just trying to put the past behind them.' Her voice kept breaking. She might have been speaking of herself. 'You know what the cops are going to do with that list. You give them the names, they'll start busting doors, bringing people in for parole violations, probation violations, bullshit charges, busting them for whatever they've got in their pockets, anything they can think of to haul someone in and lock him up. That way they can pretend to be doing something, but in reality they're just undoing all your brother's work, getting back at him for all the times he made cops look like morons. That's how you want your brother to be remembered, as a lawyer who sold his clients down the river?'

'I don't see how they can avoid taking a look at the clients. They're going to do it one way or another. Someone walked up to him in that restaurant and shot him. Tried to murder him. He's probably going to die. The police are on our side this time, Tanya. Let's try to separate courtroom rhetoric from reality, here.'

'It wasn't a client. It wasn't anyone who had anything to do with any of Teddy's cases. And the San Francisco Police Department is not on our side, and they aren't on Teddy's side, either. They're glad he got shot, but that's not enough for them. They have their own ax to grind.'

I rubbed my brow. I felt very tired. I would have liked nothing better than to stretch out on the couch and close my eyes, sleep until morning, and be on my bike as the sun came up, riding across the bridge into the hills of Marin County, or better yet, with saddlebags and a trailer heading up the Pacific Coast; I'd often dreamed of repeating that long trip. 'How can you be sure the killer wasn't connected with one of Teddy's cases?'

She tossed her head but gave no answer.

'Do you know something, Tanya?'

'I don't know anything.'

I wanted to ask her whether Teddy had been mixed up in anything serious enough to be shot over, but I didn't want to ask that question until I had a better sense of what she might be hiding. I stood rubbing one knuckle into my eye. 'Better get that list together, then.'

'No.'

'Get the list together or pack up your desk.' I felt tired enough now that I didn't really care whether I had any authority to fire her. I was no longer afraid of her, or maybe I was coming to see that her pugnacity was mostly bluster, a shield for her grief at what had happened, maybe also for her fear of what would become of her without my brother. Teddy had meant just as much to Tanya as he did to me, maybe more. In one way or another she depended on him for every aspect of the life she had now.

Her eyes narrowed, and she crossed her arms, but there was no longer threat in her posture. I went on: 'If you want to go down the list and call anyone you think might benefit from a warning, do that. But until we've got a more definite lead, the cases are all we have to go on. I want the cops to find this guy. You want it as much as I do, I'm sure. And that means offering our cooperation, even if it goes against the grain of business as usual around here. So we're going to give the police that list, and you and I are going to spend a whole lot of time together going through every file.'

I walked past her to the cabinet and tugged open one of the heavy drawers. It was so full that you couldn't have inserted a sheet of paper between any of the folders. I knew that each of the four drawers in each of the five cabinets was as tightly packed as this one. All the much-thumbed yellow file folders were raggedy with notes and documents, transcripts, and photographs. Here and there were gaps marking the smaller bulk of audio- and videotapes. To my eyes all the layers of information took on almost geologic significance as the fossil record of Teddy's career.

I slid the drawer closed and fingered the handle of another one. I felt strongly that I was in the presence of my brother's would-be killer, that somewhere in all these documents the shooter's name was written. If I just knew what to look for, his identity would stand out as obviously as if it were written in blood.

I turned back to Tanya. 'I'll also need a list of Teddy's active cases and the files themselves. For me, not the police. Someone's going to have to sit down with each of his clients in the next few weeks, if not sooner, and explain what's happened and what their options are. I suppose I'll have to be the one to do that, now that Jeanie's gone.'

She went slowly around behind the desk, sat down, and made a note. 'Okay.' A pause. 'I'm sorry about your foot.'

I nodded, preferring to pretend it hadn't happened.

I grabbed a pad and fastened the top button of my new suit coat.

'Are you going somewhere?' she demanded.

'I'm going to see Mr Bradley.'

Chapter Five

It was a ten-minute walk to the Hall of Justice. With the sun down and the fog pulled over the city's head, the air was twenty degrees cooler and so clammy that it numbed my cheeks and fingertips. We were fortunate that Ellis had been housed here during his trial, rather than at the jail in San Bruno, which was unreachable by public transportation. Teddy didn't keep a car in San Francisco, and of course I didn't have a vehicle. In the room I rented in a house with six strangers in Hayes Valley, I had a queen-size mattress, a desk, a computer, a TV and stereo, an original Nintendo that I liked to play when stoned, some books, and my bikes, but little else of consequence.

The walk brought me past the Ninth Circuit court-house, which had gotten itself stranded in this neighborhood of junkies and residence hotels. Suddenly I realized I was standing in front of the Seward Hotel, where Teddy kept a room.

I should let Anderson know about this little hidey-hole here in the city, I thought – or maybe he'd even found it without my help. A pair of squad cars was double-parked on Mission, and an ambulance with its doors open and its lights flashing stood fifty yards farther down, the driver relaxing with one elbow out the window.

I hesitated, then pushed open the heavy, splintered door, and went inside.

The dark entrance hall hadn't been renovated in at least fifty years, I guessed. To my left was a closed door and beside it a scarred window with a pass-through and a grille. Behind the window was a room with a desk, a board with hooks for keys, and cubbyholes for mail. A miniature black-and-white TV pushed up against the Plexiglas showed me myself.

The small but tough-looking man behind the desk took one look at my new suit and tie and shook his head slowly, as if this just wasn't his day. He waved me on. 'They're up there,' he said. 'Go on up. I'll buzz you through. They all got here about five minutes ago.'

I hesitated. 'What was that number again?'

'Six-oh-nine. Take the stairs. Elevator's broke.'

On the second-floor landing a single used needle lay in a dingy spill of light on the windowsill. On an impulse I touched the needle's plastic shaft. It was still warm. The tip was smeared with blood. After that I stopped paying attention to the scenery.

Only as I came to the sixth floor and heard the sounds of a woman sobbing and a man muttering something over and over again did it occur to me that the police would have no use for an ambulance crew if they were here merely to search Teddy's room.

I went out into the hall anyway.

Two uniformed officers stood outside the door of room 609 at the far end of the hallway. Only a few doors were open between here and there. Seeing a couple sitting on a bed in one of the open rooms, I stopped and asked what happened.

'She killed him, that's what,' said the man, a white guy in his late thirties in a sleeveless undershirt that crumpled over his ribs. He had unclean dreadlocks dangling above an oversize brow, a shadowy beard, and black, broken fingernails. 'Waited till he was sleeping, then stuck a knife in his ribs.' He gave a barking laugh, and the petite dark-haired woman on the bed beside him smiled like someone who didn't understand English. The man looked me over with a hungry eye, as if trying to determine which of the suited classes I belonged to.

I went down the hall to the room. The paramedics were inside. I got close enough to see blood spattered on the wall, and then one of the uniformed cops blocked my path. On the bed a naked man sat flinching while the paramedics worked on a gash in his shoulder. Contrary to what the dreadlocked man had said, he was very much alive and cut rather than stabbed. Still, there was a lot of blood. It had made a dark pool on the sheets and spattered the floor. A woman huddled in the corner with her head bowed against her handcuffed hands. 'Just looking for a client,' I told the cop and retreated, though it was difficult to tear away my gaze.

I continued down the hallway to the open door, in shock that my brother had actually lived in such a place, that he apparently considered it restful. 'You wouldn't happen to know which room was Teddy Maxwell's?' I asked the dreadlocked guy.

'Third floor. Three-oh-eight, three-ten, one of those two,' the man said. 'Hey, did he really get shot up?'

'Yeah. I'm his brother.'

His face brightened. ''Cause I've been trying to get hold of him all week. You see, I caught this case . . .'

I had already turned away and was walking toward the stairwell, hoping he wouldn't follow me. He didn't.

Three floors down things were quieter. I didn't know which room was Teddy's, and in any case I didn't have the key. I went back down the stairwell and into the lobby.

'I must have gotten confused,' I told the guy behind the Plexiglas. 'I'm actually Teddy Maxwell's brother. It's his room I'm looking for.'

The man just stared through me as if I were an apparition that might disappear at any moment.

'I'm here to pick up some things for him. He's in the hospital.'

He stirred, his eyes finally coming to rest somewhere

between my forehead and the ceiling. 'Lemme see some ID.'

I pressed my driver's license against the window.

'All you people barging in here all of a sudden, it's like I'm runnin' some kind of damn store.' He spoke with rising vehemence, his eyes sliding away from me, not bothering to look at the license. 'All I know is when Teddy was around I never knew him to have even one sibling, let alone a pair of them. Or maybe you're the kind of brother who keeps clear until a man goes down, then starts nosing around to see what he might have tucked away under the mattress.'

'Someone else came here claiming to be Teddy's brother?'

'Claiming. You the one claiming. I have half a mind to make you come back with the sheriff, prove you are who you say you are.'

'Look at my license.' I was still holding it up. 'My name is Leo Maxwell. I'm Teddy's only brother. Did this other person show you any kind of identification?'

He still didn't look at it. 'You a lawyer? 'Cause I don't talk to no lawyers. Your brother excepted, but I hear he's gonna be dead, and then there won't be a lawyer left in the world I care to talk to.' His voice lowered insinuatingly. 'Unless the name on that damn driver's license is Alexander Hamilton, we ain't got nothing to talk about.'

'What did this guy look like? Tall, short? Fat, thin?

41

White, black?' It was no good, though. He wasn't going to budge. Anticipating his demand, I'd palmed a twenty-dollar bill in the stairwell, mindful of the security camera, and now I slipped it to him through the pass tray, keeping my hand flattened so that the camera couldn't make out the exchange.

Like a fish snapping up bait his hand came down and made the bill disappear from beneath my fingers. 'See for yourself, I guess.' He buzzed open the door, his manner now one of satisfaction. 'Went up there an hour ago and hasn't come down. Room three-oh-eight. And look, I can't be responsible for all the lies people tell in here. I had to answer for those, I'd be in the jailhouse long ago.'

He reached behind him for the key and slid it toward me the same way the twenty-dollar bill had come.

'You should have checked his ID,' I said, taking it. He muttered something about lawyers coming into his place, but the closing door cut him off.

I went up the stairs slowly. I had no idea what I was going to say to the person who'd evidently impersonated me and was now searching my brother's room. Again it occurred to me that I ought to be calling the police.

At the third-floor landing I met my dreadlocked friend from before. 'There you are,' he said. He was drunk or high, I couldn't tell which, and not entirely coherent. 'I was wondering, did you go to the same law school as your brother?'

'Maybe,' I said. 'Only what makes you think I'm a lawyer?'

'You're funny,' he told me, and we shared a laugh over how funny I was. Then he got serious. 'It's just, you see, I caught this new case and the PD wants to plead me out.'

I was holding my breath against the ammonia smell of him. 'Come with me to Teddy's room and we'll talk.' Maybe I was a coward, but this way there would be a witness to whatever happened. A witness with a drug problem and a rap sheet, no doubt, but if I got my head blown off, his priors would be the DA's concern, not mine.

He started to open his mouth, no doubt meaning to tell all the details of his case, but I shushed him. We went to the door and I listened. A soft flurry of movement in the room made me hesitate, standing frozen with my hand on the knob. Then my heart started to beat again, and I pushed open the door.

The room was very dim. For a long, panicked moment I was defenseless, exposed; then she lifted her hand, and my eyes adjusted enough for me to make out a small Asian woman with bleached-blonde hair sitting up in bed as if she'd just awakened. I flooded with relief. She wore an oversize green USF T-shirt, and her legs were covered by the sheet. Her eyes were bleary, as if she'd been sleeping or crying. But if I'd awakened her I hadn't managed to surprise her. In her hand, pointed at me, was a gun.

'Come in out of the hallway and close the door,' she said in a voice that might have belonged to a child.

I came in, holding the door open behind me for my friend and guardian, but the dreadlocked man now had vanished as suddenly and soundlessly as if he'd been there only in my mind.

'I'm sorry,' I said. 'I thought this was Teddy Maxwell's room.'

'Take the key out of the lock and close the door.' She had a heavy accent that I couldn't place.

I did what she said, pocketing the key and latching the door behind me.

Like the other rooms this one contained only a twin bed with a thin mattress, a dresser, a wardrobe, and a small desk. It was all cheap, battered, and grimy. She swung her legs to the floor, pulling the blanket around herself. It was the third time in my life I'd had a gun pointed at me. The other two had been muggings. This was the first occasion when I couldn't be sure what the person with the gun wanted.

'I'm Leo Maxwell,' I said. 'Teddy's brother.'

She didn't say anything. She went on pointing the gun, relaxing her body forward so that her elbows rested on her knees.

'The cops are two floors up investigating an ax murder. You shoot, they'll be here in thirty seconds.'

She thumbed down the hammer.

'Point taken,' I said.

The silence began to drag, and I spoke again. 'I hate to be the one to say it, but this is starting to feel pretty awkward. Usually these situations work more smoothly if the person holding the gun sort of takes the lead.'

'Are you holding the gun?'

'Clearly not. Otherwise we would be talking about what I want to talk about. About who you are and what you're doing curled up with that nine in my brother's bed.'

'Maybe you should take your own advice and shut the fuck up, since I'm the one holding this and I don't really feel like talking.' Her aggression was only at the surface. These were just the words that came out, and I felt it gave her neither pleasure nor displeasure to speak them.

'It wasn't advice, exactly. It was more in the way of a general observation. There are exceptions to every rule, even where guns are concerned. I could try to guess why you're here, if you're not going to tell me.' I seemed impelled to prattle on. 'You don't look like Teddy's type of girlfriend, no offense. So I'm guessing client?'

A look of involuntary disgust came over her face. 'I'm nobody's client.' There was a shyness to her now, and maybe pride.

'I've told you my name. Maybe you could tell me yours?'

'I could tell you but I'd have to kill you,' she said through a yawn.

'I could come back. We could do this another time, when you've had your rest.'

She sucked her lower lip and looked at me pensively. 'I never heard Teddy had a brother.'

'So you know him. That's a start. Now we're getting somewhere.'

'Teddy's all right,' she said. Coming from her, this might be a rave review.

By now I'd had a chance to look around, and I'd seen enough to realize that there was nothing of Teddy in this room, not so much as a sock wadded under the bed. The door to the wardrobe was open. Inside were only a few suit hangers. A bottle of Jim Beam with an inch of liquor left in the bottom stood on the dresser beside a plastic cup; another cup held a toothbrush and a travel-size toothpaste.

I didn't let my attention wander long. She was still holding the gun, and it was still pointed at me.

Finally she looked me in the eyes and said, 'Who shot him?'

News traveled pretty fast. 'I don't know.'

'You were there.' She wagged the gun. 'I know you were.'

'White man. Slicked hair. I didn't actually see him but that's what I heard.' I hesitated, then said, 'Maybe you were in on it.'

She scoffed. 'I didn't shoot Teddy. Don't be dumb.'

'Then who did?'

She gave a laugh. 'Teddy doesn't tell you nothing, does he?'

I didn't know how to answer that. 'Tell me what?'

'Nothing, that's what.'

'I know you lied to the man behind the desk, told him you were Teddy's sister. I'd love to know why you came here.'

'I never said anything about being his sister.'

'Or his brother. I don't know what you said.'

'You don't know nothing, do you?' she repeated.

I sensed that she was beginning to lose interest. I wanted to hold her attention. 'You tell me who shot him, then.'

'Teddy thinks he's above it all. Teddy brought it on himself.'

'What's that supposed to mean?'

'If you don't know, then I'm not telling you. He's your brother. You figure it out.'

I couldn't explain that I didn't really know him, that we'd gone our own ways after our mother's death, and that he'd always been a mystery to me, a silent presence when he was home, but more often an absence, night after night, week after week. He was supposed to be my guardian, but the housekeepers he paid to fix my lunches and cook my dinners were the ones who raised me. He was just a tenant in the apartment that belonged to neither of us, that was not our home. We were merely the stranded survivors.

She tilted her head, seemingly listening for something, still pointing the gun. Too late I realized what we'd been doing here all this time: not playing a game after all but waiting for a third person to arrive. I'd heard whatever she must have heard, footsteps in the hall coming to a stop outside the door. There was a knock. 'Open it,' she said.

I opened it and found myself face-to-face with a second, much taller woman, wearing a baggy black hooded sweatshirt and extremely baggy lowrider men's jeans held on by a canvas belt. Despite the outfit, one glance was enough for me to see that she was beautiful, nearly as tall as I was, with curly dark hair, a slender nose, cleft chin, high narrow cheekbones, and smooth skin the color of scalded butter. Her face was thoughtful and serious, with all the stillness and gravity of intelligence. She had the broad shoulders of an athlete and the compact chest and waist of a fashion model.

When she saw me, her eyes narrowed and her delicate nostrils flared.

'Don't worry,' the girl on the bed said in a voice purring with pride. 'I've got him covered.'

When she spoke I'd half turned, worrying about the gun. The tall woman stepped forward, and I turned back to her just in time to see her hand come up toward my neck with a plastic object clutched in it, metal prongs glinting in the light from the window, then a blue crackle. Taser, my mind said, then a thousand teeth

48

ground in my ears, and I went down.

I was aware of the women stepping over and around me, of clothes being pulled hastily on and a cursory search for an object that seemed not to be there. When I came to my senses I was lying on the dusty floor. The door was shut and I was alone. My fingertips tingled. I figured that in about five more minutes I would feel like getting up.

On the way down I met the dreadlocked man again. He gave no sign of remembering having abandoned me at the sight of the gun, and I didn't speak of it, either. We treated each other with the utmost courtesy, and he even dusted off the arm of my suit as we walked. 'You see, the way I figure, it was entrapment,' he began as we went down together. 'I didn't have even five bucks on me. The cop offered to give me the stuff if I agreed to pay him later.'

'Did you agree?' It was easier to listen to him than to think about what had happened.

'Well, yeah. I'd never seen him before and I figured I'd never see him again. Anyone would have gone for it.'

'Let the PD plead you out. They end up getting the best deals anyway. It's called a volume discount.'

'You don't think we could prove it was entrapment?'

'Not unless you didn't say a word, didn't so much as look in his direction.'

'What if we had a witness say I walked away and he

kept following me, and he stuffed the baggie in my pocket?'

'Is that what happened?'

'What if we had a witness?'

'Then your lawyer would be guilty of suborning perjury. He could lose his license and go to prison.'

'Oh come on man, don't do me like that. Don't you never work pro bono?' On his lips the term sounded lewd. 'Your brother would help me. Your brother and I are tight. Teddy would step up, man.'

When we reached the bottom of the stairwell, I turned and slammed him against the wall, my breath coming in bursts. It was only after I'd gotten him there that I realized how much larger and stronger than me he was, even in his obviously run-down state. But I was too angry to care whether I got my ass kicked again. 'My brother would never have done what you're suggesting, knowingly put a liar on the stand. You got that?'

He looked at me in puzzlement. 'Just take it easy.'

I let go of his shoulder and stepped away, hesitating briefly to make sure he wasn't going to try anything. When he didn't budge, I pushed through the lobby door and left him.

'You have yourself a family reunion?' asked the man behind the desk, his eyes boring into mine with a lascivious smile.

'Those two look like Teddy's sisters to you?'

He shrugged. 'You all had the same last name. How

50

was I supposed to know you weren't related?'

'Hamilton. Same first name, too, I suppose. Alexander. That's some coincidence.'

His smile spread. 'Like I said, how was I supposed to know?'

'Look, you ever see either of those women before?'

'Hamiltons?' He went on grinning. 'Now and then. Not as often as I'd hope.'

I had another twenty ready. 'With my brother?'

'The taller one mostly.' He looked away as he took the bill, his face becoming serious. 'I think she must know your brother pretty well. I let her in. No non-residents in the rooms, but I let her go up. I did it for Teddy. Ain't no limit to the things I would have done.'

'You mean for Alexander Hamilton? You ever see either of them again, you give me a page, and I mean right away, and there'll be three more Hamiltons in the family.'

I wrote the cell phone number on the back of one of Teddy's cards and palmed it to him along with another twenty, the last of the petty cash from Teddy's office. I realized I should call the police, file a report, give a description of the two women, let Detective Anderson know, but I also understood that I would do none of these things. First I had to find out what they'd been looking for in Teddy's room.

I didn't want to get Teddy into any more trouble than he already was.

Chapter Six

'Legal visit,' I said to the woman behind the bulletproof glass. Behind her, half a dozen video monitors cycled through views of the jail. The inmates wore orange, the guards forest green. My voice sounded strange to my ears. I should be at the hospital, I thought. Where I really wanted to be was on my bike, pedaling up the shoulder of Mount Tam.

I slid over my ID, and after checking me in the computer the woman behind the window slid it back with a clip-on visitor's pass. 'No phones, no currency,' she said, and I traded my wallet for a grubby claim check.

Waiting for the elevator I felt disoriented, like I was wearing the wrong pair of glasses. I was in no state to dispense legal advice, but I was sure that I was doing what Teddy would want. Someone had to talk to Ellis.

From a short hallway outside the elevator I had to pass through another metal door. The deputy who opened it checked my ID, then closed the door behind me. I was now in the jail proper. An inmate mopped the concrete hall. I signed the book, gave the guard Ellis's name, and was shown to a tiny, airless interview room down another hall.

Ten minutes later a different deputy brought him out from the deeper reaches. He walked purposely but without haste, his head down, like a man crossing an open field, and he didn't look at me until he was seated in the flimsy plastic chair that went with the flimsy plastic table. He was a tall, thick man with a youthful face and a fringe of gray at his temples. Along with his jail-issue orange jumpsuit, he wore unlaced Timberland boots and half-rim reading glasses. The room was so close that I could smell his breath, an acidic smell I recognized from other meetings in these cubicles, somewhere between acetone and algae, equal parts bad nutrition, anger, and despair. It was the smell of a man digesting himself from the inside.

'This is some terrible shit,' he said.

Accepting that as commiseration, I nodded, waiting for him to be done talking about what had happened, about what was still happening to my brother and me.

'So this dude just walked in there and popped Teddy while you two was eating lunch,' he said, shaking his head.

I had not yet relived that moment in memory, and I had no intention of doing so now. I'd come here to put Ellis Bradley and his troubles behind me as quickly as possible, but he'd likely been my brother's last client. At the moment when that bullet entered Teddy's brain, Ellis Bradley's fate had been more important to him than anything else.

'You don't look too good,' Ellis told me now. 'I'm sure you need to be getting with your people, so I won't take up your time. I've been thinking about my situation, as you can imagine. I figure I must qualify for the public defender since your brother cleaned me out. No way can I pay another private lawyer to go through this garbage all over again. The DA will probably offer me some shitty-ass deal, and I'll probably end up taking the fall, doing two or three years, losing my kids. That about sum up the situation from your perspective?'

I nodded. 'The judge will probably declare a mistrial tomorrow morning and dismiss the jury. There's always the chance the DA will drop the charges, but in a case like this, where it all comes down to witness credibility, that's not likely to happen. Any case with a domestic violence label, you can pretty much expect the DA to go for blood. We might be able to argue for reduced bail, given the circumstances, the delay. But yeah, basically you're going to be doing this all over again. It's too bad. The evidence came in pretty well for you. And Teddy knows how to close a case like nobody else. Knew.' I looked down.

Ellis nodded, and I could see that the fight was seeping out of him. He couldn't bring himself to eat anything on the mornings when he had to appear in court. During the trial he'd had a tendency to react visibly, sometimes audibly, to things that were said about him. Under stress, he appeared to be precisely the angry, aggressive black man whose portrait the DA had painted for the jury. No way was he going to testify, Teddy had decided, because his discomfort would come across as guilt. Seeing him now, I knew that he'd surrendered, that the system had broken him.

'You can fight this. The new lawyer will get the transcript of what happened this time around. He'll be able to see all the weaknesses in the DA's case. The good news is you didn't testify, so they won't be able to use your words against you like your lawyer will use Lorlee's.'

He shook his head. 'I just want to thank you for coming down here this evening.'

It was time for me to leave, but I didn't stand. I was remembering the last thing my brother had said to me, with that half-serious smile on his face: 'I ought to let you close this one.' I wouldn't have to try the whole case over again, the way a new lawyer would. It was a closing argument, a speech of an hour or two pulling together the evidence, arguing to the jury how the facts supported Ellis's version of events. I wouldn't have to cross-examine witnesses or argue fine points of law, and we'd keep the same jury and the evidence as it had come in, more in Ellis's favor than not. By the end of the week it would all be over, instead of dragging out for six more months with him sitting in jail as a prelude to prison. I knew the case forward and back, and I knew the closing statement Teddy had prepared, though he was also a compulsive improviser, meaning that the statement he'd written was almost certainly not the one he would have given. Most of the jurors had probably made up their minds by now; Teddy always maintained that most made them up during jury selection, before they'd heard the facts, yet he fought as if the jurors' hearts and minds were up for grabs to the bitter end.

'Or I could do it,' I heard myself say. 'I could get up there tomorrow and give that closing argument, if you don't mind taking your chances.'

'You?' Ellis was startled. 'Don't you have to be a lawyer?'

'I am a lawyer. I just passed the bar exam.'

Now he looked embarrassed. I meant a real lawyer, is what he wanted to say. Instead he asked, 'How you going to give a closing argument?'

'I know what Teddy was planning to say. So I'll just get up there and say it. Simple as that.'

I didn't blame him for the skepticism that showed on his face. He kept pressing together his lips in an attempt to hide it, but the look kept returning.

'We'll have to persuade the judge that the jury hasn't been tainted by what's happened. No judge likes to burn a jury, not if she can help it. And you have the right to an attorney of your choice, whether it's me or someone else. I've been there all along. You just say yes when the judge asks if you want me as your lawyer, and you let me say whatever else needs to be said.'

He sat very still, staring distantly. Finally he licked his lips and parted his hands. He looked like a man who'd just been goaded into a stupid bet, his life on the table between us. 'Monkey Boy to the rescue.'

I nodded, my hand going reflexively to my shoulder with the tattoo. 'Go Monkey Boy,' I said. I reached across the table and shook his hand.

When I got back to the office Tanya was still there, working on her computer. 'They didn't take us off the calendar tomorrow for Ellis Bradley, did they?' I asked.

'No. You're still on at nine a.m. Why?'

'I'll need that list of open cases by the weekend. I'll be in Teddy's office.'

She didn't speak. She didn't look up. Probably as far as she was concerned, hell was freezing over.

Outside the window the orange streetlights were diffused by the fog. On the sidewalk whores and drunks were filtering southward. I took off my jacket and tie and sat down at Teddy's desk with the trial binders. I had Teddy's notes, along with ones I'd made during the trial and during last night's marathon practice session. I didn't intend to sleep until I figured out how to impersonate a trial lawyer.

For a while it seemed that Tanya would try to outwait

me. She worked at her computer in the outer office. On what I don't know. Her resume, maybe. At ten she ordered a pizza, but I couldn't eat, even though I hadn't had lunch. It was as if my stomach had been disconnected. Finally at eleven Tanya shut down her computer and left without saying good-bye.

Alone, I paced from wall to wall, trying but failing to make Teddy's words sound natural on my tongue. Stepping into his place was not going to be as easy as I'd thought when I made my offer to Ellis. Words that sounded tough and forceful and utterly convincing when Teddy spoke them became carping and petulant. Even his opening line fell flat: 'After forty hours of testimony and ten days of trial, we know only one thing for certain. One of these two women is a liar, guilty of perjury and seeking to convict an innocent man.'

To the jury, spoken by Teddy, this accusation would come as no surprise. But while Teddy mercilessly attacked Lorlee in his cross-examination, I had sat meekly, silently at the defense table making notes and occasionally leaning over to whisper calming words to Ellis. The jurors had never heard a word from me. I'd gained no authority in their eyes; I'd banked no trust. When I stood up in Teddy's place, even the jurors who were with us were going to wonder who I was and why I was there rather than simply listen to what I said. Trying to parrot Teddy's personality and tone was the surest way to close their ears.

It was 2 a.m. before I finally accepted that I would have to go through my notes and Teddy's notes and the evidence and come up with a new closing. I felt I wouldn't have the latitude to argue the case as forcefully as Teddy would have. I had to trust the jurors to have his voice ringing in their ears.

All the while my eyes kept going to the phone, expecting it to ring with news from the hospital. I found myself forgetting that Teddy wasn't there with me, guiding me through that wilderness of facts and law. I had only to imagine his reaction to some point I was trying to make to feel an instant, powerful surge of approval or disapproval, like a compass needle spinning to North. A minuscule portion of Teddy's legal knowledge and wisdom must have lodged like a seed in my brain, and that seed was now beginning to germinate.

Just before dawn I visited the restroom. Catching a glimpse of myself in the mirror above the sink, I saw how badly I needed a shower and a shave. My brown hair was mussed, my eyes were bloodshot, my jaw gritty with stubble. Over the summer I'd lost weight, my slight frame dwindling. Too much work, not enough biking. Washing my hands, I noticed a black gummy residue under my cuticles. I stood rubbing my hands under the water for a full minute before I realized it was Teddy's blood.

I gazed at my reflection, waiting to see if I was going

to break down. If I did, I'd be no use to anyone for a long time afterward, least of all to Ellis.

It didn't come. After a minute the hot prickling feeling in my nostrils and eyes went away, and I stopped feeling like I was going to throw up. I finished washing, paying careful attention to my cuticles and fingernails, then dried my hands.

I borrowed one of Teddy's jumbo briefcases and filled it with the trial binders, my notes for closing, a CEB practice book, and a copy of the evidence code. It was a cool, clear morning. The night's fog had disappeared, and the sky was salmon colored. It was still early enough that the lighted windows of the buildings showed brighter than the sky, and the few cars on the street all had their headlights on, their hoods and windshields beaded with dew.

I went home, took a shower, drank two cups of coffee, and put on the second shirt Tanya had bought. My roommates were stirring, but I avoided them. In my room, I called the hospital. Teddy's condition was unchanged. I was in the middle of calling a cab when I realized I couldn't possibly ride all the way out to Potrero and back. Even if I had time, I didn't know what it would do to me to see Teddy on his hospital bed with his head wrapped in bandages, breathing through a respirator. With so much on the line for Ellis, I couldn't risk the chance that it would be more than I could handle.

For Teddy's sake I had to put Ellis first, I told myself.

I was back at the office in time to organize my notes and also do some last-minute research into mistrials due to attorney withdrawal, illness, and death.

Chapter Seven

I expected Tanya to be in the office when I returned. She usually showed up every morning around seven, no matter how late she'd worked the night before. But the office was empty, the vinyl cover still draped over her computer monitor, the air as stale and worried as it had been when I'd left an hour before. The files I'd asked for were rubber-banded together on a corner of her desk, with two lists on top of them: one of active clients with contact information and/or jail numbers, the other, longer, a spreadsheet of more than thirty pages, listing chronologically all the clients Teddy'd ever represented. There was no explanatory note, nothing to indicate that I was the one who had asked her to produce these records. But there they were, waiting for me since she'd left without saying anything.

I faxed the list of current clients to Detective Anderson.

I rode the elevator down at eight o'clock and set out on foot for the Civic Center courthouse. The air was still cold enough to chill my hands, but I'd sweated through turned up McAllister.

way Teddy and I usually did, forgetting

al route would bring me past Coruna. I

nt of the restaurant when my legs stopped,

gly of their own accord.

I couldn't see inside. A heavy velvet curtain blocked the front window. Something made me try the door. It was unlocked. I pushed it open, shouldered through the velvet curtain, and walked in.

In the long, narrow restaurant all the lights were on, and I heard water running near the back. There was an empty place where my brother and I had been sitting. The floor had been sanded, and someone had hung a painting on the wall behind Teddy's seat. The smell of bleach was very strong. I guessed that by lunchtime they would be ready to open for business.

The sound of water running stopped, and a tall, bearded guy wearing a rubber apron and gloves came out from the back carrying a bucket of foamy water in one hand and a scrub brush in the other. 'We're closed,' he said. He gingerly knelt and began scrubbing at the place where the floor met the wall. He rinsed out the brush and went at it again, like Lady Macbeth at her housework. 'We don't do breakfast,' he added when I didn't move or say anything.

'What's for lunch?' I asked. 'Suicide bombers?'

It was a cheap shot. Did I imagine he was going to close his restaurant and preserve it as a shrine to my brother? It wasn't his fault Teddy had been shot there. He straightened, then got to his feet so slowly that he might have spent the last twenty hours down there. From the look on his face I guessed he was going to come over and push me out the door, but when he'd walked halfway across the room he stopped, and the irritation froze in his eyes. 'Jesus, you're the dude who was with him.' He sighed. 'I'm sorry, it's just that we're closed. But if there's anything we can do . . .'

I got out of there before he could offer me a complimentary gift certificate for my inconvenience.

A couple of camera trucks were double-parked outside the courthouse, but I didn't immediately connect their presence with my situation. I went through security and rode the elevator up from the rotunda. As I rounded the corner I saw that the fourth-floor hallway, which was normally deserted, was occupied by half a dozen reporters and a pair of camera crews. The jurors were waiting on the benches at the far end of the hallway. They were hands-off, but I received no such deference.

The outer doors of Judge Iris's courtroom were locked, and I banged on them, hoping to rouse the deputy. The reporters gathered around me and I turned, not liking to have my back to them. A TV anchor stood next to me, a woman in a pantsuit over a low-cut blouse. She stuck her microphone under my jaw and spoke in the intent auctioneer's style her kind have adopted. 'Mr

Maxwell, do you have any idea who might have wanted to kill your brother?' As she asked the question her eyes focused somewhere behind my face, behind the door. Standing so close, I saw that she was bored with the question, bored with me, bored with murder.

I just stood there like a poorly animated corpse until the sheriff's deputy assigned to Judge Iris's courtroom unlocked the door. He stared at me for a moment, as if the courtroom were the last place he'd expected to see me this morning. Then his face sagged, and he gave a little nod and let me by him. The reporters and jurors had to wait in the hall. While he relocked the doors I went on through the low swinging gate that divided the spectator gallery from the counsel tables. I had to remind myself to sit in Teddy's chair, on the side closest to the jury. I arranged the contents of my borrowed briefcase in front of me. There was a dry rasp in my throat, and a muscle in my leg kept twitching. I couldn't seem to follow any thought to its conclusion.

The court clerk came through the door at the back of the courtroom, the one that led to the judges' chambers and to the secured hallway through which prisoners were brought. 'Oh,' she mouthed, stopping short as she saw me. Without a word she turned and disappeared back through the door she'd just entered. I heard the wooden heels of her shoes clopping as she went toward the judge's chambers.

Someone else hammered at the doors at the back of

the gallery. The deputy slowly rose from his chair, keeping his eyes glued on his spread-out *Contra Costa Times* even as his body stepped around the desk. Finally he tore himself away and went to let in the assistant district attorney, Melanie McRae, your archetypical DV prosecutor, impassioned and ambitious – and very, very good. Melanie wanted Ellis in prison for the next dozen years, and the only thing standing in the way of her getting what she wanted was me – and of course the jury. Yesterday during her closing statement, she had seemed to hold the jury in the palm of her hand.

She came right up to the defense table with her briefcase and her giant tablet, which she'd used to great effect during that statement. With a fat Sharpie of the kind preferred by juvenile graffiti artists, she had written on the tablet in foot-high letters words like *Liar*, *Adulterer*, *Wife Abuser*, *Rapist*, underlining each several times.

'Mr Maxwell – Leo – I'm sorry about your brother.'

I didn't like her standing so close. 'Thank you.'

'It really isn't necessary for you even to be here, you know,' she said in what Teddy had labeled her sweet mother voice. 'All that's going to happen is that the judge will declare a mistrial. Obviously the case can't proceed. This jury is irrevocably tainted.'

'Mr Bradley has retained me as his attorney. And we're going to proceed.'

Her face changed. All the sympathy drained away. 'We'll see about that,' she said.

The clerk returned and sat at her desk. 'Judge wants to see you both in chambers,' she said to Melanie without looking at me.

If that clerk showed up in my jury pool I'd have struck her in a second. Thank you for your service, ma'am, don't forget to validate your parking.

Melanie had rounded the prosecution table. I made a show of letting her go ahead, following half a step behind down the secured hallway to Judge Iris's chambers.

I'd been back here once with Teddy for a pretrial conference. Catherine Iris was in her late fifties, a former big-firm partner regarded by the defense bar as generally fair. Unlike many judges, she seemed to care what the lawyers who practiced in her courtroom thought of her. This made Teddy uneasy. He always felt most comfortable when a judge was out to screw him. 'Because then you don't let your guard down for a second, which you might do if you start thinking of the judge as your friend,' he said. 'Never put your head in the tiger's mouth.'

Melanie knocked, and we went in. Judge Iris sat behind a desk the size of a Suburban. Her robe hung from a coat stand by the door. She wore a V-necked cream-colored sweater and gray slacks. 'Sit down,' she said, watching me with troubled eyes.

I perched on the couch in front of her desk. Melanie hesitated, then sat next to me. I moved over but I was still closer to her than either of us wanted.

'Your brother was – is – a very – skilled lawyer.' Judge Iris chose her words carefully. 'There are going to be a lot of sad faces over at the jail today. And around here, too,' she hastened to add. 'It's been an education to see him at work. All these years I've heard about the magic, but I've never had Teddy Maxwell in my courtroom until these last few weeks.'

'Thank you, Your Honor.'

'I take it you're here today to stand in for him.'

'That's right. Mr Bradley has retained me to represent him. I've had my bar results for' – I made a show of checking the date on my watch – 'six days now.'

'Your Honor, the state intends to move for a mistrial,' Melanie interjected. 'Without prejudice, of course. We'll plan on retrying Mr Bradley as soon as possible.'

'All that's left is the closing argument,' I said reasonably. 'My client wants to proceed.'

Melanie sat back and was suddenly much closer to me. 'There isn't a person with a pulse in the city who hasn't heard about this shooting.'

'We can poll the jury,' Judge Iris said.

I had no doubt that Judge Iris and Melanie were capable of this same dialogue without my participation. Still, I had my arguments prepared, and thought I might as well use them. 'The way I see it, Your Honor, there's no clear prejudice either way. The DA may not like how the evidence came in, but that's neither here nor there. This horrible event shouldn't be an opportunity for the state to take another crack at Mr Bradley. Whatever happened to my brother, it wasn't Mr Bradley's fault, and as long as he doesn't consent to a mistrial, the state shouldn't be able to try him again. He has a constitutional right to a speedy trial and not to be put in jeopardy twice for the same offense, and he wishes to assert those rights and move forward.'

Judge Iris looked at Melanie with raised eyebrows. 'Counselor?'

I felt my first ruddy flush of success, like good Scotch spreading warmth from the pit of my stomach.

Melanie shrugged. 'If Mr Bradley wants to roll the dice, I'm happy to let him. I feel pretty good about the way the evidence came in. I thought we were doing Mr Bradley a favor by offering a mistrial. If your client wants to turn down that offer, the state is content to proceed.'

Judge Iris was waiting for her to finish. 'We'll poll the jury. You can make your mistrial motion, Ms McRae, and I'll consider it based on what the jurors say, if the shooting will prejudice them either for or against Mr Bradley. I assume your advice to your client about proceeding would change, Mr Maxwell, if my polling indicates that this event has turned a significant number of jurors against your client.'

'Yes, Your Honor, I suppose it would have to change.'

'All right, then. Let's go out there, and we'll call in the jury, and I'll ask them what they've heard about the

70

shooting and whether that news will affect their deliberations in any way.'

Melanie hastened to add, 'And the state intends to request a jury instruction to the effect that the news of the shooting should not affect the jury's deliberations in any way, in the event that Your Honor allows the trial to proceed.'

I saw what she was doing. If we were going to go forward, she was going to throw it in their faces, insist so stridently that the shooting mustn't affect their deliberations that the jurors would begin to wonder if it should, whether we were hiding something important.

'We'll cross that bridge when we come to it,' Judge Iris said, saving me from having to respond.

We went back into the courtroom. The reporters and a few spectators had been admitted to the gallery, but the jurors were still outside. The moment of truth was close, and I could not remember how I'd meant to begin. I needed to review my notes. The deputy had brought in Ellis and seated him at the defense table. I gave him a thumbs-up. He shook his head, looking sick to his stomach. He had on his gray suit and a purple shirt with a black tie. Teddy had gone to his house with a sheriff's deputy the weekend before trial to retrieve a selection of clothes. The judge had been keeping them for us in her chambers.

'Okay,' I said to Ellis. 'The judge is going to ask the jury if they heard about what happened to Teddy, and whether it's going to affect their deliberations in any way. The jurors want to finish this trial as much as we do. They've been sitting here for two weeks the same way we have. So it's really just a formality. I doubt any of them is going to want to get out of it at this stage.'

'And then you're on,' Ellis said in a tense voice, one of regret and fear. He wouldn't look at me. I knew I ought to ask him whether he wanted to accept the DA's offer of a mistrial. I didn't say anything. If someone had told me I didn't have to give that closing argument, I would have kissed him on the lips.

'All rise,' the deputy said. 'The Superior Court of San Francisco is now in session, the Honorable Catherine Iris presiding.' She came in and took her place on the bench. The court clerk called the case. It was all as ritualized as a church service where the officiants have long since forgotten the meaning of the prayers. 'All right,' the judge said. 'Anyone have anything to put on the record?'

'Yes, Your Honor.' Melanie stood, resting her fingertips on the glass-covered table. 'The state moves for a mistrial without prejudice, based on the fact that defense attorney Theodore Maxwell was critically wounded in a shooting just a block and a half from this courtroom yesterday prior to the conclusion of arguments. Reports of the shooting have saturated local news media, and it is the state's belief that the jury has become irrevocably tainted.'

'Counselor?'

It took a moment for me to realize that the judge was looking at me. Thinking that we'd been through this, I feared that they were playing a trick on me, that what I had thought would happen was not happening. Perhaps the judge was going to change her mind and rule in the DA's favor. My face burned. Judge Iris said, 'We're just making a record here, Counselor. What we were talking about in chambers.'

There was subdued laughter from the gallery. Feeling my face grow hotter, I managed to blurt out something about my client's constitutional rights, a garbled version of what I'd said before.

I was barely finished before Melanie said, 'Your Honor, the state requests that the jury be polled.'

'Very well,' Judge Iris said. 'I will poll the jury. Deputy, please ask the jurors to come in and take their seats.'

I felt Ellis stiffen. I didn't dare look at him now. My eyes were on the notes I'd made for the closing argument. I was too nervous to read them, but I stared down at them just the same, willing the words to resolve into meaning. Then I heard the doors open at the back of the courtroom. I jerked upright, standing as Teddy had taught me whenever the jury came or went, elbowing Ellis to remind him to stand with me, as a gesture of respect for the jury's service and for the power they held over his life. I glanced at their faces, trying to remember which ones were likely with me and which against me, and which might be on the fence. There were fourteen, twelve jurors and two alternates. A few of the jurors studied me as they followed the deputy through the swinging gate, their movements stiff under the scrutiny of the journalists. One woman around my age gave me a little pursed-lipped smile of sympathy. An older man looked at me suspiciously, as if imagining I might have tried to kill my own brother. Dear God, I prayed, just give me a hung jury.

For Teddy, it would have been blasphemy to hope for any result short of total acquittal.

The judge polled the jurors one by one, asking them if they'd heard about the attempted murder, if they realized that it had been Teddy who was shot, if it would affect their deliberations in any way. This was the first time since selection that they'd been called on to speak. Their eyes flashed to the reporters, to the judge, to the DA, but most of all to me. After two jurors answered that they could be fair, Judge Iris began to phrase it as a leading question. 'And what's happened won't have any effect on your deliberations in this case?' she asked, and each juror answered no, though I could see a few of them wondering if maybe it should. Otherwise, why would she ask?

After the judge had finished polling the jurors she sent them back out into the hall. They filed out as meekly and mysteriously as they had entered, resigned by now to the interminable routine of entering and leaving and waiting without any explanations, their paperbacks and their knitting baskets always close at hand.

When they'd filed out she denied the mistrial motion on the record, finding that the jury had not been tainted. Beside me Ellis had begun sketching furiously on his legal pad, his usual reaction to moments of stress and tension in the trial. 'All right,' Judge Iris said, giving me a significant look, her eyebrows raised seemingly in encouragement. 'Let's bring the jury back in. If you need anything moved around in here, Counselor, why don't you go ahead and do that.'

Teddy always made a point of changing something in the courtroom before he gave his opening and closing statements, a subtle way of demonstrating to the jurors that he owned the space he was about to occupy, that he belonged in it just as much as the DA or the deputy or the judge. But that would mean my coming out from behind the defense table and wrestling with the podium or the easel. I shook my head.

'Ladies and Gentlemen,' Judge Iris droned when the jurors were back in their places, 'the defense will now give its closing argument. Since it's been a whole day I will repeat the instructions I gave you yesterday morning before the assistant district attorney gave her closing argument. What the lawyers say is not evidence . . .'

They didn't listen to the instructions then, I thought, and they won't listen now. They'll decide based on some illogical detail that has nothing to do with the facts, something they think makes them cleverer than the attorneys or the police or anyone else, some coincidence that has nothing to do with anything. She was finishing: 'After Mr Maxwell speaks, Ms McRae will have ten minutes for rebuttal. Counselor, you may proceed.'

I thought of giving the whole thing sitting down, staring at my notes. But then I was standing and moving away from the relative safety of the defense table, walking around it to the well at the center of the courtroom and turning to address the jury as I'd seen Teddy address them. I was like a swimmer who'd cast off from the edge of the pool and was treading water; now I had to put my face down and open my eyes. I had to take a deep breath. I had to swim.

'Ladies and Gentlemen,' I began, 'I want to thank you for your service in this difficult case.' I had to pause for breath. 'I'm not going to tell you how this case should come out. It's not my job to do your thinking for you. You heard the evidence, you saw the witnesses. Often in these cases we have expert witnesses who come in and tell the jury all about some technical aspect. Forensics, fingerprint analysis, that sort of thing. But in this case you are the experts. This case does not hinge on chemical analysis or accident reconstruction or any of those things. This case hinges on human nature, on basic questions like who has a motive to lie and what that person stands to gain. And every one of you, based on your lifetime of experience as a human being, is an expert in human nature.'

My pants had not fallen down. My voice had not cracked. I was starting to feel as if I could breathe again. 'The night before last I had a chance to listen to my brother practice the closing statement he was planning to give.' I waited half a beat for an objection, since I was arguably appealing for personal sympathy from the jurors, but Melanie kept her seat. 'Yesterday afternoon he was planning to stand where I'm standing now and tell you that the one of those two women, either Lorlee Bradley or Sharla Johnson, sat in that witness stand, took an oath to tell the truth, and then immediately began to tell the most fabulous lies. Now, I don't know about you, but I cringed when I heard that. I like to think the best of people. When a person's story doesn't square with the truth I like to tell myself that human memory is uncertain, that my fellow citizens make mistakes and don't intentionally lie, especially not in a courtroom when they've taken an oath to tell the truth, the whole truth, and nothing but the truth, under the penalty of perjury.

'In this case, however, it simply isn't possible that we're dealing with just a mistake, given that the testimony of these women is diametrically opposed.' I gave a summary of the differences. 'With the contradictions between these women's stories, there are only two possible conclusions. Either Lorlee invented the rape accusation to get back at Ellis and get custody of her kids, lying about it when she called the police and lying again here in court. Or Sharla Johnson came here on a matter in which she has no direct stake in the outcome, took the oath, and lied about those phone conversations with Lorlee in which Lorlee admitted making up the rape.

'Now, I'm not going to tell you who lied and who told the truth. I'm sure you can guess what I think, but that's beside the point. The point is what you think, what you heard, what you saw, and what you know. You heard those two witnesses testify. You listened to their words and you listened to the sound of their voices. You watched their faces, and you noticed the way they held themselves. With all your lifetime's knowledge of human nature, you know in your heart of hearts which one was lying and which one was telling the truth. That knowledge may sit well with you, or it may not. You may feel in your mind that my client is a scoundrel for having an affair with his wife's best friend, and it would be hard not to agree with you. But that's not what you're here to decide today, whether Ellis Bradley is a scoundrel. What you're here to decide is whether the DA proved beyond a reasonable doubt that he raped his wife and beat her on those specific occasions named in the charges.

'It's the DA's burden to prove her case beyond a reasonable doubt. This means that if at any point in the DA's chain of proof you have a doubt, and a reason for that doubt, you must vote to acquit Mr Bradley. In that sense your job is easy. If you have a doubt, and you have a reason, you're finished. That's the safeguard that's built into our system, because our forefathers decreed that before a man can be branded a criminal, the state must bring an extraordinary amount of proof. Proof beyond a reasonable doubt.'

I launched into a fairly standard set piece about Ellis's decision not to testify, explaining that he had the right to remain silent, that the DA was required to prove the case against him and that he was not obligated to prove himself innocent. Also, that neither he nor Teddy nor I had to say one word, that we could have sat there with our arms folded all through the trial. Then I talked about the other evidence in the case, showing how ultimately everything came back to Lorlee's credibility.

I'd stopped being aware of myself as a person standing in a courtroom giving a closing statement. Instead, I was wholly the words I was speaking, the jurors I was persuading; for several minutes now I had been living not in myself but in their gazes. Their eyes were still on me, some guarded and hostile, others open and frank, but all engaged, all listening. Their pens were poised over their notebooks, but they were not writing. The only person who was writing was Ellis. I heard the scratch of his pen as he furiously sketched.

'What you saw revealed here in court was an ugly situation, a situation that must fill you with distaste.

Ellis Bradley was having an affair with his wife's best friend, and Sharla was sleeping with her best friend's husband. That's repugnant. But Sharla was Lorlee's best friend, and Lorlee had no reason to suspect that Sharla would reveal what she told her in confidence. What she didn't know was that Sharla was Ellis's lover, and that she couldn't stand to see Lorlee do that to him. Remember, too, Lorlee's stake in the outcome. If Ellis Bradley is convicted, she'll get full custody of the children.'

At last Melanie rose. 'Your Honor, that's completely speculative.'

Judge Iris looked over her glasses at the jury. 'I'll remind the jurors that what the lawyers say is not evidence. Proceed.'

The objection took the wind out of my sails. I ran through a shortened version of the conclusion I'd planned, a quick summary of the points I'd made. 'When you get back there in the jury room and start talking about the evidence, and thinking about how what you've heard fits into what you know about human nature from your life experiences, I'm confident you'll come to only one conclusion. I'm confident that you'll find Mr Bradley not guilty on every charge.'

I walked back to my chair on stiff legs, feeling the way I'd once felt after I'd hiked up Mount Diablo in the heat of summer with Jeanie and had to come back down on burned-out quads, my legs wobbling every step of the way. Ellis gave me a nod, and relief flooded through me.

Melanie strode confidently around the table to the far side of the courtroom, lifted the easel and her gigantic writing pad, and carried them into a position in the well right in front of the jury, placing the easel at an angle where neither Ellis nor I could see what she wrote on the pad. I knew my brother would have taken the opportunity to move both himself and Ellis over to the gallery right beside the jurors, but after speaking for an hour I didn't have the energy to budge.

I checked my cell phone under the table. The hospital hadn't called. Teddy must still be alive. I wished, suddenly, that I was with him.

Beside me Ellis was still drawing.

Melanie was ready. 'Ladies and Gentlemen, you've just heard the defense attorney concede that his client is, in his words, a scoundrel who was sleeping with his wife's best friend and that the only witness in Mr Bradley's favor is the woman with whom for four years he cheated and lied. When you look at this situation from your life experiences, you'll see at once that Sharla Johnson is the obvious liar, the kind of woman who would chase after her friend's husband. What motive does she have to lie? To get him off the hook, of course, and to harm and humiliate Lorlee, supposedly her best friend but in reality her rival, the person who stands in the way of her being with Mr Bradley. You're all experts in human nature, the defense attorney said. Think about the attitude of a mistress toward her lover's wife. Think about the jealousy Sharla Johnson feels for Lorlee. The hatred. You all saw it in her face, the sheer ill will that comes from having to settle for another woman's leftovers.'

She went on like that for ten minutes. As she spoke, my breath seemed to die in my throat, and all the exhilaration and satisfaction I'd felt after my own performance withered away, my heartbeat slowing to a crawl. It seemed to me that Melanie had picked up my whole speech and neatly inverted it against me, showing all the points I shouldn't have conceded, showing the jurors that the portrait I'd painted of Ellis was in fact the portrait of a guilty man.

By the time Melanie finished with her rebuttal I was certain Ellis was going down, guilty on all counts. Judge Iris was kind enough, but she would throw the book at him.

Ellis was still sketching, withdrawn into his private world. It was a good hobby for prison. He would have a lot of time to work on his art.

I glanced back and saw Detective Anderson sitting in the back row of the courtroom.

All that was left now was the jury instructions. The judge had to read them verbatim. This usually took more than an hour. We had to sit there pretending to follow along while the jury pretended to listen.

About halfway through, between the instructions for the battery charge and the rape charge, Ellis ripped the sheet from the pad and pushed it over to me. It was the page he'd been drawing on all through the closing arguments, a lifelike caricature of a hero, half-monkey, half-boy, wearing an oversize suit but with bare clawed feet and a short cape embroidered with a stylized 'MB'. The monkey boy was swinging down into the courtroom with a law book in one hand, his lips parted in savage ferocity, while a sexed-up version of Melanie cowered behind the prosecution table, her easel and pad fallen beside her.

Monkey Boy to the rescue. I supposed it was his way of saying no hard feelings, Monkey Boy, you did your best.

Ellis's drawing remained in the file for over a year. Eventually I rediscovered it and had it enlarged on matte paper. I even got him to sign it and had it framed. To this day it occupies a place of honor on the wall behind my desk.

Chapter Eight

The daylight surprised me. A high wisp of cloud dispersed the light without dimming it, leaving nowhere to rest the eyes. I had to fight the urge to close mine and leave them closed.

I walked down across Market and managed to hail a cab before I reached Teddy's office. 'SFGH,' I told the driver, then let myself back into the corner of the stinking vinyl seat and closed my eyes.

I'd shaken Ellis's hand and left him to the peanut butter sandwiches and daytime television in the lockup. Judge Iris's clerk had my cell phone number so the court could call me if there was any news, a verdict or a question from the jury.

Teddy was in the neurotrauma intensive-care unit at San Francisco General. I later learned that there was no better place for him to have ended up, that he was in the care of some of the best neurologists in the country.

At the desk in the ward I told the nurse I was there to see Teddy Maxwell. I had to present an ID before she showed me to his room. She pointed out a chair, promising to be back in a minute.

My brother lay surrounded by equipment on all sides, his bulk covered by a doubled sheet. His head and eyes were thickly bandaged. An ooze of bloody fluid showed through the brown elastic overwrapping. A faint beard had grown on his neck and cheeks, and the skin underneath his stubble looked very pale. The respirator tube was in his throat rather than his mouth, connected to an accordionlike air pump on a stand beside the bed. The air smelled drily of disinfectant.

The room had a view of the building's interior courtyard and probably received no direct sunlight much of the year. With the lack of creature comforts, it seemed to me a place meant for the dying rather than the living. I pulled the chair from behind some disused equipment near the window and positioned it near the bed, wishing I'd brought something to read, one of the adventure travel guides I collected, maybe. Anything not to have to look at my brother, to distract me from that clockwork wheezing. I had the trial binders with me, but the last person I wanted to think of now was Ellis Bradley.

Teddy's chest rose and fell, rose and fell, rose and fell. The machine kept his lungs filled with air much longer than normal breathing, so that Teddy seemed to hold each breath before letting it out with a *whoosh*. With each one held, my claustrophobic dread increased.

When the nurse came back I had the evidence code open and was mouthing the hearsay exceptions nervously, compulsively, like a prayer. Studying for the bar exam, I'd learned the exceptions forward and backward. In retrospect, those months of studying seemed a happy time.

I closed the book when the nurse came in. Carol, her name tag said. She wore scrubs and sturdy white tennis shoes. She was in her midthirties, with the self-sufficient look of someone who spent most of her time with people who didn't talk back. 'You're the brother?'

'Yeah.'

'You just get in from out of town?'

'No, I live here. I was with him when he was shot.'

'What's your name?' she asked, checking the IV.

I told her. Then I said, 'He's probably going to die, isn't he?'

'I can't tell you that,' she said, taken aback. 'Dr Gottlieb makes his rounds at six a.m. and six p.m. You'll have to save those kinds of questions for him. All I can tell you is that his vital signs are stable, and they're watching the pressure inside his skull. He has brain stem function, but he scores pretty low on the coma scale. He's been unresponsive to external stimuli. But you never can tell. You just have to keep up your hope.'

She turned to walk out. I opened the evidence code again, biting my lip. Where the hell was Jeanie?

When Carol reached the door she turned back. 'You

should talk to him. Hearing a familiar voice might let him know that he's not alone, that there's something to hang on for. And even if it doesn't help him, it might help you.'

We didn't ever talk before, I wanted to say to her as she walked out. How was I supposed to start now? Was I supposed to just sit here and open my heart to an empty room while Teddy went on saying nothing in return, the way he had all our lives? What kind of deal was that?

I wasn't ready to talk to Teddy, but I would have liked to pray for him, much as he would have hated it. Unlike my brother, I believed that a higher power shaped our lives, and it had always seemed to me that this power must be subject to pleading and intervention.

For a long time I used to wonder what the purpose of my life was supposed to be. I could hear Teddy's dismissive laughter at that phrase, *supposed to*. The law drew me, but the law was Teddy's domain, and for that reason I initially avoided it. After majoring in history I traveled for a summer, then taught at a private high school for two years, but without conflict and contention I was like an engine running on the wrong kind of gas. The best thing I ever did for those kids was quit and go to law school. I figured that I'd be a public defender, that while Teddy worried about fame and money, I would dedicate myself to helping the poor and to safeguarding the Constitution. But I quickly discovered that my passion lay with the law itself rather than with any abstract principle of equality or justice. If you're the best lawyer in the room, you ought to be paid accordingly, no matter how guilty your client or how unjust his cause – that was Teddy's view, and it had come to be mine.

And now it seemed a thumb had come down and squashed him.

I wanted to stay until six, and I meant to stay until six, but the longer I stayed the easier it became to convince myself that Teddy would want me out there looking for the person who had shot him rather than sitting here like a lump beside his hospital bed. I found Carol again and double-checked that they had my cell phone number at the nurses' station.

I took a cab back to the office. The door was locked, but I'd found a spare key in Teddy's desk last night, and I used it to let myself in. Tanya's computer screen was shrouded, the lights off, the blinds down, motes swimming in the few shafts of sunlight that managed to get through. I went into Teddy's office and sat at his desk, laid my cheek on the blotter, then quickly sat up, and ran a hand through my hair. I had the voice-mail code, at least. One of my jobs over the summer had been to transcribe Teddy's messages, and I checked them now. There was one from Detective Anderson thanking me for the list of Teddy's clients. Nothing from Jeanie.

As I hung up the phone I saw the flame of a cigarette lighter and smelled smoke, and I froze. I hadn't turned on the desk lamp, and the blinds were closed, but I could see someone sitting on Teddy's old loveseat in the dimness by the door, the glow of the lighter and now the cigarette lighting his downcast face. No one ever sat there. Teddy used it for stacking file boxes.

I reached down to open the bottom desk drawer, where Teddy kept a gun.

Car's voice was hoarse and angry. 'For Christ's sake, leave the piece in the drawer.'

I lifted my hand to the desk. 'I didn't know you had a key.'

'I've been getting after Teddy to change these shitty locks.'

'Looking for something? Or did you just need a place to drink?'

In response he took a pull from the tall can of beer he was holding.

'Maybe I should call the cops? See if they can help you find whatever it is?'

'Just something I left here. Nobody's business but Teddy's and mine.'

His eyes must have betrayed him, because my gaze went to a framed photograph of the Golden Gate Bridge under construction that hung on the wall opposite Teddy's door. The picture was askew. I grabbed the gun from its place in the frontmost hanging file in Teddy's desk. Car's limbs seemed to loosen when he saw it. I rose and went over to the picture, which, I saw, concealed a safe, now ajar. All summer I'd been here without noticing it.

'Your brother gave me the combination,' Car said in a bored voice behind me. 'What do I look like, a safecracker?'

The safe was empty. 'He owe you money? Or did you just figure no one would miss it?'

'Oh, Christ. If you're going to be waving that thing around—' Car set his cigarette on the edge of the bookshelf, rose from the couch, and came toward me helpfully. Before I knew it, he'd spun me around, jerked my arm up behind my back, and made me drop the gun. I smelled the sharp odor of his sweat and the reek of alcohol on his breath.

He used his shirt to pick up the gun, as if it might contaminate him. He popped it into the safe, shut the door, and spun the dial. 'Do me a favor, don't start thinking you're a tough guy.' He drifted back toward the couch and resumed his place. 'I told him when I got him those guns, I said, "Teddy, don't ever pull it out unless you know you're going to shoot it. Otherwise you'll just get it taken away from you, and you'll be in worse trouble than you were before."'

I sat behind the desk gingerly bending my wrist back and forth, trying to figure out how Car had done that when I'd known exactly what he was going to do. With all the dignity I could muster I said, 'I didn't tell the cops about that argument you and Teddy had in the stairwell.'

'Teddy and I didn't have any argument.'

'If you say so. I only know what I heard.'

'I'm sure you hear a lot of things, Monkey Boy. But it's a pretty big leap from hearing to understanding.'

I had never noticed his accent before. Probably it only came out when he was drunk. It was Russian or Eastern European, maybe. There are a lot of Russians in San Francisco.

'I can call up this detective, tell him I forgot something. Let him ask you about it.'

'You do what you want.' Car picked up the beer and drank from it again, then retrieved his cigarette just as it was about to burn the shelf. 'Hear you gave Teddy's closing argument today. I hope Ellis packed his tooth-brush. Maybe I'll visit him, pay my condolences, put some money on his commissary account for toothbrushes. A lot closer to visit him here than in Pelican Bay. That's, what, a seven-hour drive? His kids can drive it in shifts. When they get their driver's licenses, that is. If they even remember by then that they ever had a father.'

'You think he would have been better off sitting in jail a few more months, waiting for a new lawyer?'

'Don't mind me, Monkey Boy. I get cranky when people show me guns, threaten me with police. Not that I've got anything against police. Police do good work. You got to have police. But I don't like being threatened with them. You want to call the police, call the police. I'm sure they would love to hear from you.'

'Whatever you took from the safe, the cops haven't seen it. They haven't been here yet.'

I had Anderson's card in my wallet. I knew better than to threaten Car again with calling him unless I was prepared to make good on the threat. Car gave good advice. I wasn't going to call the police. I knew it, and he knew it.

Car dropped his cigarette butt into his beer, then crumpled the can, tossed it neatly into the wastebasket, and stood, his tattoos rippling in the slatted light, the intricate foliage moving like ivy in a breeze.

I followed him through the door into the outer office. 'Car. They shot him right in front of me. If you know anything, please tell me. We've got to give the police the information they need to find the people who did this.'

Car turned. 'Maybe the cops are the ones who shot him.'

I felt a chill, facing him through the doorway. His eyes were bright in his sculpted, skull-like face. In the light of the hallway I saw how angry he was.

'Don't be ridiculous.'

From the pouch of his sweatshirt he took an envelope. There seemed to be something else in the pocket, something heavier. 'I want what Teddy wanted. I don't want to see his wishes disrespected. But maybe this concerns you somehow. You're so eager to do something, maybe you can carry out his wishes. Maybe it'll ease your mind.'

There was a malicious brightness in his eyes as he handed me the envelope. It was a sealed letter. Across the seal on the back Teddy had written 'To be mailed unread in case of my death or incapacitation – TM.' On the front, a tiny note in the upper right-hand corner read 'Affix postage here.' Just like my brother, not trusting me to remember to add a stamp.

The letter was addressed to Lawrence Maxwell at San Quentin State Prison.

Chapter Nine

Picture me sitting at Teddy's desk through the rest of the afternoon into the evening, the letter lying unopened on the blotter before me. Again and again I thought, I will open it now, I will turn on the light, I will tear the envelope and read what's inside. But my hands would not obey.

In 1983, when it happened, Teddy was twenty-two and just starting law school, no longer living at home. I was ten. In the beginning Teddy had refused to discuss the subject with me; all he would say, when pressed, was Lawrence was innocent. I didn't believe it, and he could never say who had killed Caroline, our mother, if Lawrence hadn't. In later years he would sometimes drop a comment such as Dad was being moved again, or that he'd been sick but now was better. By then I didn't want to think about him. I wanted our father never to have existed, and barring nonexistence, I wanted him to be dead. In my darkest times at the ages of sixteen and seventeen, before I channeled my anger into cycling, I used to visit the library on rainy afternoons and read the newspaper accounts of my father's trial. The stories were written with an eye for the inconsistencies of the state's case; they included jailhouse interviews and detailed excerpts of Lawrence's testimony in which he protested his innocence and insisted that he'd been framed. Fighting back a headache from squinting at the microfilm, I used to imagine how it would feel to kill him.

Around eight o'clock I finally made some kind of decision. It didn't feel like a decision. It felt more like the end of a long, unrestful slumber, the kind of half-drunk sleep where you wake up in the morning feeling more tired than when you lay down. I locked the office door, went down to the street, found a mailbox, and put the unopened letter inside it, just as Teddy wanted.

It was like putting a black hole into another black hole. I could not guess what my brother might have written in the letter, nor what it would mean to our father to open it after hearing the news that Teddy had been shot. I knew Teddy was still in contact with him, that he wrote and occasionally visited him. I never asked what they talked about, and Teddy didn't volunteer any details.

I went back to my place, changed into jeans, then tried Jeanie again. No answer. This time I didn't leave a message. I called the hospital and learned that Teddy's condition was unchanged. Then I went out, bought a six pack of beer and a pizza, and went back to the office.

My plan was to start going through the case files, put a few hours into it. I had no idea what I was looking for – a motive, I suppose, someone with a grudge against my brother or a secret Teddy had exposed. As tired as I was, I knew that if I closed my eyes I would see his body on the restaurant floor or in his hospital bed. The smell of his blood kept coming to me in unguarded moments. I kept thinking I had to get up and wash my hands again.

I opened the pizza on Tanya's desk. It was anchovy and sausage and mushroom, and the smell of cheese and oregano was strong. I hadn't eaten since yesterday evening, but I felt no hunger until I lifted the first piece. I ate the whole thing so steadily that I kept having to pause to breathe. I drank three cans of beer very fast, without registering the alcohol except as a general loosening, an absence of fatigue. My brain felt sharp. I was ready to work.

With a fourth beer in hand I contemplated the filing cabinets. So much paper. The files were organized alphabetically by clients' last names. My tentative plan was to go through them by date, starting with the open cases, working back from the present. Then I remembered what Car had said, insinuating that the cops were behind the shooting, and I felt that chill again, the rush of indignant disbelief.

The Ricky Santorez files were huge, taking most of an

entire drawer, the documents haphazardly organized into binders and Redweld folders, the binders still exhibiting the chaos that takes over in the heat of trial: pages folded back, Post-it notes everywhere, and yellow sheets of hurried, incomprehensible notes in Teddy's scrawl, nothing quite where it should be. The size of the file reflected the outsize space the case had occupied in my brother's life.

The case went to trial the summer after my first year in law school. I should have been teaching summer school to pad my meager savings when I couldn't find a paying legal job, but I'd decided instead to sit in the gallery with the reporters and the dozens of off-duty police officers who showed up in uniform each day for the jurors' benefit.

Teddy was brilliant. He'd spent the better part of two years preparing. There was no substantial dispute about what had happened, the actual events. Santorez conceded that he had fired the shots that had killed Sergeant Craig Espinoza and Officer Greg Davis. Espinoza was a twenty-year veteran, Davis a relative rookie. Both had left behind families.

The officers had been serving a search warrant in a drug case, but the address on the warrant was actually the address of the house next door. By the time the case went to trial, the police were claiming that Santorez was the intended target of the raid, but his name appeared nowhere on the warrant. To hear my brother tell it, the police broke down the wrong door. But by dumb luck they happened upon an ex-con drinking beer with an illegal assault rifle on the kitchen table in front of him, a man who'd learned in prison that the only response to violence was violence and who believed that the men breaking into his house could only be intent on murdering him.

According to the testimony of other officers on the scene, the officers announced themselves as police both before and after they broke down the door. Santorez testified that they'd said nothing, given no warning, and that Espinoza fired first, forcing him to defend himself. Under Teddy's cross-examination, one of the surviving officers admitted that he did not remember hearing any officer call out until after the shooting started, though another officer remembered hearing Espinoza shout, 'Police, hands in the air!' before the firing started. Santorez was wounded six times but lived. He was immediately returned to prison on a parole violation and would have to do time no matter what happened in the trial. The only question was whether he'd ever be able to get out.

I flipped through the trial binders. There were tabs for each of the DA's witnesses with police reports, transcripts of Santorez's parole revocation and preliminary hearings, and other prior statements for use in holding officers to the stories they'd told before, along with Teddy's notes and outlines. Nothing here was unfamiliar to me. And none of it seemed useful in identifying whether any players in the Santorez case might have had a motive for killing my brother.

The only trial materials that seemed to offer any possibilities were the redacted excerpts from the police officers' personnel files that Teddy had received in discovery, containing information on allegations of misconduct and violations of department rules. There was dirt on Espinoza, who, as it turned out, had been involved in a shooting eight years previously under similar circumstances, raiding a drug house in Hunters Point. That time Espinoza had emerged unscathed and the suspect had died. Teddy had succeeded in getting evidence of that shooting admitted at trial, through a bystander witness Car had brought back to town from LA, a former addict who'd been too scared or cynical to come forward at the time of the original internal investigation.

I remembered overhearing some officers in the hallway during a recess, clearly talking with the intention of being overheard, tossing around the rumor that Car had flown down to LA and offered ten thousand bucks to this woman if she'd tell the story Teddy wanted her to tell. The rumor took on a life of its own, and the DA cross-examined the junkie on it, but Teddy's witness denied every word and made the DA look like a fool. It didn't end there. After the verdict the DA's office filed a state bar complaint against my brother, accusing him of suborning perjury. They had no proof, of course. I figured the file on that complaint and the press clippings must be in these cabinets. One of Tanya's duties was to comb the papers and clip any article mentioning Teddy or his clients. It wasn't vanity on Teddy's part, exactly. However good or bad the coverage was, he needed to know what the papers were saying about him, what potential jurors might have heard.

None of this seemed to me a likely motive for attempted murder. I fingered back through the file. At the very end was a Redweld with a yellow smiley face on its tab and a label in Teddy's hand that read 'Death Threats'.

It was hefty. There was a log for phone calls, with summaries by each entry, and a manila envelope for threats received by mail. There was also an envelope containing all the police reports Teddy had filed, one for each threat he'd received. They were what surprised me. Teddy didn't even call the police when he got mugged outside his office.

I paged through photocopies of letters and notes. He must have given the originals to the police. Most simply suggested in various unpleasant ways that the world would be a better place without Teddy and his clients in it, yet there was one that made my skin crawl. It resembled a treasure map, with blowups around the center drawing showing details too small to include there. Everything in Teddy's life was on it.

On the right side was a miniature sketch of Teddy's unfinished house in Contra Costa County, and then a blowup insert with a diagram of the rooms showing the closets, the bathrooms, the bedrooms, and even the bed. The writer had labeled which side of the bed was Teddy's and which was Jeanie's. Beside the house were pictures of their cars, including make, model, year, license number, and VIN. From the house a line ran across the bay to a cartoon version of San Francisco and the office Teddy and Jeanie had shared, where I was sitting now. Another inset showed an accurate rendering of the floor plan.

There was nothing else, no explicit threat, but there didn't need to be. I made a copy of this one. I thought it might interest Detective Anderson, though somehow I didn't believe that the person who made it was responsible for Teddy's lying there at SFGH. Suddenly I felt I had to get out of the office, out of San Francisco, if only for a night. It was as if I were trapped, suffocated by a city that until now had always seemed an extension of myself.

I slipped the last two beers into my coat pockets, locked the door, and went down to the street, where I walked quickly, my head down, dodging drunks; the sidewalk was thick with voices and bodies in the block between Mission and Market. I went down the piss-reeking steps of the Civic Center BART and paced the yellow line, impatient to be on a train.

That time of night there were no direct trains to Orinda. I changed at MacArthur in Oakland. As I waited on the platform I watched the fog pushing up around the spires and boxes of San Francisco in the distance. The air was crisp. The Mormon temple perched on the hillside above me like a spaceship bathed in light, ready to abandon this world on a moment's notice. Cars and trucks clattered over joints in the concrete on the freeway beneath the tracks.

In Orinda I had to walk up and down the station parking lot before I found Teddy's car, a white VW Rabbit with the stereo ripped out and a 'nothing to steal' sign in the window. I'd taken the spare keys from the office, and soon I was maneuvering the unreliable little car with its squeaky brakes and stripped gears up Moraga Way toward the unincorporated community of Canyon, a network of dirt roads and footpaths in a steep valley between Moraga and Oakland, separated from Oakland's Skyline Boulevard by a swath of water-district land.

In Moraga I turned right on Canyon Road, and within half a mile I left behind all signs of civilization. I was driving through a forest of oaks and madrone that soon dropped down into the redwoods. Through the open windows the clean scent of their bark and needles filled the car. The undergrowth was all ferns, and the head-lights penetrated deeply into the woods.

Pinehurst Road runs up the valley floor through a

remnant of the redwood forest that once towered above the bay. It was one of my favorite biking roads in the Bay Area, with killer hills in both directions. San Leandro Creek runs on one side of the road, then crosses beneath it. A mile from the junction of Canyon and Pinehurst Roads are a post office and a K–8 school under the trees. The residents maintain their own roads and water system and take pride in composting, recycling, and solar power. They feed their kids organic produce and Niman Ranch beef and teach them Zen meditation.

This is where Teddy and Jeanie once tried to make a life together.

I drove across the WPA bridge above the creek into the school's gravel parking lot. Pulling over to the farthest, most shadowy corner of the lot, I put the Rabbit temporarily out of its pain. I didn't know why Teddy refused to buy a real car. Jeanie used to drive a Lexus while they were married. I cracked one of the remaining beers. I'd meant to get out and walk along the road, clear my head, but instead I let the seat back as far as it would go, about forty-five degrees, and lay there taking small sips of beer as the night sounds of the forest reasserted themselves. The outside world and all its cares and problems drifted further and further away.

I fell asleep with the beer propped between my legs and immediately slipped into a dream, in which it turned out that Caroline was still alive, that we'd been mistaken all these years. She had just been standing very still, pretending to be a statue. Look, I said to my father, turning him physically to face her, she's alive, she's breathing, feel her breath. Lawrence was in despair, and I was trying to convince him what he'd done was not irrevocable after all, that there was still time to make amends, there was always time. The past was gone, washed away, and we were prepared to forgive him. At first he didn't want to see that she was alive. Look, we kept telling him. Look at her.

Never had I dreamed of Caroline so vividly as I did that night, dozing in Teddy's car under the redwoods. I used to dream about her, but her face would always be turned away, or it would become another face when I tried to hold it in my gaze, so that it seemed she was running away from me. Now she held still. Now, sixteen years after her death, I was able to see her as she'd been when she was alive, the way her brown hair faded to downy wisps behind her ears, the softness of her skin, the smell of her, which I'd forgotten and which was like rediscovering a lost self, a younger self, me as I had been before my childhood was uprooted by her absence, me as I might have been if she'd lived.

The roar of a motorcycle hitting ninety on Pinehurst awakened me. My face felt cold in the night breeze. The beer had not spilled, and I swallowed the rest. I hadn't been asleep long. A few minutes, maybe.

I lay there staring at the ceiling of the car, getting

myself together. Then I straightened the seat, started the engine, and pulled out of the parking lot.

I drove slowly, because the turnoff was easy to miss, just a rough gravel road heading up a steep grade through the trees, not much more than a fire trail, the entrance blind from this direction. You had to look for a reflector stuck to a tree. I put the Rabbit in low gear and drove up, ignoring PRIVATE ROAD, NO TRESPASSING signs. My destination was about a mile up, past a geodesic dome and a ramshackle structure with bay windows that resembled a crouching grasshopper.

Teddy's house was set back among the trees with a view through the redwoods, just high enough that on cloudy nights you could make out Oakland's orange glow. I left the key in the ignition the way Teddy always did and walked down the footpath toward the house. A motion light came on, but even without it my steps would have been guided by the sound of plastic sheeting flapping in the breeze. The redwood needles made a soft carpet underfoot, and the scent of them filled my lungs as my feet stirred them up.

Teddy was an idiot about this house: I will say that now, so that no one thinks I was blindly on his side. It had been his idea to live up here, which meant a good ninety minutes of commuting each way. The school down on Pinehurst was what finally persuaded Jeanie; that and the steep dirt roads, the communal saunas, the yards cluttered with arcane salvage, and the neighbors who looked after one another. I believe that Teddy even promised that they would eventually move their office to Walnut Creek. A false promise if I ever heard one. He'd insisted on tearing the house down and rebuilding. A necessity, I suppose, given that the former owner had used it primarily as a set for his avant garde films. His first big mistake was to insist that they live there during remodeling. His second was to stop construction each time the cash flow dropped at their two-person, husband-and-wife firm.

For three years Jeanie toughed it out. I have to give her credit. In the end, though, it wasn't having to live in that gutted shell of a house that made her leave. That was just a symptom of deeper problems in their marriage, as well as in Teddy's heart. I don't know exactly what it was that drove the final wedge between them, but at bottom I suppose it had to be the way my brother was, because of what our father had done.

After Jeanie left, he kept the work on the house going to the point where rain couldn't get in and he had the basic necessities of life: a furnished bedroom, a functional kitchen, a back deck where he could sit late at night and think. The rest of the place remained half finished, plywood on the floors and drywall on the walls, plastic sheeting over the eaves. To reach the front door you had to clamber up onto the waist-high porch. He never got around to installing steps. He'd gone with the lowest bidder and the cheapest materials, cutting corners wherever he could. If I built a house, I would build it to last, I told myself, and if I found the right girl, I was going to hang on to her. I had Teddy to thank for showing me how not to live.

As I gained the porch I heard the phone ringing, echoing as sounds can only echo in a large, unfurnished, uncarpeted structure. I unlocked the front door, heading for a nook in the living room where my brother had set up a cheap IKEA corner desk. The instant I got to the phone it stopped ringing, and the answering machine clicked on even though the caller had hung up. The tape must have been full, because the machine clicked off as soon as Teddy's message played.

Was it possible the police hadn't driven here yet? I wondered. I remembered Anderson's promise to run down every lead, to bring the killer to justice if only to spite Teddy. Thirty-six hours had passed since the shooting, and it seemed odd that I was the first person to set foot here. Again I remembered what Car had said about the cops being involved. How many times would Anderson's name come up in Teddy's files?

I picked up the phone and hit *69, but a recorded message informed me that the number was blocked. I replaced the handset and turned away, but at once it started ringing again. When I answered, a woman's voice said in a rush, 'Teddy, thank God.' She sounded desperate, on the edge of tears. 'I knew it wasn't true,' she said to someone on her end.

'This is Teddy's brother, Leo,' I told her. 'Teddy's in the hospital.'

She gave a gasping cry and slammed down the phone.

I sat there, flipped on the light, and opened my other beer. Teddy had a lot of girls – on the sly when he was married and in the open now that he was not. I hit the PLAY button and waited while it rewound.

'Teddy, I— look, just call me.' A different voice, this one with an Asian accent. Then another time: 'Teddy, it's Martha. It's Monday evening, and I'm here with Chris. Call us right away.' Then she rang again. And again. The repetition of her pleas was mesmerizing as the messages grew more and more tense. There was also a call about a dentist appointment Teddy had missed and another from a contractor saying that he had a crew ready to start work on Monday, and all Teddy had to do was fax over the papers. Had he finally decided to finish work on the house?

All the messages had been left before the shooting. I was sure that Martha's voice belonged to the woman who'd held the gun on me at the Seward.

I sat for a while drinking beer and turning over the objects on Teddy's desk, little more than a temporary workspace a person might set up in a borrowed room. I hadn't been here since Jeanie and Teddy still shared the house. Even though I'd known more or less what to expect, its emptiness was shocking. When Teddy and Jeanie were together here there were books and music and art on the walls. I could see that it would be a real house someday. Now that illusion was gone.

I realized how little of what other people thought of as life my brother had set aside for himself. Our family had shattered when Teddy was twenty-two and I was ten. If he'd turned unremittingly to work, it must have been partly because of his responsibility for me.

It wasn't just work, however, and it wasn't my fault. There was a quality of self-indulgence in his asceticism, a neurotic's pleasure in yielding to neurosis, an aversion to feeling at home. The house, which more than any other place should have been a home, showed how completely this aversion had thwarted every satisfaction and reward that work is supposed to bring.

Documents were scattered across the desk, copies of police reports and transcripts of preliminary hearings, all of them from open cases, none of which I had yet had the chance to review. The drawers held the same assortment of alligator clips, burned-out tape recorders, and half-used tablets that had filled his desk drawers in the city. The rest of the room was empty except for a couch and an armchair – both shrouded in plastic – a stepladder and drop cloth, and a roller immobilized in solidified latex. Two of the walls had been painted, and two were plain drywall.

I wandered into the kitchen, which wasn't much more welcoming. It was finished, at least. On the stove was a pan with scum around the rim. The cupboards held bottles of tomato sauce and an assortment of dishes. The freezer was jammed with packets of frozen ravioli and Costco hamburger patties, with a few ancient-looking bags of vegetables. In the fridge I found a half-full case of light beer. I threw out my empty and opened one.

Martha, I wondered. Martha and Chris. I'm here with Chris. Where?

I went back to the master bedroom. Its sliding glass doors gave out onto the deck. Here, at least, Teddy had made a modest effort, I suppose because this room and the deck were the only parts of the house that the girls he brought home had leisure to examine. Or perhaps of all the rooms, Jeanie had taken the least from this one when she left. On the deck stood a pair of Adirondack chairs. The slope dropped off steeply, and the broad lower branches of a young redwood brushed the deck railing and carpeted the boards with needles. One of the chairs had a bare space around it, with an ashtray, empty beer cans, and a few crusted plates, but the rest of the deck and the other chair were covered with a thin layer of needles. It was clear that Teddy never went to stand by the railing, never did anything but sit, eat, drink, and smoke his dope.

I stood listening to the night birds' calls and to the creaking of the tree trunks all around me. In the forest I saw no lights. A tinge of wood smoke rose to my nostrils.

In that moment I thought I understood what it was that my brother had loved about this place and, conversely, why he kept that room at the Seward.

I was startled by a noise from the house behind me, the click of the front door latch as somebody eased it closed.

I turned back inside and went quickly to the bedside table, expecting exactly what I found when I opened the drawer: Teddy's other gun, the twin of the one in his office, and a pack of condoms. I slid the drawer closed, leaving the contents in place. No way was I going to shoot anyone.

I pressed my shoulder against the wall just inside the bedroom. I'd left on all the lights, so the intruder had to realize he wasn't alone. We were each waiting for the other to reveal himself.

Finally a woman's voice startlingly near called out breathlessly, tremulously, sounding a note beyond hope: 'Ted?'

'Jeanie!' I called back at once, my voice cracking as I sucked a great gulp of air. 'It's Leo.'

From the living room came a volley of choked sobs that stopped abruptly.

I came out. Jeanie stood three feet away with a huge barbecue knife in her hand, her face wet. I didn't doubt that she would have used the knife if she'd had to, and used it well.

'What are you doing here?' she asked, lowering the

knife to her side and giving me a hard punch in the chest with her free hand.

I stepped back with the punch, thinking I could have asked her the same thing, then moved close again. She gave a little gasp of dismay and embraced me, the knife clattering to the floor. 'Oh, honey,' I said, my breath catching with the intensity of our shared grief and my sheer wonder at holding Jeanie again.

The history of that wonder is easy enough to tell. I had self-consciously fallen in love with Jeanie shortly after she became my brother's girlfriend and moved in with us when I was fifteen. We kissed once shortly before I moved out of the Potrero apartment for college. That night we were all drunk because Teddy and Jeanie had just lost their first big felony trial. He'd said something crude, I don't remember what, and she walked out. When he wouldn't go after her, I did. I caught her within a block, and she put her hands on my shoulders and kissed me deeply. In a few weeks she and Teddy patched things up. She never told him about the kiss.

How confused I was, how alone in my adolescent throes. And Teddy never spoke up, though he must have known what was going on, and there were times when a kind word or even a harsh one from him might have made all the difference. He did the best he could, or so I tell myself now, when there is no point in accusing him or myself any longer.

Thirty-six hours after the shooting, ten years after I had first met Jeanie, she was still beautiful: a few inches taller than me, big-boned, with wispy brown-blonde hair and a freckled face, and a way of looking you frankly and directly in the eye. Her attractiveness was not in any collection of features, and it would have been easy to make her sound plain, but to me and Teddy and others she was remarkable, amazing. It was all in her quickness, in her willingness to sting and then soothe the stung place, and in her intelligence, which always seemed to be working on some knotty problem, like she could solve me if she only thought hard enough.

'Have you been to the hospital yet?' I asked.

She pulled from our embrace, swiping at her eye with the back of her hand. 'I've been in Mendocino. I didn't get your message until this afternoon. I called the hospital, and they told me how serious it was. It was too late to go there, so I thought I'd come here. I saw the lights and I saw Teddy's car, and I thought— I don't know what I thought.'

It was a pleasure and affirmation to step away from her and remember that I was a man and not the child who'd decided long ago that he was in love with his brother's girlfriend.

'I was hoping I might find something here that would help me understand what happened,' I said.

'It was just so public,' she said, like she'd been sitting on this thought during her whole drive, just waiting for someone to share it with. 'Like they were trying to send a message.'

'You're right.' I glanced around me. It would have been so very simple to shoot him here, follow him home one night from the BART and do it. 'But a message to whom?'

She turned away. Suddenly she seemed nervous, tense. 'Do you want a drink? I need one.'

I wasn't about to turn her down, though I'd had plenty already. She'd left a canvas shopping bag by the front door. I followed her as she went to retrieve it. Inside was a sweating bottle of Tanqueray gin she must have taken straight from her freezer. Jeanie liked to drink, and sometimes she liked to get drunk. I suppose that's what she had in mind.

She took down a pair of tumblers and poured two Jeanie Martinis, our old household term for ice-cold gin in a glass. Then she seemed at a loss. To sit at the kitchen table we had to clear away layers of junk mail.

'When was the last time you talked to him?'

'Last week.' She tossed her head as if to clear it. 'We've been talking all the time lately, actually. He calls me up late at night to chat about cases, throw ideas around. He keeps trying to talk me into coming back here to live with him, but we both know he's bluffing.' She took a long drink of gin, then stared straight at me. 'He's going to die?'

'I don't know. The nurse said his brain activity is

minimal.' I hesitated, then said, 'I keep wavering between hoping he'll live and hoping he won't. I mean, he'll be a vegetable, won't he? With his head half blown away?'

Her voice was stern. 'I don't think either of us can know that, Leo.' She was a Catholic, if a lapsed one, resistant to better-off-dead thoughts.

'I just can't help feeling that Teddy wouldn't want to live like that. What would he do without his work? Can you imagine him ever being forced to depend on anyone?'

'He'd want to live no matter what. Let's not talk this way, Leo.'

She seemed tense and distracted, as if only one part of her mind was participating in the conversation, and she went through her first Jeanie Martini very quickly. I poured her another, then put the gin away in the freezer. It had been several years since I'd seen her sopping drunk, and I didn't care to repeat the experience. Not under these circumstances. For both of our sakes, I wanted Jeanie to keep her dignity, which was considerable, given her stature in the criminal defense community.

'Who's the detective on the case?' she asked.

'Anderson. You haven't heard from him?'

She shook her head.

'He hasn't been here, as far as I can tell. He wanted a list of former clients. I had Tanya draw it up, and I faxed it over to him this morning. I saw him in court this morning, but he didn't stick around to talk.'

'Court?' She gave me a quizzical look.

'The closing statement in the Ellis Bradley case. They shot Teddy before he could give it. So rather than have the judge declare a mistrial and let the client cop a plea to put this all behind him, I stepped in and gave it.'

Her look deepened into an expression of worry and concern.

I was flushed, my cheeks getting hotter as I remembered how things had gone in court. 'I got my bar results Friday. It's okay.'

She brightened. 'Oh God, of course. Congratulations.' She leaned over to give me a hard squeeze, her chin digging into my shoulder, her gin breath hot in my ear. For good measure she added a kiss, a wet smack right on the eye. Everything went all fuzzy and crackly for a moment.

'Thanks,' I said. 'It's nice for someone to finally say it.'

'You mean Teddy didn't . . .'

'Nope. And it's not like I was hoping for the corner office.'

'Welcome to the club. He wouldn't let me stand in for him even in the most basic scheduling hearings when we were partners. He'd have the clerk redocket the case if he was delayed and couldn't be there, even if I was already at the courthouse for something else. He didn't want his clients to think that any other lawyer could be trusted with one of Teddy Maxwell's cases for even the most routine status report. Like he was just so much better than anyone else. I was astonished, frankly, to learn that he was letting you shadow him this summer. Because the Teddy Maxwell I know works alone.'

'That about sums it up, doesn't it,' I said, feeling the gin hit me on top of all the beer I'd drunk.

She went on, not entirely successful in her attempt to reassure me. 'He might actually have seen you as a rival, Leo, ridiculous as that may sound. So you shouldn't be hurt. You should take it as a compliment that he was too insecure to congratulate you.'

'What's so ridiculous about me and Teddy being rivals?' I snapped.

She gave me an appraising glance, then looked away again, smiling a strained nonsmile, old memories resurfacing. 'So, Ellis Bradley. You gave the closing. How'd it go?'

I pretended to quote myself, raising an arm and assuming an oratorical style: 'Ladies and germs, just because my client is a scoundrel who cheated on his wife with her best friend and probably beat her on any number of occasions, only not on this particular occasion, it doesn't mean he should go to prison.'

'You didn't.'

'And I found this great case from 1865 saying rape isn't rape if she's your wife, unless the marriage was fraudulent. I don't know how Teddy missed that in his research. I hammered that idea pretty hard.' I shrugged.

'I'm not Teddy. I'm not even me yet. As a lawyer, I mean. The jury's still out. Literally. They resume tomorrow. That closing may well turn out to be the last thing I'll ever get to do for Teddy, or so I keep thinking, and I can't shake the feeling that I screwed it up. So, basically, I'm a wreck.'

'Well, maybe not the last thing. You can figure out who tried to kill him.'

Neither of us spoke for a moment.

She went on: 'If he lives, Teddy's going to seriously depend on you. On us all, for just about everything, and I'm not talking about rides to the doctor. I mean eating, going to the bathroom, dressing himself, learning how to talk again. I've had a couple of clients with similar injuries. It's a long, long road, and you never get back to where you started.'

'That's what I'm afraid of,' I said, trying to cut off the thought of my brother needing help for basic everyday chores. 'I can't imagine him depending on me or anyone.'

She spoke sharply. 'You can't imagine him depending on you? Or you can't imagine being there for him?'

I waited until I was sure I could control my voice, and then I said, 'I owe him. Is that what you're telling me? For all those years he was stuck with me? All those years you were stuck?'

She shook her head. 'I'm not saying that. It's just that this is going to be very, very hard for all of us, no matter what happens.'

After a pause I asked, 'You think Teddy'd be pissed at me for giving up that list of his clients?'

'Yes,' she said after consideration. 'But it was still the right thing to do.'

'Tanya thinks the cops just want an excuse for harassing the clients. She probably has a point. They see them all as scumbags, getting away with murder. So why not use this as an excuse to do some mopping up?'

'Detective Anderson, you said?'

'He's the one I've been talking to.'

She thought for a moment, then shook her head. 'Doesn't ring a bell.'

Her glass was empty again. She sat looking at it for a moment, then stood, got the gin bottle from the freezer, and brought it back to the table.

'Since the police were so interested in his clients, I figured I might as well take a look at some of the old files,' I said. 'Ricky Santorez, for instance.'

'He's still in prison,' Jeanie said quickly. 'Out at San Quentin. They got him on a parole violation.'

'I wasn't thinking Santorez did it. Or any of Teddy's clients. What I'm thinking is more along the lines of witnesses, victims. Someone he humiliated on the witness stand, someone who feels Teddy screwed them out of justice.'

'Someone with connections,' she said, picking up from me without missing a beat. 'There was both a shooter and a driver, right? It was well planned, well executed. If I were on the outside looking in, I'd say it was a drug hit, but Teddy doesn't represent drug dealers. Except Santorez.'

'You said earlier that this looked like a shooting meant to send a signal to someone. What were you thinking?'

'You remember that S-and-M homicide a month ago?' she said. 'That's a case of his.' She paused, then frowned. I wondered what was going through her mind. 'Teddy had a meeting scheduled a week ago Wednesday with someone from the DA's office. His client was supposed to finger the killer and receive immunity. But the client didn't show up. He seems to have disappeared off the face of the earth.'

That would have been about the time of Teddy's argument with Car in the stairwell during the Bradley trial. 'Who was the client?'

'Keith Locke. Dad's a big-time cancer researcher at UCSF; mom's a professor of some sort. Keith must be in his late thirties now, kind of a grown-up idiot child. Teddy represented him, what, eight years ago on a charge of oral cop on a minor. He was caught giving cunnilingus to a sixteen-year-old girl on a bus-stop bench at 4 a.m. Christmas morning. Wearing a Santa hat. The girl didn't want to testify but they had him cold. We made it go away.

'Anyway. Two weeks ago, down in a parking lot near Candlestick, middle of the night, Keith was trying to push this grown man's body over the side of a Dumpster when a San Francisco police car pulls up. Cue spotlight, do not pass go, do not collect two hundred dollars. The body was this Stanford professor, Marovich. Young guy, good-looking. Made a career writing sociological papers about his sex life. He had a cord around his throat and plenty of other marks, as well. Like he'd been sexually tortured.

'Turns out that Keith's place of employment is the Green Light, that sex club downtown. Closed down now, of course. The police raided it a week after he was arrested.

'Keith calls up his esteemed lawyer and says, "Mr Maxwell, I did not commit murder, I was just stupidly trying to cover up this terrible accident, won't you please help?" And Teddy says, "Give them the real killer and you walk away." Teddy sets up the meeting, then does some fancy dancing, and gets Keith out on bail.'

'So who was he going to finger?'

'I don't know. Teddy does, presumably, but he and Keith weren't talking to anyone until Keith had those immunity papers in front of him. And Teddy certainly wasn't going to violate that kind of confidence with me.'

'So you think the person who killed Marovich tried to have Teddy murdered to send a message to Keith?' It sounded pretty dubious.

'It's a theory. It's more than I should have told you and more than Teddy should have told me. And the key points in that little bedtime story are covered by attorney-client privilege. The privilege belongs to the client, not the attorney, so it doesn't matter that Teddy violated it. You'd have to get Keith's permission to reveal any of what I just told you to the police.'

'I know about attorney-client privilege,' I told her.

She didn't acknowledge the edge in my voice. 'But to get Keith's permission you'd have to find him, and that almost certainly means dealing with his family. They might even be hiding him. Teddy hates dealing with those people. He had some way to reach Keith before all this came to a head, but I doubt he wrote it down.'

Something clicked in my brain. 'You were going to turn this place upside down looking for a phone number,' I said.

Her voice came out hoarse. 'Like I said, I doubt he wrote it down. Doesn't mean I can't look.'

'It just seems far-fetched to me.'

'Fine.' She downed the rest of her drink. 'You tell me what happened.' And then she was crying, sloppy Jeanie crying into the dregs of her martini. She wiped her eyes. 'I just had to think of a reason to come up to the house tonight, to be here. I thought it would make me feel better, but it doesn't. It makes me feel miserable. God, Leo, I don't think I can stay a minute longer.' She put her hand on mine and said woozily, 'Are you sober?'

'Sure,' I lied.

'Bring the gin.' She went back to the master bedroom

and closed the door behind her. Then I heard the bathroom door shut.

When Jeanie came out a moment later she'd washed her face and pulled her hair back into a ponytail, but her eyes were still teary. With a laugh she held her keys in front of her face, and when I reached for them she pulled them behind her back and kissed me again, this time on the cheek. 'You're sweet,' she said. 'You've always been sweet to me.'

I grabbed the keys and put a hand behind her back to steady her, but with a toss of her head she stepped away. I turned off the lights and checked the sliding glass door, but I didn't see any immediate sign of what she might have been doing in the bedroom, if she'd taken the opportunity to look for something. She grabbed her glass, tucking the gin bottle under her arm, and we went out to her car. I was grateful to see that she drove a Volvo now. I figured my chances of getting pulled over in the Volvo were a lot lower than they would have been in the little Lexus she used to drive.

'Where am I taking you? Home?'

'No, God. I'm not ready to go home. Just drive. Head up Pinehurst.' She poured more gin into her glass.

At Pinehurst I turned right, heading up the valley. The towering redwoods gave way to intimate crookings of moss-hung oak and laurel as the hillsides steepened and drew closer to the road. The road made a switchback, the headlights shining on a crumbling rock face, then into the tops of the trees on the mountainside beneath the road.

A last steep rise caused the Volvo's engine to race; then we crested the hill and turned left onto Skyline Boulevard. On the downhill side of the road only the garages of the houses were visible; the rest of the houses were beneath road level on the steep slope. Above the garages the lights of Berkeley and north Oakland glimmered. I thought wistfully of cycling. It would probably be a long time before I pedaled this route again.

I pulled over on the next curve to take in the view. The fog had enveloped San Francisco. Above its roiled ceiling, which seemed to have more definite substance than the water below, the devil-horned prong of Sutro Tower and the tip of the Transamerica Pyramid were visible. The Bay Bridge emerged from the fog like a sleeper's outflung leg. Nearer but startlingly far beneath us, Oakland's shabbiness was partly redeemed by height and distance. At the port near the bridge terminus, shipping cranes stood like vigilant sentinels, bathed in yellow orange light.

Beside me Jeanie meditatively drank.

'What were you looking for in the bedroom?' I asked.

Her reply came after a long delay. 'I wasn't looking for anything.'

'Everyone in this case seems to be looking for something. Everyone except me.'

I could have pushed harder, but I didn't want to tell

her about my confrontation with Car, or Teddy's letter and how I'd agonized over mailing it, or the women at the residence hotel.

'I wonder if you've seen this.' From my pocket I took out the copy of the hand-drawn map I'd found in the Santorez file.

Her shoulders jerked as she took it, an involuntary movement between a shudder and a shrug. 'So this is your theory, huh? This loser bides his time for four years waiting for his opportunity, then shoots Teddy in about the most public way you could imagine?'

'It's worth checking out, don't you think?'

'Car checked it out four years ago. The guy got all this information from public records. He's just a loser, one of these rent-a-cop types with an off-the-lot Crown Vic tooled up at Radio Shack. What Car did is he started following the guy, spying on him, sending little love notes detailing his personal movements. Then he paid him a visit. Car is very, very good at having difficult conversations with difficult people.'

'How'd Teddy hook up with Car, anyway?'

'I don't know,' she said, instantly withdrawing. 'Found him in the phone book, I guess.'

Again I didn't push. I'd decided not to mention Car's theory about police involvement in the shooting. Something told me that even he didn't believe it.

With one last glance at San Francisco, the spires floating higher now on their pillow of clouds, I put the

Volvo into gear and slid noiselessly back onto Skyline. Beside me Jeanie gave a snort, then jerked awake. It was after midnight, and it would soon be too late for me to make it back on the BART. But Jeanie was in no shape to drive, and there was no question of leaving her at Teddy's. So I did the gentlemanly thing and drove her home to Walnut Creek.

We followed Skyline down through Joachin Miller Park to the Warren Freeway, which I took north to Highway 24 and the Caldecott Tunnel. I kept the cruise control at sixty-five and gripped the wheel with both hands, watching for CHP, trying to convince myself that my sweating nervousness was fear of being pulled over rather than that near kiss on top of the memory of that long-ago, completed kiss and my sorry history of wanting Jeanie. I couldn't relax until she fell asleep before the tunnel.

After that I turned my head every half mile or so to study her sleeping profile against the freeway lights. The younger me would have savored these moments as an opportunity for silent devotion. He would have been deep in fantasies about what might happen when we finally got to her house in Walnut Creek, what might have originally been possible if my brother hadn't found her first. What might be possible again now.

Don't think, Monkey Boy. Just drive.

Chapter Ten

I woke up at 5 a.m. on Jeanie's couch to the clatter of a pan of eggs dropping and her saying 'fuck damn' in the tone of someone who's failed to sober up gracefully. Her eyes were bloodshot, her face pale. She was dressed for the gym and looked about as hungover as anyone ever deserved to be.

'We can still make six a.m. rounds if you get your butt in the shower,' she said.

Once again I drove, battling the early commute while Jeanie sat with her eyes slitted, her face mashed against the window. We arrived at the hospital at six and were in Teddy's room just ahead of the chief neurotrauma specialist, Dr Gottlieb, and his flock of four residents, among them the doctors who'd spoken to me in the ER.

After introducing himself and the residents to Jeanie and me, Dr Gottlieb quizzed Dr Singh on the minutest aspects of my brother's condition, forcing him to recite Teddy's roster of blood chemistry and vital signs and to conduct a Glasgow test, which involved poking a pin under Teddy's fingernail and shouting in his ear. Teddy scored a six out of fifteen, according to Singh, fifteen being full consciousness. From what I could see, my brother didn't react at all.

Dr Gottlieb asked us to leave the room while they changed the dressings on the wound.

In the waiting area Jeanie sat with her elbows propped on her knees, her palms against her brow, her hair hanging in front of her face.

'This is really happening, isn't it,' she finally said from underneath the curtain of her hair.

I nodded, feeling thick-headed but not too bad, considering. I eased back against the wall and closed my eyes.

When I opened them Jeanie was looking up at me. 'You're wrong, what you said last night. No matter how bad it was, he'd want to go on fighting.'

She seemed to think that I wanted Teddy to die and that I wanted that because it would be inconvenient for me if he lived, because I would have to be there for him in ways that would humiliate him and me. I was too wounded to respond.

The doctors emerged from the room. We made to stand, but Gottlieb sent on the four residents and came to sit with us. Leaning forward with his elbows on his knees, he looked at us in turn. 'It's a miracle he's made it this far,' he said. 'Even so, the prognosis is grim. He's in a very deep coma. There's brain stem activity, meaning that he could theoretically recover to breathe on his own. That's the good news. The bad news is that a recovery of any kind isn't likely. After a head wound like this, people usually don't wake up.'

He'd said what I expected to hear. So why did I feel an abyss yawning before me? It hadn't been real to me until now, I realized. Some part of me had expected a reprieve, as if some doctor would snap his fingers and we'd all wake up.

This one parted his hands in sympathy. His movements were gentle and deliberate. 'We have a hospice here that provides support for people in your situation. Eventually, if his situation doesn't change – and this is just to warn you, not to push you toward any kind of premature decision – we will need to ask you whether you want to continue life support, hydration, and the feeding tube. Right now I have to ask whether he had a living will, some kind of document expressing his wishes for an end-of-life situation, a situation where he wouldn't be able to make these kinds of decisions for himself?'

Jeanie shook her head. 'When we were married he refused even to draw up a last will and testament. That's the equivalent of a doctor smoking three packs a day. Lawyers are supposed to take care of those kinds of things, but Teddy hated the thought of dying so much he refused even to consider making the most basic plans.'

'These issues can be very delicate. I can promise you

that if and when we come to believe that further efforts to preserve his life would be futile, we will tell you. Ultimately, however, the actual decision to continue or discontinue life support is the family's. And I want to emphasize again that we're still quite some way from having that discussion.'

I spoke up for the first time: 'My decision, in other words.'

The doctor nodded reluctantly. 'Yes, I suppose it would be yours.'

A high color had come into Jeanie's cheeks.

'What if he does come out of it?' I asked. 'Is he going to be a vegetable? Could he ever practice law?'

Doctor Gottlieb nodded, back on what he undoubtedly considered less treacherous ground. 'Generally speaking, anyone surviving a cranial injury of this magnitude should expect to contend with some degree of permanent disability. With a frontal lobe injury, especially, there can be a huge range of impairments. You should expect memory problems, certainly, both short- and long-term, and cognitive difficulty, usually involving problem solving and planning and initiating actions. Depending on what part of the frontal lobe is injured you may see changes in personality such as pseudopsychopathic behavior, resulting from injury to the brain's inhibition centers, or pseudodepressive conditions. And there is often physical impairment, sometimes localized to one side of the body, ranging from full paralysis down to loss of fine motor skills. Again, a very wide and often unpredictable range.

'We won't have any idea, really, until he wakes up. If and when. And if he does wake up, he won't be a vegetable. There will be something there. He may improve dramatically in a few months, or he may come to a plateau and sort of tail off. As for practicing law – I won't tell you it's impossible, but it would be the most miraculous recovery from this type of injury I've ever seen. With these patients, it's considered excellent progress if they're eventually able to dress themselves, cook breakfast without lighting the house on fire, that sort of thing.'

'Sounds like a great life.'

Gottlieb shrugged. 'Relationships continue, even though people change. They find meaning in unexpected places. We're getting pretty far ahead of ourselves, but if you'd like to educate yourselves, I can make some calls, get you in to visit our inpatient rehabilitation center here at the hospital, maybe also one of the residential rehabilitation centers people usually transition to for six months to a year after they're well enough to leave the hospital.'

'I'd like that,' Jeanie said. 'It's very important to me to be able to envision what kind of life Teddy might have.'

I didn't want any part of that scene. I wanted to find the person who'd done this to Teddy, and I wanted to hurt him.

'I'll arrange it,' he told her.

'Thank you. Here's my card.'

He pocketed it and stood. 'I'll let you know when I've got it set up. I'm sure we'll be seeing a lot of each other.' He glanced uncertainly but with kindness at me, then first shook Jeanie's hand, then mine. 'Take care of yourselves. Of each other. You've got a long road ahead.'

'One more question, Doctor,' I said. 'If Teddy does wake up, could he identify the person who shot him?'

'Usually people are left with no memory of the injury-causing event,' he told me. 'I wouldn't hold out too much hope, though anything's possible.'

When he'd gone we sat in silence.

'It's not your decision,' Jeanie finally said. 'It's our decision. I don't care if that's the law or not. That's how it is.'

'We're getting ahead of ourselves.'

'Leo.' Her voice was sharp. 'Don't do this.'

I leaned against the wall again, grimacing with the agony of this discussion, the idea of it. 'We'll decide together,' I conceded. 'But I'm not going to let him be a vegetable.'

'No one's talking about that,' Jeanie snapped.

I glanced at my watch. It was seven thirty. 'Are you going into work?'

She shook her head. 'If I go into the office I'll only get mired. I came back from Mendocino early to be with Teddy, so I guess I'll just stay.'

It made me feel better to be leaving, knowing that Jeanie would be here. I could see by the disappointment in her eyes that she already knew some excuse was coming, but I was eager to be gone. I glanced at my watch again. 'I should probably get home and put on a suit in case this jury comes back today.'

'Go,' she said. 'Put on your suit and come back.'

'I thought I might keep reading through the files. Someone has to be working on this.'

'The police are working on it. Don't you think you should be here?'

'This Detective Anderson, I don't trust him. Someone who cares about Teddy needs to be out there, trying to find the person who did this. I think that's what he'd want me to be doing right now.'

I was halfway down the hall before I remembered. I turned back. 'By the way, do you know anyone named Martha or Chris?'

I went home, changed back into my suit, drank some more coffee, then walked over to the office. The phone was ringing as I arrived. Tanya wasn't there to pick it up. The call went to voice mail. I saw that there were fourteen new messages. Tanya must have been right, I thought with a sinking heart. The police must be out rounding up Teddy's clients from the list I'd faxed to Anderson.

I called the court to check in. Judge Iris's clerk

answered and told me breathlessly that they were looking for me, that they'd been calling Teddy's office, that they were getting ready to go ahead without me.

My heart stopped, then beat again. Not a verdict already, I hoped. I took a deep breath. 'Did you try calling my cell phone?'

'The jury has a question,' she said instead of answering. 'They came back with it first thing this morning.'

I tried to ask again why she hadn't tried to get ahold of me, but she cut me off and gave me an earful. I was supposed to check in with the court every morning at nine thirty while the jury was out, and I had to be within fifteen minutes of the courtroom at all times. The judge and prosecutor were waiting for me now. They could proceed in my absence, if I was willing. I almost said yes, because I had just pulled Keith Locke's file and wanted to look through it. Then I thought of the look in Melanie's eyes when she rose to make her rebuttal to my closing argument.

As I was locking the door on my way out the phone began ringing once more. I let it ring.

The sun made my eyeballs feel like they were popping out. I kept glancing over my shoulder for a cab as I walked up Sixth Street, earning myself a crick in the neck, but there weren't any. No surprise in this part of town, or in any part of San Francisco, really.

I arrived at Judge Iris's courtroom sweating and disheveled. The deputies had brought in Ellis, who sat shackled all alone at the defense table. He was still in his jail uniform.

Judge Iris was looking right at me when I came in. Apparently she'd been sitting for some time staring at the unopened doors, like a terrier at a squirrel hole.

She started speaking before I'd reached the defense table, her eyes fixed on my forehead. 'You'd better have a good reason for keeping us waiting, Mr Maxwell, but that doesn't mean I have any desire to hear it. You're aware of my fifteen-minute rule. There are no excuses for tardiness in my courtroom. I've brought your client here to witness the consequences.'

She ordered the court clerk to enter a finding of civil contempt, which carried with it a fine of a thousand dollars.

I tried to persuade myself that her heart wasn't in it, that what she really wanted to do was invite me back into her chambers, sit me down, serve me tea in slender-handled cups, and listen to all my troubles. She had her reputation to consider, though.

I hadn't said a word and didn't intend to. I felt Melanie's eyes on me but I didn't turn.

Judge Iris went on with cheerful relief, evidently feeling refreshed now that she'd managed to bleed me. 'All right, now down to business. It's ten fourteen a.m., and the jury has submitted a question form.'

Ellis made a soft clucking sound with his tongue. 'They took me away from my program,' he whispered.

'Catch the rerun.'

Judge Iris glanced at us sternly. I allowed myself a sigh and bowed my head.

She went on: 'The question reads, "If we decide that one side has committed perjury, does that mean that the other side automatically wins?"' She looked up toward the DA's table, her eyebrows raised, as if ready to defer to Melanie.

'The way I see it, there's only one way you can answer a question like that,' Melanie said. 'I think the only thing you can do is refer them to the jury instructions you've already given. One-oh-five and two-two-six are right on point. "If you decide that a witness deliberately lied about something significant in this case, you should consider not believing anything that witness says."'

'Counsel?'

'It sounds to me like they've taken two-two-six to heart already, Judge,' I said. 'The jury's question goes much more directly to the burden of proof and the presumption of innocence. I don't know which witness they're referring to, whether it's the state's witness or the defense's, but their question doesn't make any distinction between perjury by a prosecution witness and perjury by a defense witness. Given the state's burden of proof, it matters very much which side the jury believes committed perjury, and I think Your Honor should make that clear. My fear is that they're asking whether in a case of suspected perjury they can disregard the state's burden of proof and find against the defense simply as a matter of principle. I think you should reinstruct the jury that the state has the burden of proving its case beyond a reasonable doubt, and if the state fails to do so, Mr Bradley is entitled to an acquittal.'

'So the state would have me refer them to one-oh-five, and the defense would point them to two-two-zero.' Judge Iris had her big green California Criminal Jury Instructions book out and was flipping from one instruction to the other. 'Well, I'm not going to do either. The jurors have been instructed, and I'll just tell them to refer to the instructions they've already been given. I'm not going to point them toward one instruction or the other.'

She closed the book and looked up. 'Anything else?' Her eyes went to Melanie.

Melanie rose. 'Yes, Your Honor. The state would like to renew its motion for a mistrial. I've just been informed by a member of my office that the San Francisco Police Department and the DA's office were this week intending to seek a grand jury indictment against Teddy Maxwell for subornation of perjury and manufacturing of evidence in numerous cases stretching back over the past decade. After the recent tragedy, the DA's office will likely postpone those plans. Given the seriousness of these allegations, however, the state believes that a mistrial is warranted in any case that Mr Maxwell appeared in as counsel while this investigation was under way.'

'You have no specific evidence of misconduct in this case, I take it.'

'Your Honor, I have a draft copy of the investigative report prepared by the district attorney's office.'

I gazed at her with disbelief as she walked around the DA's table and dropped my copy on the defense table before me, ignoring my outstretched hand.

I stood looking down at it, unwilling to touch it. I'd heard the rumors before, of course, but never on this scale. I knew there was no justification for a mistrial. There was no proof that Sharla had lied or that Teddy knew it if she had. Ellis sat absolutely silent, absolutely still beside me. I could feel the intense focus of his attention.

'I don't see how this document has anything to do with this case,' I said.

'Me neither,' the judge said, surprising me. She addressed Melanie: 'You've made your record.'

Judge Iris stepped down from the bench without another word and without looking at Melanie, who stood just as prim and proper as ever at the prosecution table, her embarrassment revealed only by the color of her cheeks. She had finally gone too far.

Beside me Ellis remained quiet. I'd meant to give him a pep talk before I let the deputies take him back down to holding, but as I gathered up my belongings I couldn't bring myself to speak to him. If Sharla had lied, Ellis had probably put her up to it.

'I sure as hell hope Sharla told the truth up there,' I said low enough not to be overheard.

'You know she did.'

'She better have.' It wasn't him I was angry with. I could only be disappointed with Ellis, disgusted with him, even, but I couldn't be angry.

Ellis signaled that he was ready to go. 'If I were you, Monkey Boy, I wouldn't think too hard on it.' He didn't meet my eyes. The deputy handcuffed him and led him out.

Melanie was still standing at the prosecutor's table. I picked up my copy of the investigative report and walked toward her, stopping when I was a few feet away. When she looked up, I threw it at her face. The pages fluttered, spread, and missed their mark, sailing over the railing into the gallery. Melanie opened her mouth but didn't make a sound.

For anyone keeping score, that was a criminal act. Third-degree assault.

'Your brother was as big a criminal as any of his clients,' she said when I turned to walk out of the court-room. 'Suborning perjury is just the tip of the iceberg, from what I hear.'

I thought better of leaving the investigative report lying around for anyone to find, and I scooped it up as I passed the spot where it had fallen.

Melanie went on: 'You all pretend that you're serving the Constitution, but in reality you're just in it for the thrill of helping criminals break the law.'

I was too furious to respond. It was not something I normally would have done, throwing that document at her. It wasn't typical behavior.

In the hallway I thought about that argument I'd overheard between Teddy and Car. Could I have missed the fact that evidence was being manufactured under my nose? *You have to fix this*, Teddy had said. Was it that he didn't think Sharla's testimony would hold up?

If Teddy had been crooked, he must have assumed I was naive enough not to catch wind of what was going on. This realization made me as angry as anything, if it was true.

I went downstairs to the courthouse café for a much-needed coffee and croissant, which I carried out to City Hall Plaza. Straddling a concrete bench, I flipped through the Keith Locke file, holding my head to one side to avoid scattering crumbs over the pages. I skimmed the patrol officer's account of spotting a suspicious vehicle in a lot near Candlestick and coming upon Keith Locke trying to maneuver the professor's body into the Dumpster, then spotlighting him and arresting him without incident.

The official cause of death was listed as asphyxiation due to strangulation from a cord that had been wrapped around his neck. The autopsy file confirmed what the newspapers had reported, that before his death Marovich appeared to have been sexually tortured. Bruises at his

wrists and ankles showed he'd been bound. There was a picture that looked like it came from a book jacket: a man in his thirties, well built, with a broad smile. As part of his workup for the case Teddy had compiled a profile of the victim, including a list of academic publications and a CV. The professor's credits included a paper on the local S-and-M community and another on the illegal sex trade. On his CV Marovich indicated that his current research was an investigative report examining San Francisco's role in the international sex trafficking market.

A shadow fell across the file folder, and I looked up to see Detective Anderson. He stood with his arms folded and a grin on his face, as if we were friends or neighbors running into each other on the wrong side of town. I closed the folder and tucked it under my arm.

'You fucked up my crime scene,' he said without altering his grin. 'You were in your brother's house.'

'So you really are a detective.' I threw the heel of my croissant to the pigeons, who fell on it with a flurry of dipping heads and slapping wings. 'I was surprised you hadn't been there yet.'

'Every investigation has its priorities.'

I thought of the phone messages on Teddy's voice mail. 'You mean you're harassing my brother's former clients and dragging them into jail on flimsy pretexts.' The phone was probably ringing again as we spoke, the mailbox filling up if it wasn't filled already.

'I'm on my way to court to testify in another case. I just saw you sitting here and I thought, Hey, maybe I should come over and apologize for the way I acted the other day. I won't take up any more of your time.'

'Why apologize?'

'Because a murder victim is a murder victim is a murder victim.'

'He's not dead yet. In any case, apology accepted. Any developments?'

'Look, no more bullshit. You and I both know what your brother's game was.'

'I don't. I really don't.' I gazed over his shoulder toward the gold dome of city hall.

'You know,' he repeated. 'You've got it right there beside you.' He nodded down at the investigative report from the DA's office. 'And so do I, and so does everyone who knows anything in this town. Your brother bought witnesses, bribed jurors, fabricated evidence. Not just in one case, but in a lot of them. He was about as crooked as a lawyer can be, and devious as hell, so we've never managed to catch him at it. He and that investigator of his have been pulling this shit for years, and it's only recently that the DA's office has started to get on top of them.'

I could only go on gazing over his shoulder. 'You actually believe this nonsense?'

'What I believe doesn't matter. The question is, did your brother's clients believe it? Way I see it, once a lawyer gets a reputation like that – and sure as shit your brother had it even if he was clean as a whistle – he better understand that every new client is going to expect that A-one service. And when they don't get it, pow.' He made a gun of his thumb and forefinger and shot it off toward the Asian Art Museum.

'These allegations were bullshit when the DA filed that state bar complaint after the Santorez case, and they're bullshit now.' I pulled out my wallet and unfolded the copy of the hand-drawn map I'd showed Jeanie last night. 'You must have seen this. In a file of death threats in the Santorez folder.'

The detective didn't even look at the map. 'This nut job didn't shoot your brother. It was a hit. That pretty much rules out anyone who isn't in the game. And guess what?' He flicked the creased copy with his index finger. 'This guy wasn't.'

'You don't think it's worth checking out?'

'Not when this department's refusing overtime. We'll find the killer on the client list, you'll see. Some disgruntled player who thought he should be getting a whole lot more for his money.' The detective started to walk away as if I'd been wasting his time.

'Detective, you don't really think that my brother could have gotten away with a scheme like that, do you?'

He stopped. 'Kid, it should be pretty obvious by now that he didn't get away with it.'

I sipped my coffee, watching the pigeons fight over the stub of croissant that remained. One carried it about fifteen feet, but none of them could manage to swallow it. One bird would pick it up, then drop it, and the others would flock around again.

I couldn't avoid it any longer, I realized. I was going to have to listen to those phone messages.

Chapter Eleven

It was nearly one o'clock. I had a headache and my stomach felt queasy. As I walked, I thought about what Melanie had said to me. I kept at a simmer for six blocks before I was able to admit to myself that she was right, at least partially. When you got down to it, all the trial lawyers I knew – all the good ones – were in it not for the righteous purpose of defending the Constitution but for the power a skilled lawyer has over a hostile witness, the power to make a person say the opposite of what he intends, the power to sway jurors' minds, the thrill of being the center of attention. He's somewhere between the quarterback who throws the winning pass, the stage actor with an audience hanging on every word, and the gambler who puts his chips on red. The deadly serious game of it is what my brother loved, and I'd caught the bug from him.

I heard the phone ringing in the empty office as I got off the elevator. The ringing stopped as I put my key in the door. I went in, shrugged off my jacket, and lay down on the couch. I closed my eyes, willing the world to shrink until there was nothing left but my head on the cushion. In the other room the phone resumed its ringing. My eyes snapped open.

I rose, went into the other room, put on Tanya's headset and hit ANSWER. 'Lawyer's office.'

'Teddy, thank God. They taking me for a ride.' The man let out an incredulous laugh. 'They telling me you was dead. Everybody been saying it.'

'Teddy was shot two days ago. He's not dead, but he's not going to be making any court appearances anytime soon, either. This is his brother, Leo.'

There was a pause. I could hear him breathing deep and slow through his mouth.

'Are you a client?' I asked.

He let out a held breath. 'They got me in the parking lot after work, right in front of my boss. Been asking all sorts of questions.'

'Tell them you won't speak without your lawyer present. Tell them you want a public defender.'

'Nah, man, I don't want no public pretender.'

'Let me take down your name and jail number.'

I wrote down the caller's information. Alan Davis. I promised to call a lawyer I knew at the public defender's office and explain the situation. There were likely a whole lot of other clients of Teddy's picked up. 'They're looking for someone to take down for what happened to Teddy. Whatever you do, don't talk to anyone, don't trust anyone.' The San Francisco police were not above building a case on the bartered lies of a jailhouse snitch.

I wished him good luck and cut off the call, then went to the file cabinets, found his file, and opened it to the summary sheet: a murder case from five years back, with an assortment of lesser included charges, and a more recent burglary conviction. I paged through the trial binder to the copy of the verdict form, where Teddy had neatly checked 'Not Guilty' four times.

Returning to the chair, I accessed the voice-mail system. There were thirty-two new messages, and I listened to them all. It took more than an hour. Some had left names, some hadn't. Occasionally there was just breathing followed by a click. Others were rambling monologues. White voices, black voices, Asian voices, Hispanic voices, men and women, educated and not, straight and gay, the whole human spectrum. Some of the callers were in custody; some had been questioned; others had found out about the shooting in the paper or on TV. All knew what had happened but hadn't believed it and felt compelled to call. I wrote down each name along with any details provided. The line rang once more while I was working. I let it go to voice mail.

When I had finished listening, I went to the cabinets and started pulling files. I doubted that anyone connected with Teddy's killing would have called the office; on the other hand, maybe the killers had calculated I'd make precisely this assumption. For lack of a better system, I sorted the files I pulled according to the type of crime involved: crimes of passion, crimes of violence, sexual assault and domestic violence, white-collar, and property crimes. There was a whole stack of prostitution cases. Teddy had started out representing hookers, and so-called B cases remained a mainstay of the practice.

I scanned the files for names on my list. My arms were full as I flipped through the L-M-N drawer, and I almost missed it. Then I saw the name Lawrence Maxwell on a much-handled, begrimed, and faded series of Redweld folders. They took up more than half the drawer.

My father was in prison for murdering my mother. Knowing our background, most people would find it hard to believe that Teddy and I would devote our lives to defending people accused of crimes. To an outsider my brother and I must have seemed natural-born prosecutors.

I bent down to set a stack of files on the floor. My hands shook.

There is a scene in every Hollywood depiction of domestic abuse where the elder son jumps between the father and the mother and stops what is happening, but in real life I doubt it happens more than one time in a dozen. Over the summer I'd gotten the uneasy feeling that Teddy despised all victims and that this moral cauterization served him well in his work. Anyone inquiring into root causes would have to conclude that such a failure of empathy must have been born in the experience of watching our mother's bullying at our father's hands.

From the files it was obvious that they'd been in close contact, that Teddy had visited him at San Quentin numerous times over the last decade. Perhaps he'd meant to spare me by hiding his legal work on our father's behalf. In retrospect, I ought to have guessed.

The entire record of our father's trial was before me, three Redweld folders filled with transcripts, evidence logs, and docket sheets. And pictures. My God, pictures.

I didn't mean to look at them – I didn't look at them – but even flipping through them in a hurry I couldn't help glimpsing a particular piece of scroll-worked wainscoting above the threshold between the hall and the foyer of the Sunset District house where we'd lived when we were still a family. It was at the very top left-hand edge of a photograph taken by a police photographer who'd been standing at the back corner of our living room, looking toward the front door. I willed myself to see nothing, and then I was past the photographs and back onto safer ground, but it was too late: I might as well have looked at them. The glimpse of wainscoting was enough to bring it all flooding back, maybe worse than if I'd actually looked at the pictures of Caroline's body laid out on the floor where my father had finally managed to beat the life out of her, and where I would find her one afternoon when I came home from school.

Save that. Leave it for later. It does no good to describe these things, no more good than it would have done me to look at those pictures or not to look at them, once I knew they existed.

I flipped through the other folders. Almost as soon as Teddy got his California bar number he'd taken over our father's appeals, which were voluminous. My father had never stopped protesting his innocence. Teddy had also filed a civil rights lawsuit after Lawrence lost his left eye to an infection that the prison medical system had left untreated. In that case he'd negotiated a settlement for forty thousand dollars. There was a new-looking folder marked 'notes for habeas corpus petition'.

I don't know how long I'd been sitting there with the files spread out before me when the shock gave way to anger. My hands shook; my veins filled with poison. I might have been fifteen again, squinting at microfilm, stewing in rage, imagining how it might feel to kill my father, to beat him to death the way he'd beaten Caroline. If I'd learned of my brother's efforts on Lawrence's behalf while he was still whole in body and mind, Teddy could at least have tried to justify himself, explaining his reasons for what he did.

If he even felt he owed me an explanation, that is. I remembered the letter that Car had tried to hide, the one Teddy had left in the safe to be mailed in case of his incapacitation or death. I still couldn't imagine what it said, and I felt even more of a coward for not opening it.

I should have been left a letter. I was the one who deserved an explanation, not our father.

I had no desire to look at the original trial record, with its promise of a lurid trip into the abscess at the center of my life. I shut that file and put it in a drawer of Tanya's desk. That left the civil rights case and the folder labeled 'notes for habeas corpus petition'. I put the first aside, since that old, closed civil case was unlikely to be relevant to what had happened.

Paging through Teddy's handwritten notes, I understood that he intended his argument to rest on the idea that the DA had unlawfully withheld evidence suggesting that someone else might have killed our mother. Teddy had no definite proof of our father's innocence, but his argument raised the specter that the police had arrested, the DA had prosecuted, and the jury had convicted the wrong man.

I had to throw down the brief and pace the office for several minutes until I was able to see what was in front of me again. Cheap defense-lawyer bullshit was all it was, and for a quarter of an hour I shared the visceral, principled contempt that a champion of justice like Melanie had acquired for Teddy and all the rest of us, the whole sordid guild.

At last I was calm enough to return to the file. Teddy's argument for reopening the case was that new evidence had come to light. There was an unsigned draft of an affidavit in Teddy's handwriting indicating that the affiant had once worked in the San Francisco Police Department property room and that, according to old records, there had once been evidence that another man had been in the apartment with my mother the day of her murder – fingerprints on a beer bottle, blood spatters on the wall, and semen from our mother's body – but the evidence had either been lost, destroyed, or withheld. There was another affidavit from Teddy stating that none of the exculpatory evidence had come to light at trial or had ever been disclosed to the defense.

Again I had to get up from the desk. Everything here stank, like Sharla's testimony in Ellis's trial. The problem was not that Teddy had drafted the affidavit – lawyers regularly did so, but rarely before they knew the name of the affiant.

My head was reeling. I couldn't think straight.

Glancing up, I saw that it was just after four o'clock, which meant that Ellis's jury was being sent home for the weekend. I felt a shock of surprise, followed by elation. The jurors had not reached a verdict, or the court would have called. If they couldn't decide on a verdict before the weekend, there was a good chance they wouldn't be able to reach one at all.

More pertinent, the end of court hours meant that I was free to go wherever I wanted without having to worry about being held in contempt again for breaking Judge Iris's fifteen-minute rule.

Making a quick decision, I grabbed the Keith Locke

file from the briefcase I'd been carrying earlier. There was a contacts sheet with a home phone number for Greta and Gerald Locke. I picked up the phone and dialed.

The phone rang twice; then a woman with an African immigrant's accent answered. 'Yes?'

'I'd like to speak with Mrs Locke, please. Tell her that Mr Teddy Maxwell is calling.'

I don't know why I said that, except that I wanted to hear what that name would do to the mother of Teddy's wayward client.

After a moment a composed voice said, 'Teddy Maxwell was shot Wednesday morning. Now please tell me who you are and what your business is.'

'I see. Your maid must have caught the wrong name. This is Leo Maxwell calling. Teddy is my brother. I'm over here at the office trying to get his affairs in order. You see, I'll probably be taking over his practice, at least until he's well enough to return to work.' It was the first time I'd spoken the idea out loud. 'I hope you don't mind me just picking up the phone.'

'I suppose whether I mind or not will depend on the reason for your call, now, won't it?'

It threw me that she didn't offer even perfunctory condolences. She might have been talking to a plumbing contractor about some shoddy tile work that was going to have to be ripped out and done over – at the plumber's expense, of course.

'What reason could I give that wouldn't be offensive to you? Maybe we should start there.'

'I'm sorry, Mr Maxwell. I'm afraid I don't have time to play twenty questions.'

'Fair enough. I'd like to have a few words with you about your son. This evening, if possible. I can make it brief. If you'd rather not talk to me, I'll have to go to the police.'

'It isn't possible. We're having guests for drinks before the opera.'

'Bad timing for both of us. I was planning to go to the opera this evening myself,' I lied. 'We could speak at intermission. I'll buy you a glass of champagne, and we'll drink a toast to your boy Keith and all his accomplishments. I've heard great things about their new *Faust*. The soprano is supposed to be marvelous. Don't worry, you won't have to look for me. I'll find you.'

'Are you out of your mind?'

I took satisfaction in having cracked her composure. It had not proved nearly as difficult as I'd guessed. The desperate edge in her voice made her seem human. I liked her a little better for it.

'I'll be there in thirty minutes, then. I hope you'll be able to fit me into your schedule.'

I hung up the phone without waiting to hear her response. I remained sitting at the desk for a moment, nodding to myself. That was how it was done, I thought.

That was how to handle a situation where you couldn't take no for an answer.

Then I realized how stupid I'd been to say thirty minutes. It might take me that long just to find a cab.

Chapter Twelve

I was lucky. In ten minutes I was able to hail a cab, and it carried me away from downtown traffic and through the Geary tunnel without a single red light. I was at the address in thirty-five minutes after hanging up the phone.

The Lockes lived in Presidio Terrace, built in the aftermath of the 1906 earthquake and marketed then as San Francisco's only all-white neighborhood, with only one entrance, a pair of granite gateposts at the intersection of Presidio Terrace and Arguello Boulevard. Beyond those, Presidio Terrace makes an oval. The properties at the center of the oval back onto one another, while those on the outer ring turn their backs on the city. The Tudor and mission revival and Beaux-Arts houses wear hedges like insignias. On both sides of the street mature palm trees frame the California sky. The roses had been pruned for the winter. Not a blade of grass was out of line.

Oddly, the place made me think of Teddy's neighborhood across the bay in Canyon, that enclave beneath the redwoods, as exclusive in its own way as this one. The two neighborhoods probably had more in common than their residents thought.

The Lockes owned a relatively modest Tudor revival, a long lodgelike place with mansard windows, a slate roof, and three chimneys. It was probably worth only six million. To fit a house that size onto the lot the builder had been forced to put it sideways. From the street I had to proceed up a long sidewalk guarded by ankle-high hedges to reach the front door.

I don't hold anything against rich people. I am as guilty as anyone else of envying them. I'd love nothing more than a stable of bikes to ride and all the time in the world to ride them. I have this dream of traveling again the way I did after high school, seeing the world from the saddle.

The door was opened by the same woman who'd answered the phone. I guessed she was Nigerian. She wore a sleek gray business suit, and her hair was cut attractively short. 'Mr Maxwell? Mrs Locke is expecting you. Please come this way.'

The two-story foyer was immaculate, with gleaming wood floors, a huge silver mirror, and a chest of drawers that looked pillaged from a French chateau. On the floor was a massive Afghan rug. A curving staircase led up to an open hallway on the second floor.

There were signs of human life. Mail and a few photographs occupied the top of the chest of drawers, and the door to a deep closet stood open, revealing rows of coats and boots. A dog leash hung on the knob. A heavy oak door to my left was closed, and in front of me one of a pair of double doors was ajar. Through the gap I made out the back of a cream-colored leather couch and beyond that a sunlit expanse of hardwood floor.

'What do you do here?' I asked, both because I was curious and because she was beautiful.

'I'm Mrs Locke's personal assistant.' She shot me a quick smile over her shoulder as she led me through an open door to our right. 'Chloe.' She wore no perfume. Perhaps Mrs Locke had a rule against it. Nevertheless she smelled wonderful. I wanted to ask her what kind of soap she used.

'You plan on doing that for the rest of your life?'

Another look, this time with a challenge in it. 'I'm starting a joint JD/MBA program at Stanford in the fall.'

That shut me up, but only for a second. 'Give me a call if you ever get interested in criminal law. Who knows, maybe you'll need a lawyer yourself.'

She palmed the card with devastating politeness, knocked once on a door at the end of the hallway, gave me another smile with nothing behind it, and left me waiting for the door to open.

After a second it did. 'Come in, Mr Maxwell. Let's make this quick, shall we? You said it was something about Keith. You mentioned the police.'

Greta Locke was nearly six feet tall. She had silver

white hair cut above her ears, a thin gray-eyed scholar's face with a sharp nose, and a rail-thin body that still looked young. She'd had her hair done but wasn't dressed yet for the evening. She wore a man's flannel shirt and tights. She went to the couch across from her desk and indicated a matching leather chair beside her. One wall was filled floor to ceiling with bookshelves. The other wall was taken up by pictures. Behind the desk a large dormer window let in evening light through a row of shrubs.

I studied the pictures from my chair, trying to pick out Keith Locke, but my eyes locked on another face: a broad-shouldered girl in a black bodysuit with a maroon S on her chest, posing with a large red- and white-bladed oar leaning in the crook of her shoulder. I felt a jolt run from the back of my scalp down to my heels, a physical memory of the shock I'd gotten yesterday evening. That was the girl who had Tasered me at the Seward.

I looked at Greta and saw the family resemblance. 'You have a daughter at Stanford?'

'I thought you came here to talk about my son.'

'You must be thrilled. I always wanted to go there. We couldn't afford it, but the main thing was I couldn't get in. I had a rough couple of years at the beginning of high school. I did two years at San Francisco City College, then transferred to Berkeley. I was pretty proud of that.'

'Stanford was always Christine's number one pick. They have a fine women's crew.'

'Rowing, huh? I was always more partial to cycling. They don't give scholarships to cyclists, unfortunately.'

'Christine was a merit scholar and the salutatorian of her class at Choate. She is a scholar first and an athlete second. I fully expect her to become a career academic. But I don't intend to discuss my daughter with you.'

'That's right. The fact is, I think Keith may be in danger.'

'You mean more than usual?' she asked, making an effort at a smile. It was then I saw something loosen behind her eyes, laying bare years and years of anxious days and sleepless nights. She blinked and it was gone, though her expression didn't change at all. It was like a person flipping on a light to get her bearings in a darkened room, then turning it off before the light could dazzle her eyes.

'I think so. I need to speak with him. I don't need to know where he's been hiding, but I'd like him to give me a call or preferably agree to meet me someplace he considers safe. Like I said, I'm taking over my brother's practice, and there are a lot of loose ends in Keith's case.'

'That doesn't sound like life or death to me, nor like anything that concerns the police.' She waited. She knew there was more. I suppose with Keith there always was. I couldn't help thinking of the story Jeanie had told me about Keith's first brush with the law, that oral-cop-on-a-minor charge at the bus stop early Christmas morning.

Thinking of that, and of her daughter with the Taser, I felt sorry for Greta.

I got up from my chair and went to the wall of pictures. 'If you're looking for Keith you won't find him,' she said. 'There came a point where I had to take all his pictures down. I keep one in my drawer.' She went behind her desk, took out a silver-framed photograph, and handed it to me. It was a portrait of a young man in a cap and gown, sitting on a grassy lawn in front of a venerable, ivy-covered academic building. 'He never actually graduated,' she said. 'He had this taken a few months after Choate kicked him out, once it became clear that we couldn't find another school to accept him. That was fourteen years ago. He still looks just the same, and he doesn't have a single degree.'

'There's always the GED.' Keith was tall, probably six three or four, with curly brown hair, a widow's peak accentuated by the graduation cap, broad cheeks, a wide mouth, and the long fingers of a pianist. He had a face that would nakedly display every change of emotion. Seeing the smirk on it, I understood that this was a man for whom the future and its consequences were trivial things, like debts he had no intention of paying.

'Yes, I hear they can earn degrees in prison now,' Greta said.

'Is that where you think your son belongs? Prison?'

She came back to the couch and sat down. 'You said Keith was in danger. If that's truly the case, I would prefer not to be kept in suspense. If not, I don't understand your purpose here.'

'My brother may have been shot to send Keith a message.'

'A message. What sort of message?'

'Keep your mouth shut about the dead man you were heaving into a Dumpster. Don't tell what you know, whatever that may be. Do prison time if you have to. That sort of thing.'

She folded her legs Indian-style and sat looking past me with an unreadable expression. 'So you believe some-one tried to murder your brother because of my son.'

I hadn't meant to put it that way, but there it was. 'I want the police to find the person who shot Teddy, and to help them I need to give them some details from Keith's case. Some of the things Keith told my brother are covered by attorney-client privilege, and I'd need Keith's permission before I could divulge them – before I could do so ethically, anyway. My brother must have some way of reaching him, but he didn't share it with me.'

'And you think I may have some way of contacting my son. Well, I don't. It's been over a year since I've seen him. I would probably turn him away if he showed up at the door.'

'Probably?'

She gave a shrug. 'He wouldn't come here. He knows better. He wouldn't risk running into his father.'

'I guess I was mistaken, then. I figured if anyone would know how to find him, his family would.' I hesitated. 'I thought you might be protecting him.'

'I wish I could protect him. I would pay just about anything if someone would tell me where he was. You see, when you called me, I had an idea that you might know.'

'He was making a deal with the DA to provide information about a homicide. Then, just before the shooting, he disappeared. He might be afraid for his life. I think I can tell you that much, if you don't know it already. But that's really all I know for sure.'

'Well, I can't help you with any of that.' She leaned forward. 'Maybe you can help me, though. I have to see Keith. I must speak with him.' Her voice wavered, and she tilted her chin defiantly. 'I need to touch him, to hold him. He's my son, my flesh and blood. If he needs help, I need to help him. I can't bear the idea of Keith going to prison. He wouldn't be able to bear it, and that means I wouldn't be able to bear it. If that makes me soft, I'm soft. But no child of mine deserves to be thrown away like some – some unwanted dog.' She was not soft at all. She was as hard and fierce as a mother bear defending her cub.

And yet she kept his picture in a drawer. I handed her the heavy frame, and she immediately laid it facedown on the couch. On balance I couldn't blame her, though I sensed that a woman of a different class, with less money and less power, would have long since been forced to accept that her son was lost to her. I found that I admired Greta Locke for refusing to accept this fact.

'If Keith becomes my client, I'll have to abide by his wishes. If he wants to see you, I'll try to make it happen.'

She jotted a number on a card. 'That's my personal cell phone. If you call the other number, Chloe will answer.'

She rose, and I understood that I was being told to depart. Casually she added, 'If you can convince him to see me, I'll pay you twenty thousand dollars.'

I was floored. 'Thanks, but I couldn't take your money. If Keith wants to pay me for my trouble, that's different, but I'd be working for him.'

She seemed to take this in stride, obviously not believing that I'd refuse the money when the time came. I wasn't sure I believed it, either. 'Where will you start looking?' she asked.

'I was going to ask you for advice.' The door opened as we reached it.

'I wouldn't know. Our son has lived his own life for the past fifteen years. Probably nearby, in the city or close to it. Keith always was a homebody. That's what he hated most about boarding school, being away from San Francisco. Even as a teenager he used to throw tantrums when it was time to head east for the start of term.'

'Then maybe you shouldn't have kept sending him.'

Her eyes slid past me and she gave a nod to Chloe.

'See you at the opera,' I said to the closing door.

I followed half a step behind Chloe, trying to think of something to say that might charm her. Voices suddenly filled the hall ahead of us, men's voices echoing in self-satisfied merriment, women's voices climbing to that pitch of laughter that fills a high-ceilinged room. Chloe put her hand on my arm, and we waited until they were muffled by a closing door.

'You ought to have been a harbor pilot,' I told Chloe as she released me and we walked on to the foyer.

That earned me a laugh. 'Does this look like a harbor to you? This is the ocean deep, my friend.' She seemed to reach the limit of banter required in the name of professional politeness. 'Dr Locke has asked to see you before you leave.'

'What about his guests?'

Instead of answering she inclined her head toward the door I'd noticed earlier, on the opposite side of the foyer from the hallway to Greta Locke's office. Chloe led me through it into a dining room with a highly polished table. The table was ringed by high-backed chairs and overhung by a very large cylindrical chandelier glittering with silver and glass. Through another set of double doors to my right I heard voices again. We walked through the dining room and down the back hall past the kitchen. I followed Chloe through a door into a book-lined den, from which another closed door gave onto the room where the party was.

168

'Dr Locke will be with you shortly,' she said and shut me in.

Everything was dark leather and heavy shag. The doors were padded on the inside with plush leather. A massive glass-topped desk was empty except for a blotter, a green-shaded brass reading lamp, and a heavy paperweight. One wall held modern medical texts. The other was divided between antique medical treatises and modern literature, hardcovers in pristine condition with dust jackets. They were first editions, I realized, taking one down.

I was still scanning the titles when the door opened and Gerald Locke came in. I dropped my hand reflexively when he entered. 'My passion,' he said, then added: 'Don't worry, you can touch them.' He had a broad unhandsome face with a large nose and ears. He shook my hand, pulled down a book, and showed me where a small child had scribbled all over the frontispiece in crayon. 'This is a first edition of Frank Norris's *McTeague*. See what a patient father I am? In a pristine state this book would be worth nine hundred dollars. I didn't even raise my voice.'

I could guess which child had done the scribbling. He poured us each a Scotch. The cut-glass tumbler that he handed me must have weighed half a pound. Setting his own drink aside, he perched on the edge of the desk and studied me with a frown.

Through the door I heard Greta Locke regaling her

guests, followed by another peal of general laughter. 'Let's cut to the chase.' Locke closed the book. 'When my son hired your brother, I made a number of inquiries. I came to understand that your brother is one of the dirtiest lawyers in this town, about as dirty as it's possible to be in San Francisco. I have a feeling Keith knew his reputation. I can guess what you told Greta, and I won't have you repeat it to me. Neither Keith nor his case had anything to do with what happened to your brother, and I won't have you coming into my home and making insinuations that amount to blackmail. With one call I could have you arrested for extortion.'

'Maybe, but the police would release me on ten thousand dollars bond, the case would never come to trial, and you would end up standing there holding your hat.' I set my glass on a shelf of first editions. If he was too good to drink with me, I wasn't about to wet my lips. 'I'm not after your money. Whether you like it or not, there's a strong possibility that someone tried to kill my brother to send a message to your son, to intimidate him into not talking to the DA. The police ought to be looking into that possibility, but I can't approach them until I have Keith's permission to disclose what I know.'

'You don't understand. You see, my son is a – a moral coward. Among other things.' A sheen of sweat had appeared on Gerald's face. He seized his Scotch glass and drank from it.

'Is that why you cut him off?'

'He cut us off, the way I see it. Not that it makes any difference. This latest charge – the dead professor in the sex club – well, I never imagined it would come to something like this. But I can't say I'm surprised, either. If Keith thinks that talking might get him killed, he won't talk. It's that simple.'

'Then they'll probably charge him with something once they catch up with him. In that case he'll need a lawyer.'

'You, I suppose.' He went around the desk for a refill and looked me up and down with distaste. 'Are you as – as effective as your brother?'

'If Teddy was crooked, I didn't know it, and I haven't seen any evidence of it. He won trials, and he made police officers look bad, and in the process he didn't make any friends in the district attorney's office. In other words, he did his job. He was very, very good at finding witnesses and evidence that other lawyers might not have found. Depending on your point of view that's just good old-fashioned investigation, or it's too good to be true. But whatever Teddy was, I'm straight. And I intend to take over his practice until he's well enough to come back to work. For as many of his old clients as will have me, anyway.'

'The hell you're straight. You're all crooks. They ought to charge you as accomplices after the fact.' He eyed me over his glass. 'You're taking on all his clients?'

'You don't think your son should have a lawyer? Or

mount a defense? You'd like him just to plead guilty to whatever the DA charges him with, maybe first-degree murder, and take the maximum?'

'You want my honest opinion?'

I didn't answer. It's better not to, when people ask stupid questions.

'I would sleep better at night if I knew my son was in prison for the rest of his life. It's almost certainly where he belongs.' He drank again and set the glass on the desk.

From the room beyond the door came more volleys of moneyed laughter.

'Is there any special reason you wanted to see me, Dr Locke?'

He struck the desk lightly with the bottom of his fist. 'Whatever my wife offered you to track down Keith, I'll double it, and all you have to do is stay home, do some light reading, watch the boob tube, sit on your ass.'

Chloe must play both sides, if he knew about Greta's offer. 'You don't want him found?'

'He'll turn up, don't you worry. But I don't want some defense lawyer finding him first, drumming it into his head that he can wriggle off the hook one more time. And I don't want him found anytime soon.'

'What makes you think I'll take your money if I wouldn't take your wife's?' I drank my drink in one swallow as a prelude to walking out.

Dr Locke gave a little nod. He cleared his throat. 'I

feel I should inform you that my son may be a murderer. He may have killed before, and I don't think he would hesitate to do it again if you were standing in the way of something he wanted.'

I turned and looked at Dr Locke. He was pale. His hand trembled on the edge of the desk.

'I tell you this for your own safety. You ought to know what you're getting into. He was seventeen. His roommate at boarding school. The official cause of death was strangulation. One loop of the rope was around the boy's neck; the other was around his penis. Autoerotic strangulation, they ruled it. He had marks all over his body, but in the end the police decided there was no other person involved, that he'd caused all those injuries to himself. It was hushed up because the family didn't want publicity. And I don't think I can ever forgive myself.'

'How can you be so sure Keith did it?'

'All the holes in his story. He claimed he didn't know about the roommate's habits, but how could a roommate not know something like that? He was scared, and he was lying. Just call it a feeling on my part. My son is not put together like normal people. There's something crucial missing. His mother doesn't want to see it, and for years I didn't, either.' His eyes glowed with the heat of obsession. 'But there comes a time when you have to face the truth.'

I stood there looking at him, taking in his sickened

expression. 'So you think Keith tortured and killed that professor.'

For a moment it seemed like he didn't mean to say anything more. Then he looked up, and the heat was gone from his face. In its place was resignation. 'I think you should consider the possibility that my son lied to your brother about what happened that night, either with or without your brother's encouragement. I think you should ask yourself whether you want to get mixed up in helping my son evade the punishment he most likely deserves and possibly getting somebody else sent to prison in his place. You don't seem bereft of honor. I think you should ask yourself whether this is the kind of situation you really want to be involved with.'

Now I understood what he was asking of me: that I put off looking for Keith until the time for his deal with the DA had passed. 'I'm not working for you, and we've never discussed my working for you. None of what you've told me is covered by privilege,' I warned him. I should have warned him sooner, but I'd been too stunned by the things he was telling me.

'Let the chips fall where they may. I'm done covering for my children.'

'I don't want your money,' I emphasized.

'Then don't take it.' He turned his back, pretending to study the books on his shelf.

I set my glass on his desk. 'How come you don't have any pictures of your daughter in here?' I asked, taking a step toward the door and stopping. 'I can see why you wouldn't have pictures of Keith, but a girl like that, so accomplished, you must be very proud.'

His eyes flashed in my direction. 'You can see yourself out.' He poured himself another drink and went back out to the party. The noise from the other room swelled, then receded. As the door opened I caught a glimpse of curious faces and wandering eyes frozen midturn, midsmile. Then the door swung closed and I was alone.

I took the opportunity to pour myself another drink and slug it down. Who knew when I might have the chance to taste Scotch that old again?

When I walked out into the hall I found Chloe waiting. 'Interesting family,' I told her. 'I can see how working here might drive a person to law school.'

She didn't respond except to pilot me back through the dining room toward the foyer.

'You sure no one else wants to see me?' I asked when we reached the front door. 'The dog?'

'He might like to see you, but not for the reason you think. He hates young men. He'd love nothing better than to chew off your balls.' I thought her mouth twitched but I couldn't be certain.

'It's been a while since I've had a good ball licking, but I'll pass.' I turned the knob of the front door and stepped out into the chilly evening. I'd been right to pay off the cabdriver. I felt like I could use the walk.

Chapter Thirteen

I couldn't get out of that neighborhood fast enough. When I passed through the gateposts at Arguello I let out a breath I hadn't even realized I was holding. I turned downhill toward the park, the prongs of Sutro Tower and the wooded hills of UCSF before me. A mass of fog billowed around the base of the tower, the solid-seeming vapor tinted orange by the setting sun.

As I walked, I thought about what Dr Locke had said. Did I really want to get mixed up with the monster of a son he described? Did I really want people like Keith Locke as my clients?

My route brought me up Turk and past USF, where my brother had earned his degrees. It irked me that Gerald had lumped me in with Teddy. There had to be some truth in the accusations about him, but it wasn't the whole truth. Just because I'd chosen the same career as my brother didn't mean I was like him. I shared neither his anarchist politics nor his grim obsession with work. I wanted to enjoy my life, and I wanted to find someone to enjoy it with.

The lights of downtown were just becoming visible against the darkening sky. There were ethical, honorable ways to defend a man like Keith Locke, who might well have killed already and gotten away with it, who might seek my help in getting away with murder again. Despite Dr Locke's warning and my own misgivings, I intended to find Keith and convince him to hire me as his lawyer. Then I would find a way to navigate a path between the temptations that had tripped up my brother.

I caught a cab back to my apartment and changed into jeans and my hooded sweatshirt. I kicked myself now for having left Teddy's car at his house in Canyon last night. I could take the train down to Stanford, but I didn't know how long it would take me to find Christine Locke, and I didn't want to risk getting stranded in Palo Alto after the last train. I'd been running on adrenaline, and I could feel exhaustion looming. I could sleep tomorrow in a chair at Teddy's bedside. For now, I needed to learn what Christine Locke had been doing in Teddy's room.

I decided to head back over to the East Bay on the BART, get a cab to Teddy's house, pick up his car, and drive down to Stanford. I was walking to the BART when my phone rang in my pocket.

'Mr Maxwell, this is Detective Anderson calling.' His

voice was cordial, professional, as if I were merely the family member of a victim of a violent crime he was investigating.

'I've been hearing from my brother's clients that you've been pulling them in, Detective. I hope you're prepared to defend the legality of those arrests in court.'

'To my dying day. I'm calling as a courtesy, because I thought you'd be pleased to hear that the district attorney's office is on the verge of filing an indictment in your brother's case. I'm pretty confident that we've got the guy.'

My heart skipped. 'Already? Who?'

The satisfaction in his voice was audible. 'Ricky Santorez.'

I laughed sadly. I couldn't help feeling I should have seen this one coming. 'Ricky Santorez is in San Quentin.'

'Yeah, but his homeboys aren't. After Ricky got off, Teddy handled cases for that whole crew. Handled a lot of things for them, actually, according to our informant. Seems Santorez and his friends gave your brother a lot of money for safekeeping. Around a hundred thousand cash. At some point your brother started dipping into it. About a month ago one of Santorez's friends came around to make a withdrawal, and Teddy didn't have anything left to give him. I don't know what your brother was thinking. Sounds like he got greedy, and it got him capped.'

'Your wildest dreams come true. You get Santorez

and my brother with one bullet, all for the low price of one desperate snitch telling you what you want to hear.'

'Desperate, I don't know. This guy's serving life. And we confirmed the details with the bank. Santorez's client trust-fund account was emptied in a series of transactions starting about six months ago. Our guy may be a snitch, but he's legit. Seems Santorez can't do anything without blabbing his mouth.'

'You're being taken for a ride.' But, in fact, I was uncertain. He probably wouldn't lie to me about something so verifiable as a bank account balance. 'What kind of deal is this lowlife asking for?'

'He wants a shot at parole. There are no guarantees with the parole board, of course, but a letter from the DA's office should carry a certain amount of weight. In exchange for Santorez, the DA will write one.'

'Sounds like you've got the case on ice. Except for the shooter and the getaway driver. But I guess from your point of view those are minor details.'

'Santorez will give them to us. Or someone will roll over. Just give it time, Counselor.'

He sounded very satisfied with himself, and very confident, but there was something else. Otherwise he would already have hung up. I thought of mentioning Keith Locke, just to see if he was on the detective's radar screen, but I didn't want to start going down that road until I'd talked to Keith myself. And now that Anderson had Santorez, I doubted he would be interested in alternative theories unless they were backed with incontrovertible proof.

'You got a name on this snitch?' I asked, though I was sure there was no way he would give up such sensitive information.

It turned out to be the question he'd been waiting for. 'Sure,' he said. 'One desperate lowlife by the name of Lawrence Maxwell. We're taking him before the grand jury first thing Monday morning, and we should have an indictment shortly thereafter. Have a great weekend.'

He hung up.

I stood on the piss-smelling stairs down to the Civic Center BART with the taste of stomach acid in my throat. I'd heard my father's name, and the word *parole*, but for a few long minutes that was all I could process of what the detective had said.

It dawned on me that here was my chance to walk away. I could make a clean break and let the courts sort out whether Santorez was behind the shooting.

I remembered the letter my brother had left to be mailed to my father. Could it have reached him by now?

A voice interrupted my reverie, accompanied by a blast of ammonia and alcohol. 'Hey, man, you got some change?' It was a homeless guy with a cardboard sign under his arm, probably on his way to the freeway ramp.

I emptied my pocket into his palm and went down into the station. I might as well go down to Stanford and hear Christine Locke's explanation.

Chapter Fourteen

The BART got me to Orinda in an hour and fifteen minutes. There were no cabs at the station, so I had to call for one, a twenty-minute wait. Then the driver didn't want to take me up the steep gravel road into Teddy's development. I told him he wasn't getting paid until he got me to the door. Turning the cab around, he began heading back the way we'd come, muttering about dropping me off at the police station. So I paid him and hiked the half mile to the turnoff, then another half mile up the hill. A second after he sped off without his tip it occurred to me that the police might have impounded the Rabbit as evidence.

It was a dark, moonless night. As I walked the starlight allowed me to make out the road shimmering faintly beneath its strip of sky. There was none of the city's noises, just crickets and the trickle of San Leandro Creek. An engine revved somewhere in the distance, then died. The rains hadn't started yet, but redwoods make their own moisture, and the green fragrance of a flowering plant tinged the air.

It was 9 p.m. by the time I reached the house. The loose plastic sheeting still flapped in the slight breeze, each unfurling making a loud crackle. I don't know how my brother managed to sleep here, with that eerie racket, why he didn't bother to fix it, or why he didn't just finish the construction once and for all, sell the house, and move on with his life.

The Rabbit stood where I'd left it. I patted its dusty hood, then went up to the house. As long as I was here, I might as well make sure the detectives had locked up.

A Contra Costa sheriff's notice was stapled to the door, indicating that the premises had been entered and searched. The handle was locked but the deadbolt wasn't. I used Teddy's keys and went in.

The police had taken his computer, along with the client files and other documents. It looked as if they'd swept everything into a box to haul it away; the desk was bare now except for a bent paperclip and a scattering of the paper disks left by a hole puncher. I felt a spark of anger: Anderson had no business with those files, even if he'd come across them in the house, not the office. They'd taken the answering machine as well.

I went into the bedroom. The gun was gone from the beside table. No matter. It wasn't like I wanted it.

I called the number Mrs Locke had given me. She picked right up. 'What do you want, Mr Maxwell?'

184

'Could you reach your daughter tonight?'

'I could, but I wouldn't, not without a compelling reason.'

'I need to ask her some questions, and they're the kind that have to be answered tonight, in person. I'm leaving the East Bay now for Stanford. I'll be there in an hour. I'd appreciate it if you'd call her and let her know that I'm coming. I'm happy to meet her wherever is convenient. Maybe the student union?'

'No, Mr Maxwell, I won't have you disturbing my daughter. Why, you won't even be getting to Stanford until after ten.'

'Either you can phone or I'll track her down without your help. I have proof she's been in contact with your son.' It was an educated guess. 'Just ask her where she was at seven on Wednesday evening and whether she remembers having a shocking effect on anyone. Use those words exactly. Then call me back and tell me where I should meet her.'

'I hate this. I hate it,' she said with such vehemence that for a moment I thought she was about to throw down the phone. 'I hate being put in the position of antagonist to my daughter.'

She hung up. As I was winding down Redwood Road toward the freeway twenty minutes later, she called me back. Her voice was husky, with a slur that was either alcohol or depression or both. She was in a quiet place now. 'I hope you're happy. You've managed to provoke

185

a full-blown fight. She's too stubborn to back down, and I don't know how to appease her.'

I tried to apologize, but she spoke over me. 'She'll meet you at the student union.'

'Thanks. I'll try to smooth things over.'

'Don't bother. It will just make things worse.' She hesitated. 'Mr Maxwell, this is very awkward, but I'm afraid I'm going to have to ask you where my daughter was Wednesday evening and how you know about it.'

'Don't worry about it, at least not for now. Give me a chance to talk to her. Let me see what I can do. It may be that we can simply put what happened behind us.' I didn't mind leaving Greta Locke sweating a little.

'For what it's worth, she told me she hasn't been in contact with Keith.' She hung up.

I hadn't lied to Greta Locke when I told her that I'd always wanted to go to Stanford. With its palm trees, mission architecture, and open vistas, the place had stood in my mind for paradise on earth since I was fourteen, when Jeanie took Teddy and me there to show us the campus. Jeanie wore her class of '84 T-shirt, and walking beside her my brother seemed to puff out his chest and square his shoulders. I knew exactly what he was thinking: that people would notice her shirt and assume he was a Stanford graduate, too.

The student union was really a bar, with abysmal techno music blasting over the speakers. There weren't any tables open, but Christine had grabbed a booth by the rear exit. It was the girl who'd Tasered me, all right. The stunning effect was achieved this time without mechanical aids: She wore a black, low-cut sleeveless blouse and a pair of hip-hugging designer jeans with tan sandals. She had a pitcher of stout before her and was in casual conversation with a tall young man with shoulder-length red hair, a goatee, and the back and shoulders of an ironworker. He refilled her glass as I walked up, and I noticed the horny yellow calluses on his palms.

'Just keeping the chair warm for you,' he said, getting up.

Christine quickly drained what he'd poured for her. 'So you're Teddy's brother.' She emptied the rest of the pitcher into her glass. 'I can't say I notice any family resemblance.'

'Look closer. Think of Teddy, subtract about eighty pounds, add grooming.'

She looked, then shrugged. 'Now that you're here, let's leave. Too many people. Unless you want to keep getting interrupted.'

I wasn't sure I liked the idea of moving to a less public place.

'Don't worry,' she said, draining her glass again and starting for the door. 'I don't bite hard.'

'You may not know this, but people die from Taser shocks. A person could have a preexisting heart condition, you give him a shock, and down he goes. Then you end up facing a manslaughter rap.'

'Let's walk.' She paused in the door, lifting her face to the evening air. 'I feel like walking.'

I didn't, but I seemed not to be the one in charge. This puzzled me.

'So now my mother has stooped to hiring lawyers to harass me on Friday nights.'

'I'm not working for her, but I'll go to her again if I need to. I want to ask you some questions. You give me the answers I need, and she'll never have to know where you were Wednesday evening.'

'Answers for whom? For Greta?'

'For Teddy.' I bit the words off.

'One way or another, you're working for Greta. You people always are. Whether you come clean to me or not, whether you know it or not, you're just another in a long line of handlers and spies my parents have hired to keep tabs on me all these years. First the nannies, then the private tutors, then the personal trainers – the list goes on. In high school I even had a personal assistant, my own Chloe, and I wasn't allowed to fire her. If there's one thing I've learned, it's how to deal with people like you, so take my advice and don't bully me.'

'How do you deal with them? With a Taser?'

'Believe me, it would have saved a lot of grief.'

We crossed the street and came to a path under the trees. A circle of drummers was playing inept but heartfelt rhythms down the path; otherwise we were alone.

Christine took a seat on a bench carved from a log. 'Are you tracking down all the girls your brother slept with?'

I shouldn't have been surprised. I couldn't imagine Teddy knowing Christine and not trying to sleep with her. 'Just the ones that were in his room on Wednesday. You and Martha.'

'Martha's becoming a bit of a problem, actually. I didn't expect to see her there any more than I expected to see you. That's one of the reasons I didn't hang around to chat. She's a prostitute. She was smuggled into this country five years ago and she's been working ever since. At one time I thought I could help her, but it turned out she didn't want to be helped. She went right back into it. She was arrested again tonight, by coincidence. She called me about an hour ago from jail. You could post her bail, get her story yourself.'

'You were looking for something in Teddy's room. I want to know what.'

'A camera. Pictures. Videos. Okay? Do I have to spell it out for you?'

'You mean of you and Teddy? So what was Martha doing there?'

'Waiting for me. She knew about the camera. She must have figured I'd show up to look for it. Only it wasn't there.'

I turned toward her and grabbed her wrist. 'Look, stop jerking me around.'

189

She twisted her wrist with deliberate ease from my grasp. 'What is it exactly that you want?'

'I want to know who shot Teddy, and I want to know why.' If it was actually what I wanted most at this moment I wasn't being very convincing about it. I was finding it difficult to think about anything but the cleft of her collarbone.

'And you think I know something about that?'

'I think Keith knows something. And that you know where to find him. I need to talk to him. That's all. I need his permission to go to the police with some information that might lead them to the shooter.'

'So this is about *my* brother?'

'Why shouldn't it be about your brother?'

'On a Friday night you come down here looking for Keith, but instead of asking me straight out whether I know where he is you launch into all of this blackmail stuff about what happened Wednesday night.' She looked forlorn, sitting there staring off into the darkness while the drum cadence rose to a crescendo. She stood and held out her hand. 'Okay. If that's the way you want to play it, I can play it that way.' She pulled me to my feet. 'Let's go.'

'What's this?' I said, stammering, pretending not to understand.

I followed her. Her dorm stood beneath the rim of the lake just on the other side of a parking lot. As we came up to it, I started to hear what sounded like thousands of bullfrogs calling. The lot was filled with Subarus and Volkswagens and even a few BMWs and Mercedes. College students drove these cars.

Christine had a single on the second floor. She didn't look in any of the open doors we passed or say hello to any of the kids in the hall, but I saw plenty of eyes flash in her direction, eyes that snapped away as they met my gaze. Conversations stalled in our wake. At twenty-six, I was a little too old to pass for a student.

Her small room was neat, with a Persian rug on the floor and a thick duvet on the bed. I shut the door behind us. Halfway across the room Christine turned, lifted off her blouse, and threw it on the bed.

She unhooked her bra and let it fall. It was her beauty that made me look away, embarrassed at the squalor of being here with Teddy's lover, this college girl.

'Stop,' I told her, coming forward and grabbing her wrists as she began to unzip her pants. My fingers grazed the taut, bare, thrillingly warm flesh of her waist. A charge went through me. 'I'm not doing this,' I said.

She tried to kiss me, her eyes boring into my face, but I turned away and dropped into her desk chair and sat there without looking at her, afraid that even one more glance would break me.

Behind me, after a pause, I heard a drawer slide open. When I glanced in her direction again she was wearing a sweatshirt and a frown. She had out her laptop and hunkered over it on her bed.

'That might be the first time that's happened to me,' she said after several minutes. 'I've been with a lot of men. A lot of boys, actually. Prep school, college, it adds up. Most go right ahead, even if they know it's a stupid idea. Even if they work for my mother and know they're putting the knife to their throat. You being in here alone with me, you might as well have done it.'

'So this is what you meant by knowing how to deal with people like me?'

'One blackmailer deserves another.'

'I'm not working for your mother, and I didn't come here to blackmail you. I came because Teddy basically raised me, and they shot him right in front of my eyes. Didn't you care about him? Don't you even have some kind of reaction to what happened?'

She didn't say anything. I went on in a pinched voice: 'I caught him when he fell out of his chair. I had his blood all over me, his brains. I can smell it, that rusty smell. And the police don't seem to be that interested in finding the person who did it. They just want to pin it on one of his old clients, on this guy who killed two cops and got off, basically, because Teddy was his lawyer.'

'Santorez.'

'That's right,' I said, surprised she knew the name. 'They're bringing an informant before the grand jury on Monday. I don't know what he's going to say, but the police seem to think it's enough.' What could our father know, I wondered? Was he lying?

192

She was still staring at her computer. 'So you think Santorez isn't behind it. What's your theory?'

Had Teddy not meant any more to her than this, that she could sit staring at the screen while we chatted about him getting shot in the head? I went on. 'I think Teddy may have been shot to send a message to your brother not to talk about a homicide. This professor, Marovich, who was supposed to have gotten strangled in the Green Light, that sex club where your brother worked. Maybe the two of you crossed paths.'

'Maybe I had a class with Professor Marovich last year.'

'Maybe? Like you don't fucking remember?'

She didn't say anything.

'Your father is pretty sure Keith was the murderer, that when the police arrested him they got the right man.'

She closed the laptop and turned to face me. 'Did he tell you that?'

'That's what he told me when I saw him this afternoon. He said there was a boy at Choate, your brother's roommate, who was strangled to death after being sexually tortured. The same way Marovich got it.'

All the defiance washed from her face. She looked far more naked than she had been a minute ago. Then her lips parted, and hatred came into her eyes. 'Teddy and my brother were friends,' she finally said. 'Keith's ten years older than I am, so I don't have firsthand details,

193

but I guess Teddy was just getting established as a lawyer, and he represented Keith on a sex-in-public charge and got him off, and after that he sort of looked out for him. I hate to deflate my father's sick fantasies, but Keith never killed anybody.'

I was surprised to hear that Keith and Teddy were friends, but I was always surprised by my brother's tendency to form personal relationships with his clients. 'Whatever Keith has done or hasn't done is none of my business. I just want the right man arrested for trying to shoot my brother. I think Keith knows who did this, and I think I can persuade him that it's in his interest to put the heat on someone else.'

'Even if Keith is a sadistic killer?' She clearly had nothing but contempt for her father.

I shrugged. 'I just want the people who shot my brother. That's all I have time to worry about.'

'Ruthless.' She gazed at me steadily. 'What if I asked you to help me find something I'm missing? To look around for it in Teddy's things. At his office. His house. Would you have time for that?'

I didn't immediately respond. 'You mean this camera with the videos of you and Teddy.'

She nodded with a little wince, as if that wasn't exactly it, and then went on: 'Teddy isn't on them, actually.'

'Who's on them, if Teddy isn't?'

She acted like she hadn't heard the question, inclining her head, her eyes going to her desk. She pulled open one drawer, then another, and finally she came up with a sheaf of paper and clapped it against my chest. 'I've been interviewing girls for my thesis. Most of them were from Asia, girls brought over here illegally to work in so-called massage parlors. The woman I'd gotten closest to was Martha. I wouldn't want those videos to fall into the wrong hands. I loaned the videos to Teddy, because he wanted to look at them. Then he got shot. I want those videos back.'

I lifted the document she'd dropped on me and looked at the title. It was called 'Ho for a Week: One Sociologist's Journey into the Underground of San Francisco's Sex Trade'.

'I'd maybe switch the word order on this title,' I suggested, just to have something to say while my head spun. 'San Francisco's Underground Sex Trade would sound better. Or maybe San Francisco's Sex Trade Underground.' I flipped through the pages. The last chapter was titled 'Turning Tricks: One Researcher's Journey to the Other Side'.

I rolled the document in my hand and looked at her, remembering Marovich's research subjects from the CV in the file. She'd evidently learned quite a bit from this professor whose class she wasn't sure she'd taken. 'So what's on those disks? Just interviews?'

'That's right. I'm not asking you to work for free. I'll pay you. I have some money from my grandmother, and I can get more.'

'How much more?'

'Twenty thousand dollars.'

That was a hell of a lot of money for a set of videotaped interviews. But then again, her family was paying for Stanford tuition each year. 'Funny, your mom offered me the same amount to find Keith.'

'See. I knew you were working for her.' She reached for the laptop again.

'I turned her down, Christine. I'm not working for your mother, and I'm not working for your father, and I'm not working for you. I'm working for Teddy and for myself.'

'You're looking for Keith, aren't you? And Keith doesn't want to be found? And my mother wants you to find him?' Her voice paused. 'Take my advice and take her money. Take it in advance. Either way, she'll end up getting what she wants.'

'How about you pay me in advance if you want me to keep my eyes open for that disk.'

'I tried to.' She didn't even blink. 'You turned me down, too. Or are you reconsidering?'

'Both of your offers have been generous. What I have in mind is you setting up a meeting for me with Keith. In return I'll keep an eye out for the camera and the disks.' I stood and tapped the rolled-up thesis against my leg. 'We can talk about money if and when I find them. Mind if I keep this?'

'Where are you going?'

'Home,' I said.

'Wait,' she said, and now there was a breathless edge to her voice. 'I can help you find Keith. I haven't talked to him, but I'm sure he's scared to death. Usually it takes a couple of days to get ahold of him. In the meantime, do you feel like going out for a drink and telling me a little about Teddy? About what he was like when he wasn't trying to get laid?'

Chapter Fifteen

We went to a bar on El Camino Real called Antonio's, where you can eat all the peanuts you want and throw the shells on the floor. We talked about Teddy, and Christine cried a little. I didn't, but I found myself telling her about the DA's investigation of him.

I thought it would make me feel better to tell someone. But it only made me feel worse.

I kept saying it was time for me to drive her home, and she kept ordering more rum and Cokes. She was a big girl in every sense of the word; if I didn't try to stop her, I didn't try to keep up with her, either. I thought she was probably working around to saying what she really wanted to say; I kept waiting for her to come clean and tell me the real story about the videos, her professor, and Teddy.

Around midnight she went to the ladies' room, and when she came out the hair at her brow was damp. She announced she was ready to go, and I drove her home. As I let her off in front of her dorm she leaned across the seat and kissed me sloppily. A kiss was okay. I didn't object to a kiss.

I wrote down her number and drove back to the city, circled for half an hour until I found a parking place for the Rabbit, and climbed glue-eyed up to my apartment, where I fell gratefully onto my mattress without getting undressed.

I wish I could say that I slept like a baby until noon. I can't. Almost as soon as I closed my eyes I was dreaming of Christine bare-chested in my arms, the clean smell of her in my nose, the warm touch of skin on skin. I kept waking and finding myself alone, twisted up sweating in the covers, my face deep in the pillow. I would fight to stay awake, trying to claw my way back to reality, but again and again I slipped back under the surface, and each time she was there waiting for me, ready to pick up where we'd left off.

In the morning I rose as cottony and frustrated as if I'd really spent all night failing to make love.

I drank a cup of coffee and showered, then found the Rabbit and drove to the hospital. Jeanie was gone, thankfully, but the room was filled with signs of her presence: an old cup of coffee, a cardigan sweater, a fat paperback spread facedown on the floor.

As I came in, my phone rang in my pocket: one of my biking buddies, a law school classmate, no doubt calling to see if I wanted to ride with him. I switched off the phone and pocketed it.

The bandages still covered the upper half of Teddy's face. I found myself longing for a sight of his eyes, fighting an urge to peel back the tape. Still his chest rose and fell, rose and fell with the sighing of the machine. They'd turned on the bed's automatic tilt function, and with a mechanical whirring it shifted his position every few minutes, tilting him to the left five degrees, then center, then to the right, then back to center again.

I felt relieved now that I hadn't slept with Christine. Sitting by my brother's bedside, I felt bad enough about the kiss.

The nurse had told me to talk to him. 'Teddy,' I said. 'I'm going to find the people who did this to you, and I'm going to make them pay.' Hearing myself, I blushed so deeply that sweat sprang out on my scalp. What else was I supposed to say? That I loved him? I could never say it aloud, and I'm sure he didn't want to hear that.

I wondered whether anyone had told him about his situation. That was the one thing he would want to hear, how bad it was. I took a breath and leaned in close, summoning my voice from my chest. 'Teddy,' I said. 'You got shot in the head. We don't know who did it. You've got pretty bad damage, but it might be possible to recover and have some kind of life. The doctors say you'll probably never practice law again and that you'll have all sorts of problems with memory and thinking. You're never going to be the person you were. That's a hard thing to hear but I know you'd want to hear it. You'd want to know how bad it was.'

I took a deep breath, gathering myself, then went on. 'I'll be here for you, if it comes to that. If you want to live, I'll be here every step of the way. Because you were there for me, and I'll never forget it. I'm sure I won't be perfect, but neither were you. And if you want to die, if you want to let go, I understand. Go ahead if that's how you feel. It's your choice, and none of us would blame you for it. But if you want to live, we're here for you. Me and Jeanie.'

I didn't want Teddy to live because he was a fighter or because surviving was another challenge to overcome, the way Jeanie seemed to think of it. I wanted him to live because he believed he had something to live for. I wanted him to care about being there to see my career unfold, to care about me, to care about something other than himself, his lost work. But I couldn't say that.

When I looked up, Jeanie was there, standing just outside the doorway. I could see by the way she was looking at me that she'd heard at least some of what I'd said. When our eyes met her face softened, and she came in and sat down, scooping the book up off the floor. 'Are you trying to piss him off, make him want to live just to spite you?'

'Something like that.'

'I hope it works. You crack the case?'

'No.' I told her about the police focusing on Santorez

and that the DA was supposedly putting an informant before the grand jury on Monday. She didn't react with the outrage I'd expected. She just opened her book. I didn't tell her about Martha or Christine or my visit with Greta and Gerald Locke, and I didn't tell her that Lawrence was the DA's informant.

With Jeanie there every second ticked by palpably. Through her vigil she had established the hospital room as her territory, and to be there was to be under her eye.

After half an hour I jumped up and started toward the door with an excuse about needing to do some research. 'Good-bye,' Jeanie said, visibly disappointed, as if the length of my visits corresponded with my love for Teddy. By her standards, I owed him more.

I agreed with her wholeheartedly, but I couldn't bring myself to stay.

I drove home and went back to bed with a beer and Christine's thesis, which was titillating, but not nearly as titillating as going back to bed with Christine would have been.

The first section was a not-so-brief history of prostitution in the Bay Area. She'd done her time in the library – that was clear. She'd dug up old newspaper articles, arrest records, and birth and death statistics, but her analysis relied mostly on other researchers' published work. The second section was a picture of the current state of the city's sex industry. For that section she had also conducted interviews with prostitutes and johns, prosecutors and cops, sex-worker advocates and defense attorneys.

The last section was the only part of the thesis that attempted to live up to its title. Told in the present tense, the chapter narrated a week Christine claimed to have spent turning tricks. It was filled with lurid details and narrated in a tone of breathless confession, describing her supposed reaction to sleeping with a series of nameless men. I didn't believe a word of it. Maybe it was just wishful thinking that a gulf lies between ordinary sexual fantasy and actually following through with it. The same might be said for crime, but that does not mean there are no criminals.

I clipped my old bike onto a stationary trainer – basically a stand with a metal roller that provides resistance for the back tire – put on a movie, and rode hard for forty minutes, until the sweat poured off me. It was a poor substitute for the real thing, but for me exercise is like a drug, like medicine, and lately I'd missed too many doses.

I took a shower, went to my computer, and found the number for the Cartwright Center, San Francisco's largest nonprofit resource center for sex workers. Christine's thesis had described the Cartwright as the leading resource for San Francisco's sex workers, dedicated to bettering the lives of the women who filled its massage parlors and brothels or simply walked the street at night. I figured it would be open on the weekend. I told the person who answered the phone that I was a lawyer looking for some background information on a case involving an underage girl. She put me through to the social worker on call.

The center kept a database on every brothel or suspected brothel in the city, the social worker told me. The Green Light had a permit as a social club, a venue for casual encounters between consenting adults – perfectly legal in San Francisco. However, many of the female club 'members' had, in fact, been prostitutes. A number were undocumented. I asked if she knew who had put up the money for the Green Light. All I learned was that the name on the permits was Keith Locke. That was definitely useful.

I thought about the money missing from Santorez's client trust account. Keith, it seemed, had signed the commercial lease for the Green Light six months ago.

Too many coincidences. Keith, Teddy, the missing money; Keith, Christine, Marovich. Maybe Marovich's death was connected directly to my brother's shooting, or maybe it was precisely the accident it appeared to be – an accident with consequences. If Teddy had stolen the money from Santorez and invested it in the Green Light, he would have been in serious trouble when the Green Light was raided and shut down.

I typed Gerald's name into the search engine and learned that he ran his own lab at UCSF, and that his research focused on the cellular mechanisms of cancer formation. He seemed to be at the top of his field; about the only thing he was missing was the Nobel Prize. A lot of people were missing that. I didn't hold it against him. All three of his degrees were from Stanford, and he taught classes at the medical school.

I called Christine. When she answered the phone she sounded like I'd woken her up. 'Still in bed?'

'Back in bed,' she said in a hoarse drone. 'We row at six a.m.'

'I wanted you to know that I've been thinking, and you're right. Keith never killed anyone, at least not at boarding school.'

'That's the reason you're calling? I thought you were going to say you had the disks.'

'Why'd your father lie to me like that?'

She hesitated. 'There's a lot of history there, and most of it happened when I wasn't old enough to have a clue. When Keith was a teenager. A lot of history, Leo.'

'You showed me just about everything last night. We might as well drag out the family skeletons.'

She sighed. 'I don't deserve to be spoken to that way, Leo. I woke up feeling pretty embarrassed about last night. I think I could actually like you.'

'I like me, too. That's something we can both agree on, and I'm glad for it, especially now that I know you would have turned me out of bed at six a.m.'

'You could have gone on sleeping and waited for me to come back.'

'Okay, maybe I could like you,' I admitted. 'But I've got to say, I think this story you're giving me about these videos is a load of crap. I just finished reading your thesis, and it also strikes me as crap. The last chapter especially. I'm not looking to deflate anyone's literary ambitions here, but Jesus.'

'Are you jealous?'

I didn't know if I was or not. I remembered Gerald Locke's anger when I asked why he didn't have any pictures of his daughter up in his office. 'Tell me, didn't Martha work at the Green Light?'

Christine's tone was suddenly wary. 'I don't know. She might have.'

'What about you?' I asked. 'Did you do any research there?'

'Call me when you've got the camera,' she said and hung up.

I was beginning to feel that everyone was lying to me. I was paranoid, maybe, but it's hard not to feel paranoid when you're alone, isolated by a grief the world does not share, and out of your depth. Check, check, and check.

If I was going to be lied to, I decided, I might as well be lied to straight from the source. It occurred to me that I needed to go to Santorez, look him in the eye, and hear him deny having my brother shot. I wasn't so naive as to believe that I could tell if he were lying. Maybe Car could sniff out a liar, but I couldn't. Still, I thought I would be able to tell something.

My bubble of determination lasted only a few minutes. I figured out pretty quickly that there were no attorney visits at San Quentin during the weekend and that my chances of getting in to see Santorez during the week were slim.

Suddenly I remembered what Christine had told me about Martha being arrested last night. From what Martha had said at the Seward, she knew something about the circumstances leading up to the shooting. If she was still in jail it would be easy to talk to her.

It was a plan of action, anyway. It was better than sitting around my apartment smoking dope and playing Nintendo or riding my bike on the stationary trainer and trying not to think about Christine.

I dressed in my suit and drove over to Teddy's office to pick up what he called his 'jail kit', a canvas briefcase filled with all the things he liked to have with him when he met a client for the first time: legal pads, retainer agreements, waivers for release of medical records, cards for bail bondsmen, authorization forms, a digital camera, a preliminary interview sheet, a tape recorder, various court forms, and a copy of the penal code. I wasn't about to sign Martha on as a client, but the jailers didn't know that.

While I was there I glanced at Santorez's main file. On the inside cover Teddy had noted a cell number along with a recent date. He must have gotten the date wrong, I thought at first. It was against CDC regulations for prisoners to have cell phones, and they could be disciplined for being caught with one. It didn't stop them.

It was as simple as dialing. The phone rang three times before someone answered. 'You a ghost?' a man's voice asked, as if he didn't actually care one way or the other.

'Ricky Santorez?'

'Or maybe what I should ask is, are you a good ghost or a bad ghost?' He sounded as cool as if he were stretched out on a recliner in front of a big-screen TV.

'I'm calling to warn you that you're going to be indicted sometime next week for attempting to murder my brother. I found this number in Teddy's files, and I thought you deserved to know that the cops think you did it.'

'Leo, right?'

I was taken aback that he knew my name. 'Right.'

'You think I had your brother shot?'

'If you didn't, tell me who did.'

'I was hoping you could tell me.'

'They're bringing a witness before the grand jury tomorrow. I don't know what he's going to say, but the cops seem to think they'll get the indictment.'

'That's not a witness. That's a snitch.' There was a

pause. 'You know, one of these days you ought to come visit your father.'

'Visit him?' The suggestion was like a slap in the face.

'He must be getting pretty lonely over there in protective custody. He doesn't get to see any of his old friends anymore. But if he had a visitor he could maybe get some air.' Some air between the ribs was what he meant. He seemed to know already that my father was the snitch. 'He's not such a bad guy, your old man. He's made a life for himself in here. I don't know what he's looking forward to on the street. Without Teddy, there's no one who gives a shit.'

'Did my brother steal from you, Ricky?'

'You showed a lot of respect calling me like this, not to mention a lot of balls. So I'm going to be straight with you, even though the truth isn't exactly in my interest, know what I mean? I paid your brother the biggest retainer he ever earned, and the balance was supposed to come back to me on request. Your brother and I were having some ongoing conversations about that. It's true, I have a big mouth. I blabbed about him owing me, he better pay me, all that shit. Plenty of people heard me talking like that, inside and out. But we were on good terms. It was going to get resolved. Now I'm guessing it ain't.'

'You're going to need a good lawyer.'

'You're a lawyer, aren't you? Teddy told me you were waiting on your bar results.'

I felt a flush of pride. If Santorez was trying to work me, he was pushing the right buttons. 'I passed.' I hesitated. 'I could handle the arraignment for you if you haven't found a lawyer by then.'

'It's shooting your brother they'll be arraigning me for, right? Know what I'm saying?'

'There's a potential conflict of interest, sure. You can sign a waiver form. You wouldn't want me as the trial attorney on this one, not least because I'm likely to be called as a witness. You probably wouldn't even want me on the preliminary hearing if there was going to be one, which there won't if the DA gets the indictment. I'm just talking about the arraignment. There's nothing substantive to be decided. You're already incarcerated, so there's no bail. You take a bus ride into the city, enter your plea, then they bus you back to San Quentin. What I'm thinking is how it would look for you in the press if I'm the one who says, "Mr Santorez pleads not guilty", if I'm the one standing beside you, if I'm the one who goes out on the courthouse steps afterward and tells the press what bullshit these charges are and that the person who shot my brother is still at large.'

'Man, you're crazy.' He gave a laugh. 'Guess I'm crazy, too. What kind of retainer we talking?'

'I'll do it for free. Pro bono. Not out of the goodness of my heart, either, but because I want to light a fire under the cops, get the press to realize that they're going after the wrong man. And frankly, the publicity wouldn't be half bad for me as I'm starting my practice.'

I was playing a dangerous game. I thought Santorez was telling me the truth, but I couldn't be sure.

'Shit, man, it's probably the cops who shot your brother. Because of what he did for me, the verdict in my case. Two for one. Knock Teddy off and at the same time make sure I never get out of San Quentin. I got two of theirs – you know they want revenge.'

The pride in his voice made me feel sick to my stomach. 'I'm working on that possibility,' I said, though I didn't even know how to begin to run it down. 'The grand jury will convene on Monday. The proceedings are sealed, which means no one but the DA, the witness, and the jurors gets to be in the room. If I hear anything about what happens I'll give you a call.'

'Yeah, holler at me. Just leave a message if I don't pick up.'

I gave him my cell phone number and told him to call anytime.

'Don't forget about what I said about coming to visit your pops,' Santorez told me in parting. 'Honor thy father, that's what the Bible tells. You got to make peace with the past.'

The peace of the grave, is what I thought he meant.

After pulling a parking ticket off the windshield, I fought inexplicable Saturday afternoon traffic down to San Bruno. All for nothing. After arguing with the deputy at reception I finally persuaded her to dig deep enough into her computer to determine that Martha had posted bail a few hours ago and been released. To me the implication was obvious: A pimp had bailed Martha out.

I sent Christine a text message, asking for Martha's address. A few minutes later she texted me back. The address was a second-floor apartment on Sycamore Street, an alley off Mission not far from the Sixteenth Street BART. People like Gerald Locke probably still thought of the Mission as dangerous, but it was pretty much like the rest of the city, now filled with trendy restaurants and coffee shops replacing bodegas and bars. It wasn't the neighborhood that made me nervous. It was one thing to interview Martha behind bars, quite another to seek her out on her home turf, where she likely lived under the protection of a dangerous, violent man.

If she'd been one of the girls at the Green Light, she would know what had happened to Marovich. Maybe she could tell me if it was an accident or if he was killed because he'd been researching sex trafficking. She'd been in my brother's room waiting for Christine, and she needed to explain that, too.

The entrance to her duplex was guarded by a metal grate. I rang. No answer. I pushed the grate, and it creaked loudly. I called hello up the stairs. Hearing nothing, I started up, my heels echoing on the bare wood. The door at the top was ajar.

I paused at the open door, then stepped cautiously into the living room. A canvas wing chair was parked in front of the television, with an ashtray overflowing with butts on the floor beside it. In the next room an enormous jade plant towered above a green painted dining table. There was a smell of cat piss.

I clicked my tongue, and a young energetic black cat appeared with a friendly chirrup from the bathroom. She arched her back and rubbed against my shin; as I bent to stroke her, my eyes settled on the string of rust-colored prints that trailed behind her, the four-toed impressions as clear as printer's ink on the tiled threshold of the bathroom, fading across the rug.

Her muzzle was wet. Smelling the ferric sweetness of whatever she'd been dipping into, I straightened. There was a streak of what looked like blood on my hand where I'd brushed her cheek. I stomped my foot wildly and she galloped into the dining room, continuing to trail an ever-fainter series of prints.

I stepped forward. The bathroom window was half-open, revealing the hinged frame of a fire escape. More bloody cat prints came and went on the sill. Beneath the window lay the body of a young Asian woman – Martha.

Her bathrobe had come open to reveal her breasts and a pubic bush like a tight snarl of thread. She'd been shot in the face at least twice, and the blood had pooled on the floor. Brains splattered the window frame. One eye was a hole and the other was squeezed through the socket, giving her a look of inconceivable surprise, but she hadn't been surprised by the shot. She'd locked herself in the bathroom and had probably just gotten the window open to climb onto the fire escape when her attacker kicked in the door. She lay half-twisted against the tub, as if she'd been in the process of turning to face him when he pulled the trigger.

On the counter by the sink a gun lay as casually as if it were a tube of toothpaste. The air was heavy with the mingled smells of gunpowder and blood, but the feminine odors of shampoo and incense lingered.

I turned into the kitchen, just managing to make the garbage before I threw up the contents of my stomach in one long retching heave.

After a while I went back to the bathroom and looked in again. This time the gun caught my eye. I recognized it as one of Teddy's. The police had taken the one from Teddy's bedside table, or so I assumed. That left the other one unaccounted for – the gun Car had taken away from me and locked in Teddy's safe.

Car.

I suddenly felt very cold. The room began to spin. I fled the bathroom again and dropped onto the sofa. Take the gun and get out of there, my brain said, throw it off the fishing pier into Mission Bay.

She couldn't have been dead long. I forced myself to stand and walk back into the bathroom, lean over the pooled blood, and feel the arm that was flung up over the rim of the clawfoot tub. Not warm, but not cold. Not too many hours, probably, but I was no pathologist. I went back out to the kitchen sink, washed the vomit taste from my mouth, and scrubbed my hands. I went on washing them long after all traces of Martha's blood had disappeared.

I dried my hands on a dish towel, then searched the apartment halfheartedly, using the towel to open drawers in her dresser and in a desk that stood under the window in the bedroom, always with the sense that Martha could hear me going through her private things. But, of course, my secret observer was not Martha but the police, who would soon be here.

One dresser drawer was filled with economy-size packages of condoms and lube. The rest of the drawers and one closet contained the most shocking assortment of sexual torture instruments I'd ever seen. There were collars and whips, elaborate harnesses, chains, batons, and a set of strange hooks connected through a system of elastic cords. It took me a moment to realize that these hooks were meant to be inserted in the skin. There were prods and dildos and just about every instrument of mingled pain and pleasure you could imagine.

Incredible that no one had called in the gunshots, but maybe someone had. Maybe the police were on their way.

I knew the gun had only my fingerprints and Teddy's on it, and certainly not Car's – I remembered him holding the gun by the edge of his shirt when he'd picked it up off the floor in Teddy's office.

I was going to need a lawyer. I should have dialed Jeanie, but something kept me from calling her: embarrassment, I guess, and also the dismal certainty that she wouldn't believe me if I told her that I suspected Car.

I still had Anderson's card in my wallet. I don't know what I was hoping for – a miracle of understanding, I guess.

Anderson answered on the third ring.

'It's Leo Maxwell.'

I heard the cries of seagulls and the throaty grumble of a marine engine.

'Hold on.' The background noise faded. 'You get your memory back?'

'I'm afraid I've made a pretty grisly discovery. I'm in an apartment at the corner of Sycamore and San Carlos in the Mission. A woman's been murdered.'

The tone of his voice didn't shift. 'You're the one who found her?'

'That's right.'

'Hold on.' I heard the static crackle of a radio and Anderson's voice in the background saying something; then he came back on the line. 'They'll have someone there in less than ten minutes. Don't touch anything. You didn't touch anything, did you?'

'No,' I told him in a hollow voice.

217

'Well, don't. I'm out fishing, but I'll be there when I can. And you better be ready to tell me everything.'

He hung up, and I sat on the couch, letting my head sink into my hands. I was still sitting that way when I heard sirens approaching from at least two different directions.

As the police cars pulled to a stop outside I shook the tension from my arms and composed myself. Things began to happen very quickly. I heard feet clomping on the stairs, and a uniformed officer appeared with his gun unholstered but down at his side. He called for me to stay where I was and to keep my hands where he could see them.

'She's in the bathroom,' I said, and saw myself as he must have seen me, the killer caught red-handed, an angry boyfriend or john resigned to being led away in handcuffs.

'I'm a lawyer,' I told him as he poked his head in the bathroom, then glanced back at me. 'I came upstairs and found her.'

Another uniformed officer came up the stairs and went through the dining room into the bedroom, his gun also drawn, checking to make sure the apartment was empty. Then he came back into the living room and told me to stand, face the wall, and place my hands against it. He frisked me, then brought down my arms one at a time and cuffed them behind my back.

I'd never been cuffed before. The steel was cold

against my wrists. 'She was dead when I found her. I didn't kill her.'

Finally he spoke, but with great reluctance. 'Come on, pal, it's none of my business. You talk to me, I got to make a report. I make a report, and someone might decide they don't like something that's written there, and then it's why the hell am I talking to the guy in the dead girl's apartment? So do me a favor and keep your mouth shut until someone shows up who actually wants to hear it.'

I kept my mouth shut, and they took me downstairs and put me in the back of a squad car. More squad cars appeared, jamming the alley along with an ambulance and a pair of unmarked Crown Vics. These had to be moved to make way for the ME van, piloted by the same two guys who had shown up at the restaurant on Wednesday.

By the time Anderson arrived an hour later I was relieved to see him. 'I have to get someone to open this,' he said, and came back a moment later with the uniform who'd handcuffed me and put me in the car.

'He said he didn't do it,' the officer said as he opened the door. This was a joke to him.

'You swab his hands?' Anderson asked the cop, who gave him a funny look.

'Word was wait for you, so we waited.'

'I'm taking him to Southern,' Anderson said. 'We can do it there.'

He didn't speak as he maneuvered his unmarked car out into traffic. I tried to keep my mouth shut. I'd read enough police reports to be aware that it would be simple for Anderson to deliberately misconstrue my statements or put words in my mouth, if that was his intention. That's why Teddy advised all his clients that they should never under any circumstances talk to the police. 'No detective is your friend,' he would say. 'If he's acting like your buddy or your shrink, it's because he's trying to hang a felony on your neck.' To me he explained, 'You'd be surprised how many clients will put their heads in the noose for a little human under- standing. They're guilt-ridden and afraid and they let themselves care what the cop thinks of them. They're desperate for understanding and respect, and the detective's the only person who can give those things to them, because the detective is the only person there. But the only way to get understanding from a detective is to confess.'

Easy for Teddy to say. He never sat in the back of an unmarked police car under suspicion of murder. He was so used to dealing with guilty clients, it probably never occurred to him that the best way for an innocent man to clear his name is to talk. The need to somehow mark myself as different from all the killers who'd sat where I was sitting was too powerful to control, and as we turned off of Mission onto Bryant I said, 'That was Teddy's gun in there. At least it looks like the gun he used to keep in his office. If it is Teddy's gun, it's possible you're going to find my fingerprints all over it.'

'You wash your hands?' Anderson asked, like somebody's mother at the dinner table.

'Yeah. I petted her cat and got blood all over my hands from its fur. Fucking cat was lapping up the fucking blood.'

'Too bad. See, if you hadn't washed them, or if you'd said you hadn't, we could have done the swab test, and if it comes up negative, that's evidence you didn't fire the gun. But since you say you washed them, a negative wouldn't mean a hell of a lot. We can still do it, though. A lot of times people wash their hands but they don't manage to get the residue off. A positive still works for us. Negative won't do you much good, though.'

The Hall of Justice at 850 Bryant Street houses both the criminal courts and the police department's Southern Station, which serves as police headquarters. Anderson parked in the subterranean garage, and we took the elevator up to the fifth floor. I'd been up there a few times that summer to serve subpoenas for Teddy in the court liaison office at the end of the hall. Thankfully it was a Saturday and we had the elevator to ourselves – on a weekday it would have been packed with attorneys and cops, jurors and witnesses and defendants.

Anderson walked straight ahead out of the elevator, seeming to take it for granted that I'd follow him, and I did. Much as I feared and distrusted this new pose of reserved silence, I believed that my fate depended on his believing me. Barely five months from the bar exam, I'd forgotten that there were such things as judges and juries and prosecutorial discretion, and that I was a lawyer and had the right to remain silent and the right to remain free unless I was placed formally under arrest. From the elevator we walked to a plain door with a frosted glass window. A placard above the door read HOMICIDE. We went in.

The large office was filled with desks. Despite the open floor plan, the supportive square columns that alternated with the desks gave the room a claustrophobic effect. In the wall beside me were tinted windows looking into what I supposed were interview rooms.

A few heads turned as Anderson led me into the one nearest the entrance. I was dressed more nicely than your average murder suspect; otherwise, there was nothing remarkable about my presence. Another day, another murderer with a better than even chance of walking away, was probably what they were thinking. I'd seen enough cop shows to know that the interrogator always leaves you alone in the interrogation room to sweat and fidget and stare at your reflection while he drinks a cup of coffee and watches you from the other side of the glass.

He left me alone, and I sweated. I fidgeted. I wriggled out of my coat but then was reluctant to drape it over the back of my chair, knowing that if I did I wouldn't be able to stop worrying about it sliding off. I ended up just putting it back on again.

The first thing Anderson did when he came back into the room was read me my Miranda rights. He got through them before he finished pulling out his chair, and he sat down heavily, as if making that recitation had been laborious. 'I'll talk to you,' I told him. 'I'm the one who called you, for God's sake. I told you driving over here that you might find my fingerprints on that gun. It looks just like the gun my brother kept in his office.'

I kept insisting on this fact as if it exculpated rather than inculpated me.

There was a knock on the door, and in walked a slender, graying man in jeans and a T-shirt with a name tag around his neck. No badge. Anderson told me to put my hands on the table. The man swabbed my hands with a pad and cleaned under my fingernails with a plastic scraper that screwed into a bottle of preservative. 'I have a couple of toenails that could use some work,' I told him, but my hands were shaking. He turned to walk out, but Anderson stopped him and told me to remove my jacket and shirt.

The so-called technician took my shirt and jacket away with the samples, leaving me there in my white T-shirt.

Anderson had a notepad on the table before him. 'Your brother have a permit for that gun?'

I told him I didn't know. 'The last time I saw that gun

was Thursday afternoon. I came back to Teddy's office after court, and Teddy's investigator, Car, was there with the lights off. He had Teddy's wall safe open, and he'd taken something out of it – he wouldn't show me what. He startled me, and I grabbed the gun from the drawer. He took it away from me and locked it in the safe. He was careful not to touch it. I don't have the combination to the safe.'

Halfway through this recital Anderson began shaking his head, and he capped his pen and set it on the table without writing a word. 'Look, Leo. We could charge you now, but I was hoping you might give me your side of the story. You told me yourself, your fingerprints are on the gun. I want to help you get through this, but you've got to give me something to start the wheels turning. Give and take, Leo. Why not tell me what you were doing there at the apartment, to start.'

'She was one of my brother's clients. I was over at County Jail Five asking about her this morning. Deputy Lopez was kind enough to help me at the lobby window. Check with her. She'll remember. I was a big enough pain in the ass.'

Again Anderson wrote nothing. 'So what happened when you got to the apartment?'

'First check what I just told you, Detective. Deputy Lopez. Cee-Jay-Five. Call her up.'

With a scowl he rose and went out. He was gone five minutes. I didn't move a muscle.

'You get through?' I asked him. I could see in his face that he had, but I wanted to hear him say it.

'Yeah. For what it's worth. Not much, in my book, but if it makes you feel better, sure, Lopez confirmed that you were a pain in the ass.'

I told him about the street door being ajar, ringing the bell, getting no answer, and finally going upstairs, petting the cat, seeing the blood, and finding the body in the bathroom.

'And you didn't touch anything, and you didn't know her. That's your story?'

'I never saw her before,' I said, and flushed at this lie I hadn't even known I was going to tell. 'I touched her leg to see how warm she was. I puked in the garbage and washed my hands. I touched the cat.' I shrugged. 'I poked through some of her things. Dresser drawers, desk drawers, her closet. A lot of curious stuff in there.'

His brow furrowed. 'You knew she was a prostitute before you went in there, right?'

'Of course. I was going to try to get her to hire me as her lawyer.'

'We have a witness that can put you and the victim together in your brother's hotel room Wednesday evening. Cut the bullshit. I'd rather be fishing, believe me, but here we are, so stop beating around the bush. It's nothing to be ashamed of. Human sexuality is a mysterious thing. Believe me, working in this city, I've seen it all. It'll all come out sooner or later. It always does.'

I doubted that the front desk clerk had talked. I couldn't imagine that guy remembering anything when the police were the ones asking the questions. Maybe it was him, though. Maybe Hamilton wasn't his favorite founding father. He could have been a Benjamin Franklin man.

Then I thought of the junkie with the dreadlocks who'd followed me downstairs, the one who kept trying to tell me about the case he'd caught and about all the magic Teddy would have worked for him. I could have been nicer to him, I supposed.

'Okay, so I saw her before,' I admitted. 'She was in Teddy's room when I went there to look through his things.'

He gave me a smile of perfect sweetness, as if he expected me to break down and confess.

'I'll tell you two things,' I went on. 'One. Santorez didn't shoot my brother. He had no reason to. I'll be representing him at his arraignment, and I'll be talking to the press afterward. That's how confident I am that you've got the wrong man. Two. Car killed that girl. He shot her with the gun he took from Teddy's office. What he didn't count on was me being the one to find the body, and he definitely didn't count on me coming clean, telling you the gun belonged to Teddy. He messed up there, and if you're any kind of detective you ought to make him pay.'

Anderson just sat there with the smile on his face.

I stood up. 'Book me now, or I'll assume I'm free to leave.'

He didn't say anything. I walked out, feeling the flesh crawl up and down my back, expecting Anderson to grab me, shove me against the wall, cuff me. My shirt and jacket were lying across an empty desk. Seeing them, I felt my cheeks burn. He'd never had any intention of testing them; he'd never seriously believed I was the shooter. This was just a game he was playing with me, an elaborate prank. I grabbed both articles of clothing and stopped to thread my arms through the sleeves of the shirt. I didn't try to button it. My hands were shaking too badly for that. Now that I knew there had never been any danger, the fear hit me powerfully. My quadriceps cramped, but with my jacket over my shoulder I managed to walk out.

It was nearly four in the afternoon.

Chapter Sixteen

I caught a cab, retrieved Teddy's car, bought a twelve-pack of beer and a pizza, and spent the next five hours getting drunk and winning Super Mario Brothers 3. In those early Nintendo games everything is always the same, down to the pixel. Sometimes I think I could play it blindfolded.

When I had defeated Bowser for probably the thirtieth time in my life, I put the remaining six beers in the fridge and switched to water, took a shower, and finally let my mind begin to turn over the day's events. It was clear to me that Anderson had meant not only to humiliate me but also to warn me that I should stop digging, stop finding bodies. Whether he was trying to thwart me from discovering the truth or merely protecting his turf remained unclear.

Had Car bailed out Martha, then killed her? No one else had access to the gun in Teddy's safe. Had someone been to Teddy's house after I was there and before the police, taking the matching gun from Teddy's bedside table? It occurred to me that Jeanie might have had time to take it. I could have checked her purse after she passed out Thursday night, but I hadn't thought of it.

Or maybe my fingerprints on the gun were Car's insurance policy. Except the gun connected him to Martha's murder as much as it connected me.

I went out and walked up Powell from Market into the heart of the Tenderloin. The girls were out in force, wearing a thin overlay of boredom to mask the nervous energy of danger and drugs. I'd never paid for sex before, though I knew it was a cash service like anything else, available just a short walk from home.

After recrossing Market I found myself at the office. The door was locked, and inside everything was as it had been. The door to the safe was closed, and the safe was locked.

All my theories had collapsed now that Martha was dead, and Car was most likely her killer. Car was plenty tough and plenty smart. Working for my brother all these years, he could have built up quite a stable of prostitutes from Teddy's clients. And he could have learned plenty about trafficking, if he wanted to bring in girls from Asia or Eastern Europe – young girls, not hardened by the street; girls who would have depended on him for everything, girls like Martha must once have been.

'Fix this,' Teddy had said to Car in the stairwell, within a week after the Green Light was raided and shut down. What had Martha known? That Car shot Teddy? Or had she known what Teddy knew, about Car's role in the Green Light and the source of the money Car put up and lost?

I went to Tanya's desk and took the files marked 'Lawrence Maxwell' from the drawer. I decided to go through the case from beginning to end, including the original arrest report and the trial transcripts, continuing through the motions, appeals, and lawsuits my brother had filed on our father's behalf and the notes he'd compiled for the habeas brief.

I had known one version of the story – the story that was told by the prosecution in court. Then when I was a teenager prowling through microfilm I discovered another, my father's strident, half-coherent protestations of innocence and conspiracy. Now I confronted a third.

My conscious, willing memory stretches back to a few weeks after her murder; before that, the images swim and run. Whenever I think about my mother's death it is the years afterward that come most readily, those lonely years living with Teddy, taken care of by a succession of nineteen-year-old girls.

This is to say that much of what I was reading felt new to me, though at the same time it hit home with all the shock of memories uncovered and relived.

The story the file told was an ugly one. In a few notes Teddy had sketched out an accurate portrait of the final period of my parents' marriage: periods of calm alternating with explosions of rage, my father's paranoia and violence, and my mother's disenchantment.

I remembered my father as always angry. He would sit at the kitchen table for hours nursing a grudge. The whole world was in on a conspiracy to keep him from getting what he wanted, which was always something other than what he got.

Teddy was the only one who was able to talk to him. For Teddy, Lawrence would let his bitterness melt, and I could see how he might have been. But he was never like that with me. For me and my mother, the ones who lived with him, because Teddy had moved out when he turned eighteen, the violence was always right under the surface, and the more he drank the more it would build, until he would accuse Caroline of terrible things.

She would lash out, tell him how worthless he was, and he would make a show of controlling himself, not reacting, but of course what he was doing was provoking her, and he knew it. The angrier she got the more beautiful she seemed. She would grab his hair, pull as hard as she could, or take a swing at him with a bottle. That was his green light. She'd fold and crumple, but he wouldn't stop until he'd worked it out of his system, all the hatred. I'd hide in the bedroom until it was over and she came to me.

Those fights were a shameful secret. I would tell Teddy about them, but he did nothing, and I took my cue from him. I never talked about them to anyone outside the family. Now, reading the file in astonishment, I wondered what Teddy had known then about her secrets.

His notes outlined the missing evidence, all of it tending to show that my mother had been with a man besides my father the day of her death – information the defense never had. My first reaction was indignation. How dare they? Along with the affidavit from the former property-room attendant, the file contained photocopies of receipts for what appeared to be samples from the crime scene, blood and semen and fingerprints, none of which had been turned over. If it was true, it was a shocking miscarriage of justice.

I felt my world shifting beneath me, as if the ground had begun to slide. Reading Teddy's notes, giving way to them, I felt the excitement a lawyer feels when he realizes he has a case, mixed with the dread of the angry teenager I still was deep inside, living in a prison of my own making. Holy shit, I thought. The old bastard might actually be innocent.

And in all these years I hadn't even been to visit him. If what I was reading was true, I had made a colossal, wrongheaded mistake. I couldn't face it, not all at once. I wanted to go on blaming him. I didn't want to owe him anything.

The notes made no attempt to articulate a theory of innocence. They pointed to no new suspect. My father had been convicted by a jury, and the conviction had been upheld by the appellate courts, despite Lawrence's continual clamoring for justice. I couldn't figure out what Teddy was hoping to achieve with a habeas corpus writ, if he wasn't able to point to the real killer, who'd gone free.

I closed the file and pushed it away. As I did, I dislodged an envelope I'd somehow failed to find before, made of stiff yellow cardboard. It contained glossy five-by-sevens, high-quality darkroom prints that had faded only slightly with age.

My hands trembled even as I opened it. I wanted to go no further. Let it stop now, let the past stay put, a voice protested. I didn't want to see what the envelope held, but I'd come too far to put the pictures away.

The first was a wide-angle view of our old house in the Sunset, showing a man walking up to our door. I gave a cry of pain and astonishment as I recognized a younger but already imperious Gerald Locke. No, I thought. This cannot be, it simply cannot be.

Another astonishing photo had caught Gerald and Caroline on the grass in the park, leaning close together, their faces clearly visible, my mother's bare legs youthful and trim, though she must have been over forty. There were ten pictures in all.

For more than an hour I studied them, the smallest details striking me like fists, a poison I remembered from adolescence filling my veins, the muscles of my neck tightening as they'd used to ache when I spent long

234

afternoons in the microfilm room, my adolescent rage now turned on its head. How could she? I thought, stoking the same rage Lawrence must have felt. How could she – with Gerald Locke?

I didn't want to believe it, couldn't believe it, but no matter how long I sat staring at the pictures, it was his face, his hand, her smile as she looked at him. Was Teddy right? I wondered. Was it all her fault, the beginning of their troubles? Where could Teddy have discovered these pictures after all these years?

Nothing about my mother having an affair with Gerald Locke had come out in my father's trial. The DA's case had focused narrowly on the recent history of abuse in the marriage. My father's prints had not been found on the baseball bat she was beaten with. There were no witnesses. If and when my father's writ of habeas corpus was granted – and it remained a long shot, though the pictures gave them a fighting chance – and if the DA retried my father, Teddy must have planned to make that courtroom ring with Locke's name. And if Locke knew what Teddy was up to, he had a motive to silence him before Teddy could file that habeas brief.

After a dreadful hesitation I flipped to the crime scene and autopsy photographs. I had been the one to find the body, but if I had any memory of what I'd discovered, I'd blocked it out. Now I saw how savagely she'd been beaten. The killer had used one of my aluminum baseball bats. As I looked I again felt the anger that had crippled me during my teenage years returning to its proper focus, not on Caroline but on the person who had done – this. I went through the stills again, studying each one carefully. I opened myself to the anger, taking it in like an alcoholic taking his first drink after fifteen years.

I remembered what it felt like to love her and need her, to want to be with her, but the truth is I did not remember her at all.

Santorez was right. One of these days I was going to have to visit my father.

Chapter Seventeen

There were so many things I needed to do before I could hope to prove or even be certain in my mind that Gerald Locke had killed my brother – but on Sunday, paralyzed by the weight of my suspicions, I did nothing to further my search for the shooter.

In the morning I went for a purging, punishing ride starting at the Rockridge BART. I climbed to Skyline Boulevard on the ridge of the East Bay Hills, followed it for several miles, then dropped over into Contra Costa County. I wound through grassy hills before crossing the coastal range again and ending up at the Richmond BART, my legs cooked.

Anderson had wanted to scare me, and I was scared. I was in the unenviable position of knowing more than I wanted to and suspecting worse. What good did it do me to suspect that Gerald Locke was behind the shooting, I asked myself, if I could never prove it? He would likely escape justice now just as he'd done fifteen years ago, if he had, if it were possible to believe that such an astonishing secret could have lain undisturbed all these years.

I got to Teddy's room by eleven and found Jeanie established with her paperback in the chair by the window. A glance at her tired face told me nothing had changed. Still the bed automatically turned him, and the respirator deeply wheezed. If she saw me pause in the doorway, she gave no sign.

I went home, avoiding my roommates, and went to my room. I had some marijuana that Teddy had given to me over the summer; he'd simply dropped it on my keyboard like a turd in a bag. I smoked some of it on the back porch, had lunch, smoked some more, then fell asleep on the bedroom floor where I'd lain down to stretch.

It was dusk when my phone rang in my pocket.

'Leo.' Jeanie's voice. 'Did I wake you?'

I checked the time. Twelve after five. I'd slept for three hours. 'Yeah,' I said, so thick-headed I almost dropped back to sleep.

'I just got one of your old messages. I thought maybe you were calling to tell me why you've been avoiding me. Why you can't be in the room with me, with your brother.'

Jeanie always wanted to talk, even when she knew it did no good. 'I can't sit there and pray for a miracle, hoping everything's going to work out great when I know it isn't.'

'So what did you do today? The same thing you've been doing all week?'

'I went for a bike ride. Then I got stoned and fell asleep on the floor.'

'Jesus, Leo. I need to feel like we're in this together, but right now I feel like, I don't know, like you blame me somehow. Blame me for what, I keep thinking? What have I done? Can you tell me what I've done?'

'Nothing. It's me.'

'I'm at the hospital all day, and you're off God knows where, chasing God knows what. And then when you do show your face, you see me and you turn right around and walk out, and you don't come back. How's that supposed to make me feel?'

'It has nothing to do with you. I thought I could handle being there today, but I realized I was wrong.'

There was a long pause I couldn't bring myself to fill. I wanted to tell her about everything that had happened, but I didn't know where or even how to start. Maybe it was better if she thought I was off getting stoned every day.

'I'm coming over there,' she finally said. 'We need to talk.'

'Not here,' I said, not wanting to be trapped with Jeanie in my place, with my roommates around. 'How about I meet you at Teddy's office?'

'Fine,' she said and hung up.

On my way over there I picked up a bag of ice and a

fifth of gin. I stuck them in an empty wastebasket and sat behind Tanya's desk with my father's files spread before me.

It wasn't long before I heard the elevator churn its way down to the ground floor, pause, then come rattling up.

Jeanie must have brought a change of clothes to the hospital with her. Her eyes moved immediately to the file folders on the desk, took in the name written on their tabs, then looked away.

'For what it's worth, I always said that he should tell you what he was doing,' she said. 'You were bound to find out sooner or later.'

'Well, now I've found out.' I took the gin out and poured some for her into a coffee mug. 'Why did you and Teddy split up?'

'The marriage or the practice?'

'Were there different reasons?'

'What are you driving at, Leo?'

'They're convening a grand jury tomorrow. I told you, they've got a snitch from San Quentin who's going to testify that Santorez was behind the shooting.'

'And : . . ?'

'I don't know what his testimony is going to be. Only that the detective on the case, Anderson, seems to think it'll be pretty damning. Supposedly Teddy stole a lot of money from Santorez.'

She blinked, then knocked back a slug of gin. 'If that's

true, then the Santorez idea suddenly makes a lot of sense.'

'You told me before you thought it was this other guy, whomever Keith was covering for. His partner, I guess.'

'Maybe it was.' She watched me over the rim of her mug.

'Teddy was putting together notes for a habeas brief for Lawrence.' I opened the file, took out the stiff envelope, and opened it. My voice wanted to quit on me but I went on. 'These pictures were in the file. That's Gerald Locke going into my parents' old house. That's Gerald and my mother in the park.'

'This would be Keith Locke's father, I presume?' Jeanie studied the prints as if she'd never seen them before. Maybe she hadn't. 'You've got to hand it to Teddy,' she finally said. 'Imagine the odds of something like this turning up after all these years.'

'Teddy obviously was going to argue that the police knew another man had been with my mother the day she was killed. If she'd been having an affair with Gerald, that'd make him suspect number one. But why wasn't he? There was evidence of her having been with another man, evidence that was either lost or deliberately destroyed and never disclosed to the defense. When Teddy filed that brief, Gerald's name was going to be all over it.'

She started to say something, then didn't.

I put the pictures back in the envelope. 'Do you think these are real?'

'As opposed to figments of our imagination?' She tried for a smile.

'We both know that Teddy has a reputation for fabricating evidence. That's what I was getting at when I asked why you split up. Was it because you found out how dirty he was?'

'If you believe that, you're just as bad as the rest of them.' She was pale with anger. She went on: 'This stuff about your brother fabricating evidence and putting on perjurers started in the DA's office. The truth is that Car went out there and pounded the pavement and found the witnesses Teddy needed to win tough cases. He's the best investigator in the city. And Teddy's light years better than any other defense attorney in town. He's smarter and he works harder. He has no life. That's the reason we broke up, if you need to know.' She took another swallow of gin. 'I wanted a life. I still do.'

'Car killed a woman yesterday. A prostitute named Martha.'

'What?'

I told her a simplified version of my activities without mentioning Christine Locke. I said that I'd met Martha at the Seward and that I'd gone to her apartment and found her shot to death with Teddy's gun. I told her about my interview in the homicide office at 850 Bryant. Someday maybe it would make a funny story, how scared I'd been. For now I could only tell it straight.

'And why do you think Car would have killed her?'

'She knew something about why Teddy was shot. Either that or she knew whatever it was they shot Teddy for knowing.'

'So Car killed this prostitute, and Gerald Locke had Teddy shot. Have you got any kind of theory that makes sense of all this?'

'Teddy was shot for a reason, right?'

'That doesn't mean they were shot for the same reason.'

Remembering the message on my brother's home answering machine – Martha's voice, *This is Chris and Martha calling* – I was sure that Christine hadn't told me the half of her relationship with my brother. I was working on the assumption that the person who'd killed Martha had shot Teddy, too. *Fix this*. The gun in Martha's apartment, the money missing from Santorez's trust account – it all seemed to come back to Car.

Jeanie went on: 'For me the chief thing is that Teddy's lying there in the hospital. I'm not in the business of solving crimes, Leo. I'm not a lawyer on this one, and I'm certainly not a cop. I'm just someone who cares about your brother. My ex-husband.'

Maybe it didn't matter to her who had shot Teddy, not the same way that it mattered to me. She'd spent her adult life undermining assumptions most people took for granted – that it was possible to say for certain that this event had happened, that this person was responsible, and that he should suffer this penalty for his crime. The human world was about chaos, her weary gaze seemed to warn, and it was the worst kind of foolishness to believe that we could impose order on it.

She paused. 'Maybe the police are right,' she said. 'Teddy might have stolen the money from Santorez. After all, it's hard when you're in a solo practice. One year there's money, the next there isn't, but the bills keep coming. And that big fat client trust account is just sitting there. Maybe he figured he could take some out, then put it back when he caught a big case. It wouldn't surprise me if he'd done it before and gotten away with it.'

'No one else had access to the gun,' I said. 'It had to be Car. On Thursday he was here when I came back to the office. I pulled it and he took it away from me, locked it in the safe. I didn't have the combination, but he did. He'd already opened it and taken something out. I'm sure that was the gun in Martha's apartment, the one she was shot with.' I didn't mention the twin in Teddy's bedside table.

Jeanie said, 'I think we should go out for pizza rather than sit here and drink all this gin.'

She rose. I had no choice but to follow. I knew of nothing else I might say to hold her in that chair.

We cut through the empty financial district to North Beach, Jeanie keeping half a step ahead of me. I tried to draw abreast of her but she only walked faster. It was a long walk.

The entrance of Tommaso's was crowded with people waiting for tables. I had to edge through to put our names in. When I returned I half expected her to be gone, but she was leaning outside the door holding two glasses of wine.

I found that my appetite for asking unanswerable questions had passed. Right now it seemed enough to be with her, waiting for a table, sharing our grief over Teddy, even if that grief expressed itself in each of us differently.

I'd told the host we wanted a booth, because we'd have no privacy at the long communal tables. We drank two glasses of wine each before being seated. Tommaso's had always been our place, hers and mine and Teddy's.

'You don't actually know it was Teddy's gun in that apartment,' Jeanie said when we'd sat down. 'The police nodded, they acted like what you were saying was very interesting, they took down your completely insane statement, and then they let you walk out of there when they got bored.'

'The gun might not have been registered. They had no way of knowing.'

She spread her hands on the table. 'Leo, Car didn't do this. Hurting women isn't really his style. Much less murdering them. Trust me.'

'You must know what kind of man he is, Jeanie.'

'What kind of man is he?'

'He's a pimp. Keith's partner. It's probably Car that Keith thinks he's hiding from, if he's hiding from anyone. Which I'm beginning to doubt.'

She was laughing now, so hard that she blushed in embarrassment. 'The Green Light? You think Teddy would've allowed that?'

'Car was recruiting Teddy's clients, setting up his operation. They had an argument the week before Teddy was shot. That was when the lid came off. Teddy must have finally figured out what Car was doing.'

This time she didn't try to suppress her laughter. 'Half an hour ago your prime suspect was Gerald Locke. Now you're saying Car killed Teddy?' Her tone was exasperated.

My head swam from the wine. A wave of dizziness washed over me. 'I don't know what I'm saying.'

She went on more gently: 'If Car was doing what you say he was doing, Teddy would have known. And if Teddy knew, then either he would have had to be in on it or Car would have been gone. I'm not saying Teddy wasn't in on it. He cared about helping clients. He didn't particularly care how they made their living. If he saw a chance to get some girls off the street and improve their quality of life, maybe he would have gone for it. But Car couldn't have done it alone without Teddy knowing what he was up to.'

She was right: Teddy was too familiar with his clients

for something like that to escape him. He would have known.

The pizza came. It was Jeanie who broke the silence, once we'd stopped eating. 'I think prostitution should be legal. So did Teddy.'

'Obviously, if he was in on the Green Light. With Santorez's money, no less.'

'Come on, Leo.' She paused again. 'Look, I should have told you this sooner, but I'm going back to private practice. I'll be taking over the lease on the office and representing most of Teddy's old clients. I imagine that Tanya and Car will work for me, but, of course, they're free to do what they want. There's still an empty desk. You could use it until you get on your feet.'

I just stared at her, thinking of all that I'd learned about my brother in the last four days. I thought about her refusal even to entertain the thought that Car might have been the one to kill Martha, cleaning up loose ends. And then the disappointment hit me. I should have known it was too ambitious to be true, my own plan to take over Teddy's practice. There was no question of going up against Jeanie. If you were a defendant searching for representation, who would you prefer, Monkey Boy or Jeanie Napolitano, with two hundred jury trials under her belt?

I took a deep breath and let it out. 'In that case, I guess I should let you know that I'll be representing Santorez at his arraignment for attempting to murder Teddy.

Assuming the grand jury returns an indictment. I expect it will.'

Now it was her turn to stare. Then she dropped her eyes and lifted another slice of pizza. 'You want to be disbarred for harboring a conflict of interest, you go right ahead. But if I were you, I'd try to hang on to that bar card now that you've got it.'

'He'll sign a waiver. He has a right to the attorney of his choice, and I won't be representing him in any substantive proceeding. What I'm going to do is enter a not-guilty plea; then I'll march out of the courtroom and inform the press that the DA's charged the wrong man. I can't prove Santorez didn't do it. But even if Teddy did take that money, it doesn't feel right.'

She chewed slowly. She wiped her mouth, drained her glass, and signaled the waiter for our check. 'It doesn't *feel* right,' she echoed skeptically. 'Just don't make the mistake of thinking you know what you're doing.'

I'd imagined Teddy saying much the same thing to me. Without warning there were tears in my eyes. She reached across the table and touched my hand, then quickly withdrew the touch. I grabbed the bill when it came.

During our long walk back through the financial district I racked my brain for some neutral topic of conversation but quickly realized we had nothing more to say to each other, a feeling that came to me like news of the death of someone I'd known long ago.

At her car Jeanie touched cold lips to my cheek. 'Try to remember you still have a brother,' she said. 'I'm afraid someday you're going to wish you'd spent more of this time with him. I'm not judging you.'

I looked away, impatient to be gone. I knew she was right, but I couldn't tell her that. She drove off, and I walked home and fell into bed.

Chapter Eighteen

Monday morning found me once again standing in the doorway of Teddy's hospital room. It was early, too early even for Jeanie. I'd passed a restless night. I'd kept dreaming that he was dying and I couldn't get to him. I ran up and down stairways and halls in a building more sprawling and labyrinthine than any hospital in existence – but always I found the last door locked. Meanwhile the alarms sounded *code blue, code blue*.

The arrival on rounds of Dr Gottlieb and his four residents prodded me into the room, if only because I knew they'd quickly kick me out. Teddy had gotten a shave but otherwise looked no different, maybe slightly gaunter, like something that had wilted in the refrigerator.

I went down the hall to wait in the lounge. I kept expecting Jeanie to show up, but she hadn't arrived by the time Dr Gottlieb came down the hall to talk to me.

'I was hoping I might catch you this morning,' he said, sitting down by me. 'How's the legal profession?'

I was dressed for court. 'It won't ever be the same

without my brother.' I steeled myself. 'Where are we at with what we discussed?'

'In regards to that conversation I told you we might have? Nothing's changed. Your brother's condition hasn't improved; but at the same time, it hasn't gotten noticeably worse. Of course, lack of improvement is itself a concern. At this point we can only wait and hope. Every day that passes without improvement, however, makes the prognosis slightly worse.'

'I can't stand having him like this,' I heard myself say. 'I can't stand it. I know he'd hate it. I don't want this – this suffering – to go on a second longer than it has to.' It was not what I'd meant to say, but I'd said what I meant.

'Whose suffering – yours or his?'

'What kind of life is he going to have?'

'You can see for yourself. I've arranged for both you and Ms Napolitano to tour the rehabilitation facility.' Gottlieb's face showed the barest tic of impatience.

'I'm not interested in the rehabilitation facility.'

'That's your choice.' He stood. 'To answer your question, yes, at the point where I deem that it has become medically futile for this stasis to go on, I will inform you.' His voice was suddenly very, very weary. He seemed on the verge of giving me a bit of fatherly advice, then apparently thought better of it, pressed my arm, and walked out.

I went back to Teddy's room and stood looking out

the window toward the sliver of the bay that was visible. My father must be on his way to the city by now, I realized. It made me slightly queasy to think of him on this side of the water, still in custody but perhaps one step closer to freedom. Soon he'd be on the witness stand, taking an oath he probably didn't mean to keep. What would I do if he lied his way to freedom before the grand jury? Would I have to see him?

I sat at Teddy's bedside deep in my own thoughts. At some point he must have stopped respecting the oath my father was about to take. Defending the guilty must have drained away his respect for the truth. Gerald Locke's words returned to me, and I wondered what I might do to keep my father in prison – to catch the person who shot my brother.

On my way out an hour later I ran into Car, who was walking in with Jeanie. Seeing me, Car grabbed my arm and spun me around, throwing me off balance. 'Ho, Monkey Boy.'

I kept going, but he was there beside me, matching my stride. I glanced back. Jeanie was standing uncertainly near the elevators. 'Teddy's upstairs,' I said to Car. 'He was asking about you.'

'Yeah?' Car's face was perfectly blank.

'You and Keith Locke. I caught both names.'

'You talking to Keith? Say hi to him for me.'

'Why, you looking for him?'

We were outside on the broad front entrance plaza of the hospital. 'See, I told your brother at the beginning, this kid's no good, he has no common sense, let him wet his dick with some other lawyer.' Car gave me a push. 'I hear you've been saying I murdered people.'

'That girl, Martha.' My voice came out hoarse. 'She worked at the Green Light.'

'Not for me, she didn't. Nobody worked for nobody at that place, but definitely not for me.'

'Maybe not anymore. She was shot yesterday with Teddy's gun. The one you locked in the safe. The police may not believe me, but as far as I'm concerned, you were the only one who could have pulled the trigger.'

Car looked bored. 'Sorry to hear it. I suppose I shot Teddy, too. If I did that, you'd have a bullet between the eyes. But hey, you're still breathing. Know why? Because it's all a joke. You're a joke.'

'I know what you and Keith were into. With Santorez's money, no less. What's going to happen when someone tells Santorez the whole story?'

'I told you, I didn't have nothing to do with the Green Light or with Keith, either. See, Monkey Boy, your trouble is you don't know smoke from fire. What happened to Teddy didn't have nothing to do with Keith or anyone else. It was Santorez all the way. Teddy tried to hang on to some money he didn't earn. He probably figured Santorez was in the pen, what could he do about it? Ricky reasoned with him for a while, then he saw he wasn't going to get his money back, so he had Teddy shot, sent a big loud message.'

'You were Keith's partner, and Keith was going to talk,' I countered. 'Teddy was just about to set the deal up for him. Then Teddy got shot, Ricky got blamed, Keith got the message to keep his mouth shut and do whatever prison time comes his way, and you walked off into the sunset. You and Jeanie.'

I saw the look in his eyes and was suddenly aware of my surroundings, no one around, no pedestrians passing, not even a cat to track through my blood if Car spilled it. His narrow Slavic face grew pale, bringing out the redness of his lips. His muscles knit together beneath his hoodie. Then his eyes narrowed in a catlike smile, and without any visible relaxation the tension was gone. 'You ought to forget the law. There's no money in it. Screenplays, that's where the money is. An imagination like yours, you could make bank. Safer too, way things are going.'

'I'm trying to find my brother's shooter.'

'Yeah, but you're trying too hard.' He took a piece of paper from his pocket and handed it to me. 'Be seeing you, Monkey Boy. Don't forget to say hi to Keith.'

I didn't drop my eyes to see what he'd given me until after he'd walked back toward the hospital. Then I unfolded the sheet of paper and saw that it was a printout showing a series of photographs, grainy from the quality of the printer, a night scene with the camera looking in the open front passenger door of a car. Car had a fancy digital camera, I knew. It took me a moment to recognize Christine Locke as the woman in the foreground; then a shock ran through me. It was Teddy's Rabbit in the photo, and the man kissing Christine was me.

Clearly a threat or a warning – if there was even a difference with a man like Car. Or perhaps he hadn't been following me. Perhaps he had a reason for following her. That could only mean that he knew something about Christine's relationship with Teddy.

Something was printed on the back of the page, just a line at the top, easy to miss if you were in a hurry – an empty page with a footer, 'page 4 of 4', like the extra page you get when you print something. It hadn't been printed at the same time as the pictures. Instead, someone had fed the sheet into the printer upside down so that the blank backside could be used. Jeanie's habit of reusing paper used to drive Teddy nuts. More than once, I knew, he'd filed a brief with some e-mail or map fragment appearing between the pages.

I'd meant to drive back to Teddy's office, but instead I merged onto the interstate toward the Bay Bridge, following a wild hunch that I would find something more at Jeanie's to help me catch the trail Car seemed to think he was following.

Jeanie kept a key under a flowerpot at her townhouse. Twenty-six minutes later I used it to let myself in.

The blanket I'd wrapped myself in two nights ago

still lay in a heap at the foot of the couch. Two glasses stood on the counter, and there was a faint reek of smoke. Half a dozen filterless cigarettes were stubbed out on a plate on the counter. I stood looking down at the saliva-stained, half-folded butts. Jeanie didn't smoke. Car did.

I took a tour of the place and saw more cigarettes stubbed out in a cup on the bedside table. It shouldn't have bothered me that Car had been there, but it did.

I started opening drawers in her home office – an alcove off the kitchen beneath the stairs – but they were crammed to overflowing with old checkbooks and bills. I was stymied, but then I remembered how paranoid Jeanie used to be about hiding her drugs – not paranoid enough, as it turned out, because eventually I'd found all her hiding places. She prerolled all her joints, and I would take them apart and reroll them smaller, skimming off her stash.

Her most effective hiding place was so obvious it was brilliant. In the apartment where we had lived during my teens, where I knew every nook and cranny, every loose floorboard and grate, there hadn't been many places a person could conceal the tin in which Jeanie kept the drugs she and Teddy shared, marijuana and hash and occasionally something stronger. It stared me in the face every day, but I didn't have eyes to see it. I never took out the garbage, pig that I was, so I'd never thought to wonder whether there

257

might be anything underneath the bag.

The wastebasket underneath the desk was nearly empty and too light to contain anything substantial. I tried the kitchen garbage: nothing under the bag, but in groping the outside of it I felt something hard edged and heavy inside. I got a pair of tongs from the drawer and fished around among the coffee grounds and melon rinds until I came up with a small digital video camera and disks sealed in a double layer of freezer bags.

Twenty thousand dollars in my hands, if Christine Locke was as good as her word. Not that I planned to sell them. Tucking the bag with the camera and disks under my arm, I murmured a silent apology to Jeanie and put to rights the few items I'd disturbed.

I was back on the freeway to San Francisco ten minutes later when my phone rang in my pocket.

'Verdict,' Judge Iris's clerk said simply, and I could hear by her voice which way the clerk thought it would go. 'They're bringing your client up. Can you be here in fifteen minutes?'

It was going to be more like thirty, but I told her I'd make it as soon as I could.

I drove fast, but not too fast, trying to think what I'd say to Ellis if the verdict was guilty. By the toll plaza of the Bay Bridge the words still hadn't come. Sorry just wasn't enough when the man you were apologizing to would likely be sentenced to fifteen years in prison.

Maybe he was guilty, and maybe he wasn't, but that wasn't the point.

Sorry was going to be the best I could do.

I parked in the underground lot, then walked up the stairs to Civic Center Plaza and across the street to the courthouse. The clerk was stamping documents and threading them into a gigantic civil docket. Seeing me come in, the deputy yawned and put aside his *Contra Costa Times*. It was all the same to them, whatever happened to Ellis. It was just another day, another case, another set of administrative tasks. 'You want me to bring him out right now or wait for the DA?' the deputy asked.

'Now, please.'

I ought to take Car's advice, I thought as I waited, and forget about a career in the law. Imagine a lifetime of this feeling, I thought, swallowing back the acid that kept rising to my throat, hunching my shoulders at the tickle of sweat in the small of my back.

The door at the back of the courtroom swung open, and the deputy followed Ellis, who looked both sleepy and hyperalert, his gaze darting around the courtroom but seeming to pass right through me, as if I were no longer entirely present for him. Indeed, there was nothing left for me to do but plead with Judge Iris for a lenient sentence if the verdict went against us.

'What do you think my chances are?' he asked, moistening his lips.

I shrugged. 'Just have to wait and see.'

'Pretty good, I'm thinking. They don't reach a verdict Friday. That means the ones on my side are standing firm. They go home over the weekend, spend a few days thinking it over, verdict right away Monday morning. You don't hold out over the weekend to give in Monday morning, do you? No way. They came back today holding firm. The others, the guilty votes, they're the ones who caved. It's better to vote not guilty than to risk convicting an innocent man. That's what they said to each other, I'll bet. Your words. I'm optimistic.'

His voice trailed away. He wet his lips again. He didn't look optimistic. He looked like he had a lifetime of dread and fear clamped onto the back of his neck.

'Whatever the verdict is, don't react.' It was what Teddy always told his clients. 'If it's bad news, be stoic.'

'Easy for you to say.'

'The judge is the one who sentences you if you're guilty. She's going to be watching you when the verdict is read. If you get angry, if you act sorry for yourself, she's going to notice, and she'll remember.' I wondered if I was going to be able to live up to my own advice.

Melanie came in tight faced and nervous. Her skirt was so tight, a seam creaked when she sat down at the DA's table. She opened a binder and began to scrawl notes on a pad.

She must be in trial on another case already, and I felt a stab of envy, knowing that the only antidote to losing a case is to lose yourself in the next one. I envied the lawyer who was going up against her in whatever trial she was prosecuting next. A few hard-fought cases against an opponent like her would make me into a lawyer.

Judge Iris walked brusquely into the courtroom. 'Sit down, sit down,' she said. 'Anyone have a record to make before we get started?'

She was looking at me. After a moment I realized that Melanie was, too.

Judge Iris went on more gently: 'If you want to ask for a mistrial, now is your last chance.'

The judge went on looking at me steadily, and I realized that she'd grant the mistrial if I asked for it. I couldn't look at Ellis, but I was very aware of him breathing beside me with deep, almost unbearably slow breaths. I noticed a Bible on the table. His hands rested close to it, just his fingers touching the red-stained edges of the pages, the soft leather binding.

'We'll hear the verdict, Your Honor,' I said.

'Let's bring in the jury, then.' She nodded to the bailiff. He went out and a moment later came back in with his face transformed, as if he'd been dipped in a vat of solemnity. He held open the door for the jurors as they filed past him, one fumbling with his jacket, another scratching her neck, the lot of them generally looking about as uncomfortable as it is possible for a group of people to be who are not facing prison time themselves.

I could make no sense of where their eyes went and

where they didn't. Each of the jurors avoided looking at Ellis: a bad sign. None looked at Melanie, either. Two of them met my gaze with flashes of curiosity before their eyes flitted away, as if repelled by the naked entreaty they found there. There was something splendid in their isolation. For these few minutes they knew what no one else knew.

The judge waited until the jurors had filed into the box and taken their seats; then she addressed them. In her voice I heard a respectful withdrawal, as if even she partook of the awe that gripped me. 'Ladies and Gentlemen of the jury, have you reached a verdict?'

'We have, Your Honor,' said a woman from the back row, a software engineer Teddy had identified immediately as the foreperson and whose signature had appeared on each of the jury's notes.

'The bailiff will now retrieve the verdict form.'

He crossed the courtroom, the solemnity beginning to wear off him now but still clinging in patches. He reached across the front row of jurors, took the verdict form, glanced at it, then delivered it to the clerk, who stood from her computer, scanned the form, and read aloud: 'As to count one, we the jury find the defendant, Ellis Bradley, not guilty.'

I was tingling all over, and I heard a rushing sound in my ears.

'As to count two, we the jury find the defendant not guilty.'

Ellis was on his feet, waving the Bible and shouting 'Praise Jesus.'

The judge sat looking at him with a grim little smile. 'The Lord came down into this courtroom,' Ellis said. 'The Lord was back there with you in that jury room.' As if only now remembering that I was there he turned to me and pumped my hand, pulling me half out of my chair. He smelled strongly of sweat with the release of his fear. I'm sure I was worse.

'The Lord Jesus came down into this courtroom today,' he said, faltering a bit, still grinning, half standing over his chair, smiling blindly at the judge, the jury, the prosecutor. 'Yes he did.'

He sat down and slapped my shoulder with excess force, as if he were drunk. The clerk laid aside the verdict form, sat back down at her desk, and reached for her mouse. Just another day, another verdict, another docket to update.

'You have now completed your jury service in this case,' Judge Iris read from the official jury instructions. 'On behalf of all the judges of the court, please accept my thanks for your time and effort.'

As she dismissed the jury, I basked in the feeling of having won. It was better than sex, booze, anything. I wondered if it was like this every time, if there had still been sweetness in it for Teddy after he stopped expecting to lose. I felt like a brilliant lawyer; I felt newborn. My misgivings drained away like water after a storm. I would do anything to have this feeling, I thought in the rush of the moment. Anything.

It was one of those few moments in a life when one door closes behind you and another opens ahead, and you step forward to take your first definite possession of the life that will be yours. After the Ellis Bradley verdict, for better or worse, there was no going back.

It wasn't until we'd parted, Ellis a free man, me wandering down the windowed hallway toward the stairwell, that I remembered it was Teddy who had tried the case, Teddy who'd put on the probably perjurious testimony that had gotten Ellis off.

Chapter Nineteen

I ended up in the basement cafeteria. I had a splitting headache and needed caffeine. When Teddy was in trial he used to send me down there for a double espresso during every break. The espresso was bitter and burned the throat, like swallowing a coal, and always left me feeling parched and quivery. I don't know how he could stand the stuff.

As I stood in line staring at the menu board, wondering if it was worth the wait for a sandwich, someone tapped my shoulder in an expert straight-fingered jab right where the bones knit together. I turned and saw Detective Anderson smiling at me.

'This must be some place for doughnuts,' I said, my heart jumping as my body remembered that interview room where I thought he was going to nail me for murder.

'Come on, Leo, if you're going to follow in your brother's footsteps you're going to have to come up with something more original than doughnut jokes.'

It was my turn to order. 'Double espresso for me and a glazed, please.'

I paid. Anderson ordered two coffees.

'Extra one for dipping,' I suggested. 'Good thinking.'

The woman handed me the doughnut in a fold of waxed paper and I took a quick bite, just in case Anderson thought he was going to get it. His eyes narrowed.

My coffee came, and so did Anderson's. I was about to walk out of there when he said, 'I'll give you one guess who this second coffee is for.'

Something in his voice froze me.

'I don't think I want to,' I said, but didn't walk away.

'Want to see him?' He shook packet after packet of creamer into one of the coffees. 'You'll be the first defense attorney to get a peek inside that door. The first on my watch, at least.'

He smiled, showing me once again that I was in his power, and I knew I couldn't just walk away now as I'd done for so many years. I was tired of being afraid of my father and what he'd done – what he was supposed to have done. I knew that sooner or later I'd have to face Lawrence, now that he was evidently trying to leverage Teddy's shooting into a get-out-of-jail-free card.

I gave Anderson a nod. We went toward the jury assembly room at the end of the short hall. Walking beside him, I remembered my old fantasies of killing my father. I'd rehearsed patricide in my imagination so often that I believed that I knew the feel of my flesh impacting his flesh, my skin tearing his skin, my bones breaking his bones. I'd stopped believing myself capable of murder, but as I followed Anderson through the cavernous room I once more breathed in the fury that had long been my only alternative to loneliness and fear.

As we approached the unmarked door at the far end, Anderson handed me one of the cups. I didn't have to ask whose coffee I was holding. It was for my father, I knew. Anderson knocked and the door was opened from within. At the end of a short hall I saw a room with a jury box not unlike the one in a criminal trial court, only this one had more chairs. There was a witness stand, a court reporter's and clerk's table, and one for the prosecution. There was none, however, for the defense. At the witness stand sat a slight, lean man in an orange jumpsuit and plastic-framed glasses, bald on top with gray hair cropped close at the sides of his head.

Two alarmed-looking sheriff's deputies barred my path. In no uncertain terms I was told to step back, that I had no business here. Anderson stood watching. Over the deputies' shoulders my eyes locked with my father's.

I could not tell whether he recognized me; the glance we shared was too brief. His face changed, however. His eyes hardened, and I recoiled. What they seemed to hold was not apology but accusation, as if all these years I'd been the one in the wrong.

For the first time I wondered why he hadn't sought me out, sent me a letter. All these years he'd spent trying to convince the world that he was innocent, he hadn't wasted even a single breath trying to convince me.

The last thing I saw as they shoved me out the door, my father's coffee sloshing over my hand, was Anderson's face creased in amusement.

Chapter Twenty

All the thrill of my triumph in the courtroom had melted into the exhaust-laden air, and my headache was worse than ever.

I wandered up Market Street toward the Ferry Building. Ellis Bradley was past; now only one case mattered. I didn't really believe that Car was the one who'd shot Teddy. I wanted to believe it, because I didn't like how close he'd gotten to Jeanie, but I couldn't.

Or maybe Car had been working for Gerald all along. That might explain why he was taking pictures of me with Christine Locke. Yet there were no apparent connections between my brother's shooting, Marovich's death, and Martha's murder. That seemed wrong to me, not least because it required entertaining the idea that my father was innocent. Gerald was the wild card.

I had to find out what was on the disks, but first I owed it to Teddy to tell him about the Ellis Bradley verdict.

I caught a cab out to the hospital. Except for Teddy, the room was empty. I pulled a chair up to his bedside. 'The jury came back not guilty,' I said. 'Ellis yelled and waved his Bible around and walked out of there. I gave the closing argument for you last week. I didn't want to tell you before, in case we lost. But we won. Not guilty, Teddy.'

I held my breath. I took his hand. I couldn't remember the last time we had touched before the shooting. 'If you understand, squeeze my hand.'

The bed whirred and tilted him away from me. Teddy's breath wheezed in and out, in and out.

I stayed for half an hour, then went back to the office to watch the disks.

When I opened the office door I found myself facing Tanya over the barrel of the Saturday night special she'd just withdrawn from her purse. She held me in her sights, then put the gun down. Her eyes dropped to the desk, as if I'd ceased to be of any interest once I was no longer a target. The lights were off, the blinds half-slatted.

I waited for her to say something. Finally I let out my breath and said, 'Jesus, you might have killed me.'

'Be glad you were you.'

I dropped Teddy's briefcase on the waiting room chair. 'What rock have you been hiding under?'

'I just came to pick up a few things.'

'Don't be too hasty about leaving. If you stay you won't be working for me, you'll be working for Jeanie. She's taking over Teddy's practice.'

'I could never work for a woman,' she said.

She could never work for a woman who'd been married to Teddy, is what I sensed she meant.

'What are you going to do?'

She shrugged. 'Your brother always promised I'd be taken care of. I don't suppose that means anything now.'

I glanced into the inner office and saw the safe hanging open. Of course she'd had the combination. If she'd opened it earlier and taken the gun, there'd be no reason to open it again, and if she'd taken the gun, there was no way she'd admit it. I decided not to say anything. 'You must have known Teddy was going to file a habeas brief for my father,' I said.

Her face closed down.

'I saw the file. He's been representing him for years.'

She stepped around the desk and moved toward the door.

'Tanya,' I said. 'Listen to me. *I have to know*. Does Teddy really believe my father is innocent?'

She turned, screwing up her face with deep offense. 'What the hell does that matter?'

'You must see that it would matter to me. We're talking about my mother's murder.'

'I just put in the line numbers and the headings and file them with the court. I don't ask Teddy what he *believes.*'

'But you must have some idea.' I wanted to ask her about Gerald Locke, but I didn't know how much she knew of what Teddy had known.

'If you think so then you don't know Teddy. It never mattered to him if they were guilty or innocent. Never. And he never speculated. With your father it would be no different. A client is a client is a client. That was Teddy. He was a *lawyer*, Leo.'

She was radiant with the pride of possession, a possession somehow more complete now that Teddy was on his deathbed. She looked ten years younger, and I was shocked to see that under all the accumulated detritus of hard living, under all the damage that had been done to her, a furtive beauty remained.

For an instant I wondered whether she and Teddy—

No way, I told myself as she walked out the door.

I moved the little TV down from the bookshelf to Teddy's desk and connected it to the camera to see what Christine was willing to pay twenty thousand dollars for.

You could call them interviews, I guess. Interviews of the wordless kind. The clips all took place in the same room dominated by a four-poster bed hung with mosquito netting. One wall of the room was painted with an amateurish mural of a beach complete with naked sunbathers. Fake palm trees stood in the corners. It had to be the Green Light.

Whoever put that camera in the room could only have had extortion in mind. Each clip showed a single session, and in each Martha played a leading role. The men were mostly older, wealthy-looking. I noticed how the camera would catch the glint of a wedding ring, the way Martha would make sure to turn them toward the camera at crucial moments.

I fast-forwarded through the clips just looking at faces, but none of the men was Marovich. Stupid girl, I whispered as I watched, you stupid, stupid girl. But she had aspirations, I had to give her that; she wasn't content with her place in the world. She probably made the mistake of thinking her power over those men was real rather than a disguise they put on and stripped off again when they walked out. Maybe she thought she could handle them in the outside world the same way she handled them in the Green Light.

I sealed the videodisks into a padded envelope, and I got another, larger envelope, putting both the pictures of my mother and Gerald Locke and the videodisks inside it. I used the office meter to print out postage fifty cents short and addressed it to myself. Anyone who wanted to retrieve that package would have to wait in line at the post office for at least an hour to pay the postage due, and even then the clerk might not feel like looking for it, if my experience with that dysfunctional bureaucracy was any guide. It was the safest place I could think of on short notice.

I dropped the envelope into the same mailbox in which I'd dropped Teddy's letter to my father.

I went back to my apartment and called Christine's cell phone. She didn't answer, and I didn't expect her to. I left a message saying I'd found what she was looking for and that she should call me back.

She called within an hour. Her voice sounded different, more privileged and with assumed sophistication, more like her mother's voice than her own.

'I assume you've watched the disks.'

I didn't reply.

'My offer stands.'

'Which one?'

'I'll take you to dinner. If we end up not sleeping together I'll write you a check for twenty thousand dollars, but if you fuck me you don't get a penny, and I get the disks.'

I couldn't tell whether she was kidding. The put-on sophistication was still there in her voice. This from a girl who'd stuck a Taser in my neck three days ago. I wondered if she knew about Martha yet, if she'd shrug off her death as easily as she'd shrugged off Teddy.

'And if the check bounces?' I asked.

'Somehow I don't think it will come to that.'

I agreed to meet her. I even decided to let her pay.

It hadn't escaped me that Christine's last lover had ended up shot. Right in front of me. Gerald Locke might have ordered it for no other reason than to keep her away from the son of the woman who'd been his mistress fifteen years ago, the lover he may have murdered. He might take the same attitude toward me if I strayed where Teddy had strayed.

My curiosity was too strong for my caution, though. I had no intention of sleeping with Christine or of taking her money, but it thrilled me to think of spending the evening together.

I met her outside the Caltrain station at Fourth and Townsend, a half hour walk from my apartment. The walk and the darkness did me good. After a difficult day, there's no tonic like the fall of darkness, especially when dusk brings the anticipation of meeting a beautiful woman.

Christine wore a short black dress with tights, a wide black round-buckled belt, a shawl, and flat-heeled shoes. Her hair was back and her neck was damp with sweat when she kissed me. It must have been warm on the train. She smelled like shampoo, and she carried a purse and a small bag that might have been an overnight case. I asked if she was planning to spend the night at her parents'. She laughed.

The first cab to see us did a U-turn through traffic and rocked to a halt. I opened the door, Christine slid across, and I followed suit. She gave the cabbie the name of the restaurant.

My principled resolve crumbled with one casual touch of her hand on my thigh. Before the cab reached the first stoplight we were kissing. She had slid down beneath the level of the window. I had one small breast free and was sucking it while with my free hand I flipped the elastic of her panties aside. I wanted my tongue between her legs but thoughts of the cab driver kept me above water.

When we reached the restaurant the driver wouldn't take the money from my hand. 'Just put it on the seat,' he said angrily. He was Indian or Pakistani, young but not hip. I threw the twenty on the floor of the cab.

On our way to our table Christine stopped to chat with an older couple. With nothing more than a toss of the head she'd pulled herself back together, showing only a slight color in her cheeks. I was sweating and disheveled, holding her little case in front of my groin.

Before we had even sat down she had ordered a first bottle of wine, telling the sommelier to open a second and let it breathe. I ordered a martini with a twist. Only a very skilled bartender can accomplish a Jeanie martini without producing a drink that is at least one quarter meltwater. The bartender that night was one of this rare breed. The gin was just how God made it, about fifty degrees colder than the gin in the bottle on the shelf. The outside of the glass was frosted.

We were sitting together in a corner, and the tablecloth hung below our knees. As soon as my napkin was in my lap I felt Christine's hand creep underneath it. I pretended to study my menu, watching concentric ripples widen, then come back together in my gin. Then there was a pool of spilled gin at the base of my glass.

I cleared my throat and said hoarsely, 'The bet was that you could get me to sleep with you.'

'Now you're ready to go longer than half a minute.' She withdrew her hand and let the napkin drop to the floor. 'In five minutes I'm going into the bathroom, and two minutes after that you'll join me. Don't worry, I'll still pay you.'

'You underestimate me.' I appreciated what she'd just done for me, but it wasn't anything I couldn't have done for myself.

'No, sweetheart. You underestimate yourself.'

The waiter was hovering near the wine rack, and I pointed at my martini glass. Twenty thousand dollars – a tempting offer, but I was no gigolo.

She rose and walked off toward the bathroom. I waited. Eventually I began to tell myself that in just a moment I would go to her, make nice, ask her to come out. Other diners tried the bathroom door and were turned back. I couldn't have sneaked in there now if I'd wanted to. Another drink, maybe, and I might manage it.

She was gone twenty minutes. When she returned

she seemed made of ice. Our food had arrived, and I'd dug in. I was two martinis and three glasses of wine to the bad.

The strength of her anger took me by surprise. She didn't speak, nor did she touch or even seem to notice her food. She just sat staring unwaveringly at the table, giving off a charge of violence. I flinched at each adjustment of her posture. If she could jerk me off here, she could surely punch me in the nose, slap me in the face, or shoot me. Then I began worrying she might leave without paying the bill.

Eventually she reached for her glass. The movement brought a palpable sense of release. Though we still didn't talk, we drank together. I wasn't a fool. I knew she was going to give me hell.

When she broke her silence there was something new in her tone, something hard and ominous, something she'd been holding back. 'You still don't have any idea why Teddy was shot or who shot him.'

We were drinking cognac. The bill was on the table but I wasn't going to touch it. It was probably more than the limit on my credit card. The place was half-empty, filled with diners lingering over the dregs of their dessert, sipping strong sweet drinks.

'You lied to me about what was on those videos,' I said.

She shrugged. 'Now you know. My offer still stands.'

'I don't do bathrooms.'

She looked away. 'I doubt your apartment's any bigger.'

'I kind of thought we'd end up at your parents' place. Isn't this whole show tonight for your father's benefit? You turn up at the restaurant where your parents' friends eat, then bring me home, we parade in arm in arm, straight up to your bedroom? You think everyone in here hasn't noticed what's going on? You think your father won't soon know about it?'

'So what if he hears?'

'He's already accused me of extortion once.'

'My sex life is none of his business.'

'Oh, I'm sure you've made that abundantly clear.'

'And I'm still not sure that you're not working for him.'

'Sorry to break it to you, but Gerald hates me already. One hand job more or less isn't going to make a difference.'

'Don't call him that.'

'You mean Gerald? Isn't that his name?'

'Just fucking call him something else.'

'Would you prefer Daddy?'

'What do you want from me, Leo?' Her face twisted. There were bitter tears in her eyes.

'You promised to set up a meeting with your brother. I think he knows who shot Teddy. That's why I'm here. Everything else is just what happens between then and now.'

'I want those videos. That's why I'm here.'

'You're not going to get them. They're in a safe place, and they'll stay there. When this is all over I intend to destroy them. They've got nothing to do with your so-called research, and you've got no business wanting them.'

She pursed her lips and glanced away. 'Do you practice talking that way in the mirror?'

'How's that?'

'Like you think you're a tough guy who can turn down any girl he wants, because he's always going to have another one coming along? When was the last time you got laid?'

'What makes you think I'd keep up my end of the bargain?'

'Because you would.' She looked me in the face. 'I know I can trust you.'

'Here's a tip. In these kinds of situations, take your payment in advance. Because after the magic is over, all bets are off.'

I wanted her to set up the meeting with Keith but I wasn't going to trade those disks for it. 'I'm not very good at waiting,' she said. 'And I don't ever intend to be.'

'You ever happen to see any photographs of your father taken on the street over in the Sunset, in Golden Gate Park? When Teddy got shot he was just starting to make notes for a habeas brief that was going to mention him and include those pictures. Does anything I'm saying ring a bell?'

She made no acknowledgment or denial. But I realized at that moment that she knew everything.

'How did you meet Teddy, anyway?'

'Keith introduced us.'

'Did you go after him? Or vice versa? If things just happened between you two, that's one thing, but if he came after you and shoved all this in your face, used it to get in your pants, maybe to get some kind of revenge, then that's something completely different.'

She ought to have thrown her drink in my face. She didn't deserve the grief I was laying on her, but her feelings were not my primary consideration. I was beginning to guess that they hadn't been Teddy's, either, and that she had recognized as much. When you're born rich and beautiful, real human sympathy comes in far shorter supply than most people suppose.

'He came after me.' All the anger had drained from her voice. 'About a year ago.'

'Was Teddy involved with Keith in the Green Light?'

'I don't think so. It was all very mysterious.'

'Do you think your father's the kind of person who could have had Teddy shot to keep him from filing that brief?'

A look of panic. 'I don't know.'

'Did you take those videos?'

Her voice was small. 'I think Martha must have put

the camera in there.' She wouldn't meet my eyes. 'I met her through my research. You're right, she was working for my brother. After they caught Keith with the body, Martha came to me. She was scared. She was afraid that the police might try to bring her into it, because of the videos. She wanted to know what to do with them. I told her to give them to me, and I gave them to Teddy.'

I nodded, relieved that she was finally coming clean about something. If she *was* coming clean. 'Here's how I see it going down. Tell me if I'm way off. Teddy puts Santorez's money in the Green Light, figures he'll get his investment back in a few months, then return the money to the account, no problem. He has Car in there looking over Keith's shoulder. Then, shortly after the club opens, your professor ends up dead, either because he forgot the safe word or because he was helping Martha make home movies on the sly and someone didn't like it. The Green Light is the Red Light unless they can make the body disappear. Keith gets caught dumping Marovich's body, and the club is raided and shut down. Then Santorez's men contact Teddy looking to make a with- drawal, and all he can tell them is that the money's gone.'

'Teddy would never have been stupid enough to go into business with my brother.'

'Tanya,' I said after a pause. 'It must have been Tanya.' Who else knew the combination of the safe? Who else had access to the client trust account? I remembered what Tanya had said earlier today, that Teddy had promised her she'd be taken care of; she must have emptied the trust account and put the money into the Green Light as Keith's partner, figuring she could replace the money, that Teddy would never know. Who else had the acumen to run a prostitution ring and the audacity to tell Keith to throw a professor's body in a Dumpster? Who else might Keith be sufficiently afraid of to obey? That was what the fight on the stairwell had been about. Teddy had figured out that Tanya was the one who'd stolen his money. Fix this, Teddy told Car.

I'd drunk far too much. Sweat dripped under my shirt. I was breathless. I rose from the table, holding out a hand as if to ward off further revelations, and made my way to the front door of the restaurant through a darkening tunnel. I reached the sidewalk, breathed the chilly night air, and blinked the lights of the city back into being as the darkness receded and my lungs released their clawed grip. I leaned against the wall of the restaurant, taking breath after breath.

'It was Tanya,' I said when Christine found me outside a few minutes later. 'Tanya stole the money from Santorez right under Teddy's nose, and she was Keith's partner in the Green Light. They lost everything when Marovich turned up dead. And she must be the one who killed Martha.' And shot my brother, I couldn't bring myself to say.

Christine gave a little gasping cry of surprise. 'Martha's dead?'

Chapter Twenty-One

In bed Christine traced the outline of my Batman tattoo. She was fascinated by it. I didn't like her touching it, but I didn't say anything.

'Poor Martha,' she kept saying drunkenly. 'Poor, poor Martha.' All I could see was the top of her head, a murky fog of hair. 'Did you tell the police about me?' Her voice was dreamy, as if asking a question so unimportant that she'd already forgotten it.

'No,' I said. I'd already given her a brief account of my interrogation.

'So Tanya shot Teddy and Martha?'

'Maybe not. Or maybe only Martha. I think she stole the money from the trust account and lost it. If Santorez had him shot, it was Tanya's fault, but I don't think that's what she intended.' My eyes sprang open as I remembered that I'd agreed to represent the man.

'So you're a cyclist,' she said after a pause. 'Once again I've broken my resolution not to sleep with any more demented athletes.'

'It keeps me from going crazy.'

'Have you won any races?'

'I don't enter many. I just like to get out and ride.'

She scoffed. 'So you're one of those people. I should have known.'

I reached down and goosed her. She gave me a tug, and that got us started again.

Afterward I fell deeply asleep, and I didn't awaken until the screaming of the shower pipes started at 8 a.m. I lay in bed for a minute, then got up to join Christine in the shower.

I made toast and peanut butter for breakfast, with coffee. It was all I had. 'I talked to Keith while you were asleep,' Christine said while we drank our coffee and munched on the toast. 'You still want to see him?'

'Okay.'

'We'll have to drive. I don't know where he wants to meet, only that it's in the city. He's going to text us with directions.'

Finally, progress. We finished breakfast and went down to the street to Teddy's car. There was a new parking ticket, and I tossed it in the glove compartment with the others. The police would come with the boot soon enough, but I couldn't imagine that the car had much life left in it, anyway.

Christine's cell phone chimed, and she glanced at it. 'Head west on Geary.'

The fog was spilling over the Twin Peaks toward the

bay as we crested the Geary hill and dropped down among endless rows of stucco houses perched above single-car garages, the same basic design repeated from here to the beach and selling for upwards of five hundred thousand dollars. I'd spent the first ten years of my life in a house just like those. Living downtown, I tended to forget that the outlying neighborhoods still exist. When I saw the sea, it was usually from the saddle of my bike along the coastal and mountain roads in Marin.

I was starting to feel bad about last night, the kind of guilt that gnaws at you. Not that Christine had meant anything to Teddy, or he to her. I knew there was only trouble at the end of this road.

A few more chimes of Christine's phone circled us through the Sunset. Then we ended up on the Great Highway heading north along Ocean Beach.

'Those pictures you mentioned last night,' Christine said. 'It's true, I've seen them, but Teddy didn't show them to me. They were in a drawer in my mom's office, and I found them snooping when I was a kid. Keith told me the whole story about ten years ago. He said I was old enough to know the truth. The truth according to Keith Locke, that is.'

'Ten years ago?' Keith's choice of a lawyer must have been no coincidence; he must have known who my brother was before he sought him out. 'But you didn't believe him.'

'It's very convenient for Keith to believe that my

father is the villain of all villains rather than face responsibility for his own crummy life.'

'Now you're beginning to sound like your father.'

'Teddy's basically got the same complex as Keith. He doesn't want to believe that your father murdered your mother, just like he'd never believe that the people closest to him, the people he trusted more than anybody else, could have betrayed him. For such a cynical person, he was very, very trusting. But that's probably what happened, if what you're telling me is true. Tanya must have either shot him or gotten him shot.'

There was an eerie certainty to her voice. 'You sound a lot more sure than I am,' I said.

'Just don't swallow one of Keith's conspiracy theories the way Teddy did. That's all I'm saying.'

'How can you be so certain I'm right and Tanya was behind the shooting? Did Teddy tell you something?' My voice became shrill. 'Have you been holding something back?'

'No, I've told you everything.' She stared out the window. 'It's just the logical conclusion. And I don't blame Teddy for what he was trying to do to my father. I kind of liked screwing someone who was out to screw my family.'

Her cool rationality was almost convincing. Almost. Yet last night when she was drunk she hadn't been able to hear her father's name.

'Come on, Christine. Very little of what you've told

me has turned out to be true. Look at what's happened to Marovich, Teddy, and Martha. The only thing that connects the three of them is you. I don't think it's a coincidence. You're going to have to explain yourself at some point. I want to help you out of whatever mess you're in. But you have to talk to me.'

Her voice was a knife. 'You just don't want to believe that Teddy could have betrayed your little cult of hating your father.'

We crossed the west end of Golden Gate Park below the Cliff House and continued north on the Great Highway toward Sutro Heights and Point Lobos. I wondered what the idea behind the telephone directions was. The messages added an element of surprise, but if anyone was trying to follow us he would have had an easy time of it.

'He wants to meet out here?' I asked as the Great Highway climbed onto the cliffs at the end of Ocean Beach. I didn't like that at all.

She didn't answer.

Something made me say, 'I'm not the only one who has seen those videos, just in case you're wondering. I got them from Car.'

When she spoke again her voice was calm, not with indifference but with serious concern. 'Has anyone else seen them?'

'Why don't you tell me whom you're protecting?'

'Where are the disks now? At your place?'

'You would have found them if they were, I'm sure. Tell me why you want them.'

'I just want them, that's all. You made a deal with me – now you have to hold up your end.'

'I told you last night the deal is off.'

'You don't have all of the disks,' she said, and smacked the glove compartment. 'Jesus. You're missing one, and that one's the only one that matters. You think you're holding all the cards, but you don't have shit.' She turned to me and shook her head in disbelief.

'So Car has it,' I said after a pause.

'Maybe Teddy destroyed it. You knew you didn't have it. You knew the whole time.'

'Don't you realize that those other videos that you don't even care about probably got Martha killed?'

'I thought Tanya killed her,' Christine said. She wasn't responsible for anything, and nothing was her problem.

'When Teddy told you what he was planning with that habeas brief, you really were glad?'

'Fuck Gerald,' she said. 'Whatever my father gets is less than he deserves.'

She sat wedged against the door with her shoulders hunched, turned so drastically away from me that she might have suffered from a spinal deformity – the outward expression of how her hatred for her parents had crippled her.

Crippled her, crippled me. But fuck Lawrence, I

found myself thinking. Hatred was survival; that's what I'd learned, and that's what I knew. With my father on the cusp of freedom, I once again clung to the belief that my anger made me strong.

I pulled as directed into the parking lot on the west side of Fort Miley above Seal Rocks Beach, just south of Lands End. The beach was two hundred feet below; we were atop the cliffs. A guardrail rimmed the parking lot. On the other side of the rail was a row of pole-mounted binoculars, like mouthless faces. Christine's phone chimed again.

'He wants you to go down the path to the left. I'm supposed to wait.'

'I thought the whole point was that you were coming with me.'

'I guess the parking lot is far enough. We can leave. You're the one who was so hot to talk to him.'

'We're staying,' I snapped, though I knew I might be walking into a trap.

'Can you leave the keys at least so I can listen to the radio while I'm stuck here waiting for you?'

I left the keys. As I walked away from the car, looking for the path, my cell phone rang. I glanced back at Christine, saw her absorbed in the radio dials, then turned my back to the wind, and answered the call. It was Santorez. 'I got my court hearing this afternoon. I couldn't believe it, but that's what they said. They're rushing this thing along. One thirty, Department

Twenty-two. You gonna be there, or should I have my boys call someone else?'

He made even that sound like a threat, or perhaps it was just my fear coupled with what I'd put together last night about Tanya stealing his money, making Santorez a much more promising suspect. 'I'll be there,' I heard myself say. Turning again, I took in the foggy view of the ocean, the waves crashing on bird-whitened rocks below, the Golden Gate Bridge in extreme foreshortening to my right. The air was frigid, the fog clammy, my fingertips chilled. A few tourists wearing shorts and windbreakers huddled together with their cameras at the other end of the guardrail. Nobody visiting San Francisco for the first time ever brings the right clothes.

I knew in the cold, hungry pit of my stomach that I was putting my professional reputation – not to mention my bar card – on the line before I had even gotten started and that the odds were against me. I was beginning to see why the police had focused on Santorez from the start. I felt a flash of anger at Anderson. I knew he hadn't trusted me because of this, because of the game I was playing with his suspect, a game he'd foreseen and headed off.

I would have to decide whether to talk to the press after Santorez's arraignment, and what to tell them, but there was no time to think about that now. If Keith Locke had his way, maybe I wouldn't ever have to think about it. After the flush of my victory in the courtroom, I foolishly believed that all I had to do was talk to him, and he would listen.

I pocketed the phone and started down a wide path through a grove of wind-sculpted cypress. Below, the ocean crashed and boomed, sounding now right next to me, now distant.

I don't like the ocean, not at this latitude. There is simply too much of it out there beyond the Golden Gate, and it is too violent and too cold. My dislike of the sea is one of the reasons I could never imagine living in one of the city's far western neighborhoods, where the air is perpetually tinged with salt and fog.

Ahead of me I saw a thin figure standing on a rocky promontory with the tumbling ocean behind him, silhouetted against the guano-stained bulk of Seal Rock. He wore tight black jeans ripped at the knees, hiking boots, and a green jacket. As I watched, he dropped from his perch and disappeared down the other side. I stumbled and swore.

In a few minutes I stood on the rock where Keith had been standing. Below was a large overlook area atop the cliffs, thirty or so feet above the surf. To the south was a magnificent view of the Cliff House and the entire length of Ocean Beach, the peninsula stretching away arrow-straight into the distance. Immediately below me were the ruins of the Sutro Baths, once a glass-enclosed swimming pavilion, now little more than a tidal pool half-blocked off from the ocean by an artificial breakwater.

For a moment it seemed that Keith had disappeared. Then, catching movement to my left, I saw him hiking down a trail that led inland from the vista point, then seaward to the ruins.

'CAUTION', a sign warned as I descended. 'Cliff and surf area extremely dangerous. People have been swept from the rocks and DROWNED.'

In the old bath foundations pieces of twisted iron jutted from the ground among graffiti-covered remnants of crumbling walls. I skidded on the loose gravel, and when I looked up Keith was gone. There was nowhere to hide, yet he'd vanished as completely as if the earth had opened up and swallowed him.

Then I remembered there was a cave, an artificial tunnel connecting the baths with Point Lobos on the other side of the hill. I knew that I should turn back from this desolate spot, but I went on, still convinced that I could make him tell me what he knew.

'Leo!' a voice called from the cave as I approached.

The floor of the entrance was soft sand. I could see the round opening at the other end a hundred feet away, silhouetting Keith's head and shoulders. 'I just want to talk,' I said into the sudden silence as I ducked inside, my voice strange to me after the din of the waves.

'Come on down here where it's a little lighter and we'll do that.'

It was my one chance to talk to the person who might know why Teddy had been shot. I looked for weapons on him but didn't see any bulges. He wasn't much bigger than I was. I came forward slowly, giving my eyes time to adjust. He was standing at a railing near a hole in the floor through which I heard the surf crashing on the rocks.

'Your sister's waiting in the car,' I told him.

'Yeah.' A pause. 'I hear you're fucking her.'

'Keith, your mother offered me twenty thousand dollars to convince you to see her. It's all yours if you want it. I didn't come here because of her, though.'

We stood facing each other for a moment; then Keith turned. 'Come look at this hole, man. It's pretty wild.'

I took half a step closer but no more, keeping my knees slightly bent, ready to move. Through the man-size hole beneath us I dimly saw surf washing over sand.

'I'm not interested in your mother's money. The reason I wanted to talk to you is that when Teddy got shot, he left your case up in the air. I want to pick up where Teddy left off. I think we can beat this murder charge, but first you have to turn yourself in. There's no way to clear your name when you're on the run.'

'You want to be my lawyer?' Keith asked.

'Yes,' I lied.

'Everything we talk about is secret, then?'

'That's right,' I said with reluctance.

Keith grabbed my arm. He tugged me on into the tunnel toward the light at the end. I jerked free of him, then followed, trying to keep out of his reach. 'You've got to see the view out here. It's primeval.' As we approached the mouth he spun, quicker than I thought, and slid sideways along the wall until he was behind me, a neat reversal.

I tried to move away but there was nowhere to go. The sea was at my back, and Keith was between me and the tunnel. I tried to follow my script but my voice kept sticking. 'All you have to do is tell the truth. Whatever you know about Marovich, about Teddy, about Martha. You tell the truth and cut a deal and walk away.'

'The truth will set me free.'

'Who shot my brother?'

He blinked. 'Who brought you here?'

'You're insane.'

'Daddy's little girl. The apple doesn't fall far from the tree. That whore pal of hers, Martha, drove the car. Christine walked right into Coruna with the gun in her hand. She's a pretty hot number, I know, but she can play the man when she has to. Bang, bang, then out the back. Cool as a cucumber.'

'You shot him, didn't you, Keith,' I said. 'You're the one who did it.'

'I'll tell you what I told Teddy. I don't need a lawyer cutting me any deals, because that would mean testifying against my own sister, and that I will not do. In confidence, though, she was fucking her thesis adviser. She went too far, maybe on accident, maybe on purpose. He was an asshole anyway. She called me, I came to the rescue, and I got busted. That's how it went down. So you going to represent me? We got a deal?'

Keith was still between me and the tunnel.

'Teddy knew too much. Then Martha knew too much. And now you're the one who knows too much,' Keith said.

My hands shook and my chest was heaving. I took a half step closer to him, away from the end of the tunnel, then glanced back. Just below us a wild landscape of waves swirled and thrashed and climbed the rocks, as if the waves themselves feared the ocean and were seeking desperately to break free.

He held out his hand, and I took it. Not because I wanted to be his attorney but because I felt a need to reassure myself that he was not some whirling figment of a madness into which I was descending. Because there was nothing else to grab.

Then we were breathing in each other's faces, our feet scrabbling for purchase on the sand. With a convulsive heave Keith broke free and pushed me out the mouth of the cave, and the water seemed to leap up at my back.

Chapter Twenty-Two

I should have died from the fall. As I lost my balance I saw the rocks coming toward me, one in particular the size of my torso and jutting like a rhinoceros's horn. I managed to twist in midair and take the brunt of the impact on my hip, sending a searing shock through my body. The collision absorbed the energy of my fall, and I crumpled and rolled into the water. Then the cold grabbed me by the nuts and throat, and the waves sucked and churned around my face.

This is how the ocean kills you, I thought as I caught a wave in the face, then another, and felt a third slam me against a rock and drag me down, each from a different direction. The sea's victims are found with their skin stripped off, faces pulped by impact, lungs filled with seawater, throats packed with sand.

I've never been a strong swimmer. As a kid I never even learned to tolerate putting my face in the water – not that being a good swimmer would have mattered. I had as little control over my fate as an ice cube in a cocktail shaker.

It was a tiny, V-shaped cove filled with dangerous rocks, and I owe my life to the fact that the notoriously strong currents outside the Golden Gate quickly swept me free of it. My shoes and pants weighed me down, but I was no longer being thrown against those rocks. With every convulsive, gasping breath I choked on seawater. I hadn't seen Keith Locke since the instant I'd fallen. I wasn't sure that he hadn't fallen, too.

I was just about to go under when someone shouted, and then there was a splash, and strong hands grabbed my arms. I flailed, thinking it was Keith coming to push me under, finish me off. Then I felt a surfboard being shoved under my elbows. 'Take it easy, take it easy,' the surfer was shouting.

I was shivering so violently that it was all I could do to hold on. The guy wore a full wet suit, and he stayed in the water, guiding the half-submerged board. The lower two-thirds of my body was in the water, and the cold touch of it continued to terrify me.

'We have to get through the break here,' he warned. 'Try not to drown. When I tell you to hold your breath, hold it until we come up.

'Okay. Now,' he said, and I felt the sea turning over beneath us, as if someone had decided it was time to roll it up and put it away. We were gaining speed, then the wave left us behind and water pounded down on top of me and I was turning over and over, and then there was no more up or down. I lost my grip on the board, and the surfer lost his grip on me, and I felt my face press the sand. In surprise I gasped, and seawater filled me. Inside my lungs and stomach the water was cold and completely hostile to the continuance of my life, but after a while it started to feel okay. I drifted and the breeze warmed my back. Roll over and breathe, a voice urged, but I let my head fall onto the pillow.

Just five more minutes, I promised, then I'll get up.

When I came to I was lying on my side vomiting seawater.

The current had swept us about half a mile down Ocean Beach, and it took me a minute to get my bearings. The surfer was on his ass next to me without his board. Behind me I heard the waves crashing. The sound made me shudder. I didn't turn to look.

The surfer was breathing hard. Evidently he had just dragged me onto the beach. He was in his midthirties, with a bleached ponytail and a face lined by the sun and wind. 'Next time try the bridge,' he said, getting to his feet. 'At least out there in the gate you won't be fucking with anyone's break.'

My awareness kept fading in and out. When it returned he was walking away down the beach. His board turned and slipped in the foam about two hundred yards down. He stalked up to it, retrieved it, and turned angrily back toward me. A few people were standing around asking if I was okay, if I needed help. A motorcycle cop still in his helmet kept saying, 'How did you end up in the water, sir? Can you tell me what happened?'

'I'll tell you what happened,' the surfer said, walking back up with the board under his arm. 'Fucker took a swan dive from the Point Lobos cave. Try the bridge next time, asshole. It's a sure thing.'

He sat down near the surf line, and I saw that he was fixing the leash between the board and his ankle. Before anyone could stop him he was wading back out. The cop shouted at him to wait, but the surfer had already gone prone on his board and was paddling through the surf.

'Who was that masked man?' I asked through clattering teeth, but no one laughed.

It took me the better part of an hour, sitting wrapped in blankets in the open back of the ambulance, to convince the cops and paramedics that I hadn't tried to kill myself. I could see that they didn't believe my version of events, which was that I'd leaned out for a picture from the cave mouth and slipped, but the surfer didn't reappear to contradict my story or to say he'd seen a second person up there, and eventually one of the cops agreed to give me a lift back to Teddy's car. It was still there, but the keys were gone and so was Christine. I pretended I'd lost them in the water and got the cop to drive me home.

It frightened me to think how I'd walked into danger,

thinking all I would have to do was talk to him; maybe the police weren't so far off in assuming I was suicidal. Why had I done that, kept putting one foot in front of the other when I knew where the path would lead? Simply because I didn't want to go back to the car and face Christine, because I knew she wouldn't be there?

My phone was waterlogged and useless. I took it apart and set it on the radiator to dry, then with difficulty stripped off my jeans and T-shirt and got into the shower.

The hot water stung my wounds. I had scrapes running the entire length of my body from the fall. My hip felt like a red-hot poker was buried in it, but nothing felt broken. Blood oozed from the worst abrasions at my hip and shoulder and elbow. I'd been in a few nasty bike crashes, though nothing quite this bad, and I knew that for weeks the slightest movement was going to be excruciating. After patting myself dry and slapping adhesive bandages on the worst places, I sucked air through my teeth and then as quickly and gently as possible dressed myself in my best suit, the one Tanya had bought at Nordstrom. The damaged skin and strained muscles had begun to tighten, making it hard to bend at the waist or reach behind my back. It was going to be a chore getting out of the suit later, but I tried not to think about that.

Luckily my face had not been injured. I was still pretty for the cameras. With my suit on, the only visible injury was an abrasion on the back of my hand, and I was able to cover that with a large bandage. I couldn't stop shivering even after a shower and half a microwave pizza. I was so sleepy I kept having to pause and let my eyes close for a minute while I shaved, standing at the sink with the razor poised at my face. When I told myself in the mirror to get on with it the words came out thick. I should have crawled into bed and stayed there about eighteen hours.

Instead I went down to 850 Bryant to represent Ricky Santorez at his arraignment.

Chapter Twenty-Three

The doors hadn't been unlocked yet, and the hallway outside Department Twenty-Two was filled with reporters. I sidestepped my way through the bodies and nearly made the doors before they recognized me. Then it was all 'Leo, do you have anything you'd like to say to Ricky Santorez? Do you have anything to say to the man who tried to kill your brother?'

When I reached the door I turned, at the center of the throng. I waited for silence, and then I said, 'Since Mr Santorez is my client, anything I might have to say to him is confidential. After the hearing I'll have a few words for the press.' I turned and banged on the door with my fist, ignoring the reporters' questions, trying to ignore the hands tapping me on the back and shoulders, though the contact against my grated skin brought tears to my eyes.

The bailiff opened the door a crack and peered out at me. 'I'd like to go back and speak with my client,' I said, raising my voice over the din. 'Santorez. He's on the arraignments calendar.' He nodded and opened the door just wide enough for me to slip through, then closed and locked it again.

As I walked in I felt sure neither of myself nor of my purpose in the courtroom. Even after what Keith had told me, there was a good chance that I'd offered my services to the man who'd ordered my brother killed and that in doing so I was subverting the proper course of justice. Still, I wanted very much to be right. I wanted to be the one who stood in front of the cameras and told the world that the police had arrested the wrong man. I wanted to be the hero, the lone voice speaking out for justice.

I told myself that Christine had killed Marovich, had shot Teddy, and had set me up this morning: She was the guilty one. Or, if not Christine, then her father, or Keith – anyone but the obvious candidate, my client. Purging my mind of reasoned skepticism, I was intensely focused on showing as publicly and dramatically as possible that Santorez's indictment was ridiculous and that the real shooter was still out there.

I was escorted through a reinforced door into the holding pen, which was crammed with defendants in prison orange, many wearing slip-on shoes. Someone had backed up the toilet, and the stink made me gag. I was just going to have to suck it up. At 850 Bryant, there were no cozy conference rooms for lawyers to speak with their clients.

Santorez sat in a corner of the bench that ran the perimeter of the room, as far from the unscreened toilet as you could get. I recognized him instantly among yesterday's catch of the drunk and addicted and homeless. He wore an orange CDC jumpsuit, for one thing, rather than the usual county jail overalls, and he was the only inmate granted a two-foot radius of empty space.

I felt a churning in my stomach, thinking how Santorez had gunned down those cops, how someone had gunned down my brother in that restaurant right in front of me. 'Just bang on the door when you want out, and keep on banging until someone comes,' the deputy told me. 'Sometimes things get busy out here.' With a smile he clanged the holding-cell door closed, locking me alone with the inmates in that stinking, windowless, tile-floored space.

With the ease of a habituated prisoner Santorez stood and pumped my hand. 'Man, you don't look nothing like your brother. Or your father either, come to think of it.'

I didn't say anything to that.

'I just want you to know, first of all, no matter what happens out there, I'm not forgetting about the money your brother owes me. And I don't intend to forget it.'

'I understand. You've got to pay your phone bill.' The phone would be up his ass, or up someone's ass. Probably a man in his position had a body cavity bitch. 'We were talking pro bono, but if that's your attitude we should probably discuss a retainer.'

'You already got my retainer. In the trust account, remember?'

'I don't know anything about it. That's between you and Teddy and whoever drained those funds.'

'How about you get me off and you don't owe a thing.'

'I don't owe you anything anyway,' I heard myself say.

He gave me a hard stare that didn't have any trace of human feeling in it.

'I wouldn't talk about the money in here,' I went on. 'That's supposed to be your motive, remember. You're being charged with attempted murder. If Teddy dies, the charge will be murder.'

'I beat that charge once already. And that time I actually pulled the trigger.'

'You think that means you've got nothing to worry about this time?'

'Not if you do your job.'

Teddy and I had never really talked about the Santorez case, but I knew it caused him more sleepless nights and stomach acid than any other he'd tried. I'd never seen him so relieved as he'd been the day the verdict came back. Now I understood why. Even Teddy could let only so many implied threats sail past before he began to sweat a little.

I meant to discuss case strategy, go over my reasons for doing what I was doing, make sure Santorez knew what he needed to know. 'I'm only representing you for this hearing. I'm doing it because I think publicizing your innocence is the surest way to make the police start looking for the person who actually did this. I don't expect them to drop the charges today, and after today you'll have to find a different lawyer. I'm not experienced enough to handle a serious felony. Besides, there's a conflict of interest. I think I explained all this to you over the phone.'

He held up a hand. 'I don't want to hear any bullshit. Whatever you need to say, I'll say you said it. Just show me where I've got to sign to shut you up.'

I took out the forms: first, the one informing him of the conflict of interest in my serving as his lawyer; second, the limited retainer form establishing that I was acting as his lawyer for today's hearing only, and that I would do nothing more than assert his right to a speedy trial and enter a plea of not guilty.

Making a show of not reading anything that was printed on the forms, Santorez signed his name quickly. 'Get me off and you don't owe me a penny,' he said, handing me back the forms. 'That's not written down here, but that's our deal.'

And if you're found guilty? I wanted to ask. 'No lawyer could get you off today. But if things go well out there I don't think you'll have any trouble finding an attorney. A good one.'

'Flies to shit, man.'

I slid the signed forms into a file folder and stood, but

Santorez wasn't done. He beckoned me closer, and like a lackey I bent to hear him. 'I didn't kill your brother, but I could have,' he said in a voice not quite low enough to be a whisper, his lips two inches from my ear. 'I know you think you're pulling a fast one on everyone, but you're not pulling a fast one on me. You try to fuck me on this, I can hurt you, and I will. Anywhere, anytime. You remember that, Monkey Boy.'

As I straightened, my skin felt on fire, and the room tilted around me. For a moment I was back under the churning surf, being pummeled against the rocks. Then I regained the moment, though chills ran over me where the fire had been.

Without looking at Santorez I turned and walked to the door, banged on it, and waited for the deputy to open up.

Monkey Boy he'd called me. The anger didn't come until I was safely out of that cell.

The clerk called Ricky Santorez's case at two fifteen, after a string of short hearings scheduled for the convenience of the public defenders and DAs who had business in other courtrooms. I watched the public defenders with curiosity, wondering if I'd soon be joining their ranks.

'Counsel, please state your appearances.'

The DA had sent down one of his top prosecutors, Lou Ferrino. Beside him sat a young assistant DA and Detective Anderson.

When I stood and said, 'Leo Maxwell on behalf of Mr Santorez, Your Honor,' the courtroom was all hushed attention.

Judge Dowling looked directly at me, then turned his eyes away. A conscientious judge would have called a recess and summoned us into chambers. Dowling wanted no part of it. As curtly as if this were an ordinary case, he asked if my client would waive instruction and arraignment. I said yes, just as I'd seen every lawyer before me do.

'We'll send the case to Department Seventeen for a trial date and put it on for a status conference there in one month.'

'The real show's outside,' I told Santorez as I gathered up my folders. 'Catch it on the news.'

He didn't take his eyes off me as the deputies led him away, back to the bullpen and San Quentin. I couldn't tell what his scrutiny signified. It was menacing, but there was vulnerability in it, as well. I wondered if he regretted threatening me. Then the door closed and he was gone.

Before I could move away from the defense table Detective Anderson came up. 'You ought to join me outside,' I told him. 'You'd make the perfect prop. They'd probably even put your picture in the paper.'

'Please don't do this,' he pleaded. 'You know we've got the right man.'

'I don't think so.'

'Then tell me who we should look at. Tell me who, if not Santorez. Jesus, Leo, your brother stole the man's money. You don't steal a hundred thousand dollars from someone like that and expect to walk away without consequences.'

Another attorney had approached the defense table. The court clerk called the next case. 'I can't help you,' I said. I was thinking of Christine again, of our night together, of what Keith had said.

Anderson walked with me toward the exit. 'Can't or won't? That's the question I've been asking myself all along. Because it seems that if anyone knows what's going on, you do. The question is whether you've got the guts to bring justice for your brother.'

'This conversation is over,' I told him as I pushed through the doors.

His words had stung me, though, and the sting would linger longer than the sting of the wounds on my legs and back.

The reporters were waiting for me in the hallway, milling around. I could tell they were thinking they must have missed me. As I came out, they converged, cameras held aloft, a dozen questions at once. I ignored them and stuck to my script.

'I have appeared on behalf of Ricky Santorez today because I'm one hundred percent confident that he is innocent of these charges. I would be dishonoring everything my brother stood for if I failed to speak out on Mr Santorez's behalf. This is not the time for the police department and the DA's office to be settling old scores. The person who shot Teddy Maxwell remains at large, and I urge the police and the district attorney's office to abandon their farcical prosecution of Mr Santorez and focus their efforts on finding the person who actually pulled that trigger, just as they would do in any other case of attempted murder.'

It was considerably less than I'd meant to say, and my voice lacked the stridency I'd intended it to have. I wanted Santorez to be guilty and I didn't. I wanted Christine tonight and every night; I wanted her behind bars. If only I could know whether she'd set me up, whether she'd waited for me to return from my walk down to the baths.

I walked two blocks blindly back toward my apartment, thinking that I would go to the hospital next and spend the rest of the day with Teddy, when an obstacle appeared in my path, a person standing rooted in the center of the sidewalk. I veered around him, and it wasn't until he grabbed me by both arms that I recognized Car. 'Let's go for a ride, Leo.'

I saw Jeanie driving slowly along the line of parked cars at the curb beside me, hunched over the steering wheel. Something in Car's face made me break free and run.

He caught me in five steps and wrapped me in a bear

313

hug, killing our shared momentum with a few heavy-heeled steps. The Volvo was there. Jeanie came around to open the back door.

I let him shove me into the car.

Chapter Twenty-Four

'Consider this an intervention,' Jeanie said from the driver's seat. 'No more press conferences, no more court appearances, no more bodies, no more breaking into people's houses and digging through their garbage. You're going to spend the next few days lying low.'

I didn't have anything to say to that. We were on the Bay Bridge crossing toward Oakland. I stretched out across the backseat and promptly fell asleep.

When I awakened after a dreamless interval we were on Pinehurst winding down through the oaks and madrone from Skyline Boulevard. We rounded the last switchback and were beneath the redwoods on the valley floor beside the creek. The afternoon light hung like a golden haze within the darkness of the trees.

The undercarriage of the Volvo scraped against ruts as we made our way up the steep gravel road. The plastic sheeting still clattered on the roof, and the Contra Costa sheriff's notice was still stapled to the door, the paper wrinkled from the dew.

'God, what a dump.' Jeanie dropped her keys on the kitchen table.

It was cold in the house. Jeanie was in the kitchen making coffee. Car had gone through the bedroom to the deck and was smoking, staring broodily at the trees. 'I offered a dozen times to finish it for him,' he said. 'No sweat, couple weeks work.'

'You called this an intervention.' I waited a beat. 'So intervene.'

Car stabbed out his cigarette. He went to the car and came back with a camera case. It was the one I'd found in Jeanie's garbage. I'd left it on Teddy's desk. He bent over the TV and plugged the camera into it. He was evidently going to show me what was on the missing disk, the one Christine wanted.

Jeanie handed me a cup of coffee, and set one on the floor for Car. 'Leo, I can't even begin to tell you what a huge violation that was, breaking into my apartment. I'm so angry with you about it I can hardly look at you. I was tempted to go to the police.'

'Call them up now if you want. I'll admit it. Of course then you'll have to tell them how you got the camera, and the disks might turn up, and they might look at them and ask difficult questions. Like what were you planning to do with them?'

'Enough BS, okay? Nobody's calling the police, nobody's blackmailing anybody. We brought you here to have a serious conversation.'

'Isn't it funny how people use that word, have? Have sex, have a baby, have a fight, have a conversation, as if it's just something that happens by itself?'

Car's face puckered. He turned on the television. The screen was blue; then it flickered and showed an empty room with a bed, a room I recognized immediately as Martha's, a different setting from the other disks, which had been filmed at the Green Light.

The image was muzzy, as if some thin material were hanging in front of the lens. Car fast-forwarded through an empty twenty minutes, then slowed the tape to normal speed as a woman and a man walked into the room. They were kissing. The woman was Christine, and the man was the college professor Marovich. I recognized him from the picture in Keith's file.

They seemed practiced with each other's bodies, sure of themselves and of their responses. The camera angle was a bit off for how they were lying, showing them only from the waist up, so we were spared a direct view of their coupling, but the camera saw enough, more than enough. It made me feel excited, embarrassed, and ashamed to watch a woman I'd just made love to make love to another man.

Marovich said something, and she tied his wrists to the bed, then slipped a cord around his neck and began to draw the slip knot tighter. She rode him faster, and I saw her come but keep going, shudders running through her as the motion of her hips became spasmodic. The

317

veins on his neck stood out from the cord, and his eyes bugged; then his hips convulsed. Christine ground to a halt and let herself collapse forward on top of him.

A moment passed before she sat up, looking down at him. Her breathing slowed. He was unconscious, and still she waited. An agony to watch. She began scrabbling at the cord with her fingernails. Her hands were shaking almost too badly to undo the knot, but it loosened and she yanked it off. She sat motionless, then gave a scream, and brought her fists down on his chest.

Marovich coughed once, twice, then his eyes opened and he twisted, gasping, and she touched him tenderly on the side of the head.

I was flooded with relief. 'She didn't kill him,' I said. My pulse was racing. It was hard to catch my breath.

'This time,' Jeanie said.

'That was Martha's apartment. He died at the club.' It was a non sequitur, I knew. Marovich could have died anywhere.

'I was the one who opened the package when it arrived,' Car said. 'Completely anonymous, no markings, no nothing, sent directly to the office. No note. And then we watch the videos, and lo and behold here's this clip that seems to exonerate Teddy's client while hanging Christine up by her twat hairs. And since Teddy is Keith's lawyer, it's his job to string her up.'

'You really think Christine killed Marovich?'

'The point is not what she did or didn't do,' Car said. 'The point is what she'd do to keep that video secret. Teddy knew she was Keith's sister and he confronted her about it, let her know he was going to turn it over to the prosecution. Then someone puts a bullet in his head.'

We all sat in silence for a moment. I was guessing that Christine's relationship with Teddy had begun more recently than she'd implied – probably right after he confronted her about the video. 'I think I could use one of your martinis,' I said to Jeanie.

She seemed about to tell me to fix it myself, then changed her mind, and went into the kitchen. She came out with three glasses of cold gin.

'Christine said that she had a class with Marovich. She was helping him with his research and writing her thesis about prostitution. Keith said the guy was her thesis adviser.' I left out the part about Keith telling me she'd killed him. Part of me still wasn't ready to admit it.

'We want to be able to prove she shot Teddy,' Car said. 'To do that we probably have to prove she killed Marovich. Before we go to the cops we need to have her case tied up neat. Because she's going to have a lawyer every bit as good as Teddy was. We build the case against her, then hand it all over. We do their job for them, and we do it right, and then – only then – we go public if they drag heels. You have the proof, you have the power. Until then you're just pounding sand. What you did this afternoon, you might as well have been jerking off in public.'

'So I guess you didn't kill him. I probably owe you an apology.'

'Sorry to disappoint you, Monkey Boy. Your brother was my bread and butter. See, I like working for winners, and Teddy was a winner. Now I got to go back to working for lawyers who can't find their dicks without a compass. No offense to Jeanie. You're a winner, too, aren't you, babe?'

Jeanie frowned. I wanted to ask Car whether he and Teddy had ever manufactured evidence, whether they'd knowingly put a liar on the stand in Bradley's trial. For an instant I wondered if Car could have faked the video he'd just shown, pasted Christine's face onto another body. I felt a surge of hope and fear that died away as soon as it was born.

Then with renewed energy I said, 'It doesn't stop with Christine. It's the whole family. Now we know Christine's father was sleeping with my mother before her death and that Teddy was accusing him of murder. Trying to exonerate our father, who suddenly pops up as the snitch against Santorez. That's right,' I said, noticing the astonished look on Jeanie's face. I was coming unmoored again, losing my bearings, the way I'd felt just before Keith pushed me, as if the world was dissolving around me and taking me with it. 'What was I supposed to do, just let them frame Santorez?'

Neither of them said anything. I went on wildly: 'Christine knows that Gerald killed my mother. She's known it all her life. Keith knows, too. That's why he went to Teddy, that's why they became friends. Because Keith was curious about the son of the woman his father had been having an affair with, the woman he killed while letting her husband get sent away for life. Everything that's happened has grown out of Locke's beating my mother to death and getting away with it. Except he didn't get away: Now Teddy was about to expose him.'

Car took a drink and made a face like he'd swallowed broken glass. 'Leo, it's a black hole,' Jeanie said. 'It nearly swallowed your brother. He was obsessed with proving your father innocent. Be thankful he spared you. It was heartbreaking to watch a great lawyer like Teddy fall again and again for Lawrence's scams and keep chasing down leads that proved to be bullshit. Your father's a master manipulator who had Teddy wrapped around his little finger. But you and I both know that Lawrence was far from innocent, that even the best defense lawyer in the world couldn't change that fact. In Teddy's mind, though, the truth was whatever he could make people believe, whatever story he could convincingly spin. It was all very, very sad.'

I said, 'But don't you see, everything grows out of that. We can't get justice for Teddy without getting it for my mother. We have to go back to the beginning. We have to finish the job Teddy started.'

'That's your business, kid,' Car said. 'You don't want to help us nail Christine, you don't have to. But you do have to lie low until we do what we have to do.'

I sat back into the couch cushions, cupping my drink. 'What are you going to do?' I was almost in tears with frustration at their refusal to listen to me.

'Get back on her tail for one,' Car said. 'I had to let her slip to grab you this afternoon. Believe me, I didn't want to do it, but we had to make you see sense.'

I stared at him, wondering if he'd been there this morning, if he'd known what was going to happen to me but had held back, preferring to let me take my chances rather than to show himself to Christine. He stared back at me. I ran a hand over my eyes, pressing down on them. 'How long did she wait for me in the car this morning?'

'You tell me, kid.'

'Weren't you there?'

'What's he talking about, this morning?' Jeanie asked.

'Christine took me to meet Keith at Sutro Baths and I ended up taking a swim.'

'You must be a pretty good swimmer,' Car said. 'You say hi to Keith like I said?'

'Wait, are you saying Keith pushed you?' Jeanie asked. 'And Christine set you up?'

'Something like that,' I told her.

'I wasn't there, kid. I wish I could say I was, but I went home to take a shower.'

I gave a sigh, as if I could expel my tremendous fatigue. 'What do you want me to do?'

It was Jeanie's turn: 'Call her up. Bring her here. Get her to confess and get it on tape.'

'Pretty simple, really,' Car said.

I found Christine's number in the sheaf of credit cards and bills I'd taken from my sodden wallet, now stored in a plastic bag in my pocket. I went out on the deck, closing the door so Car and Jeanie couldn't listen in.

'Do you still want that missing disk?' I asked when she picked up.

'Leo?' was all she could say. She was surprised about something. Either that I was alive or that I was calling her – or that I had the disk. 'What happened to you?' She recovered her breath. 'I waited for nearly an hour.'

'Really? And then?'

'Then I had to get to class. I left the keys under the seat and took a cab to Caltrain and took Caltrain to Palo Alto and took the shuttle to Stanford and walked into lecture ten minutes late without my books.'

I hadn't looked under the seat. 'Do you want the disk?'

'Yes, but you don't have it. You told me so this morning.'

'I have it, and I've seen it, and I'm ready to deal. Just so that you know I have it, the video was taken in

Martha's apartment. You probably didn't know the camera was there, or you would have untied that knot a lot sooner. Maybe you waited a little longer the next time. Maybe one of those times you waited a little too long and had to call your brother to come rescue you. That's what the police would probably suppose.'

She gave a plaintive sigh. 'I want it.'

'Good. Then meet me at Teddy's place in two hours. And bring your checkbook.'

After we'd hung up I remained standing on the deck, looking out into the watery daylight under the trees. After the initial surprise in her voice she'd recovered quickly, as if nothing had happened beyond what she'd claimed: that she'd waited for me, gotten annoyed, then made her own way down to Stanford. Maybe that was exactly what had happened. Maybe Teddy's house would lift up off its foundation and float away to the moon.

Back in the living room Jeanie lay on the couch holding her drink. Car was sitting on the floor with a briefcase that was all foam rubber inside with notches to hold what looked like eavesdropping equipment. 'Booty call successful?' he asked.

'She'll be here in a couple of hours. I don't suppose one of you would mind taking me back to the city to get Teddy's Rabbit, so she doesn't wonder how the hell I got over here?'

They shared a glance; then Jeanie put her drink on the floor and sat up. 'I can take him. Unless you trust me to get this place wired for sound.'

'You go,' Car said without looking up.

Chapter Twenty-Five

'I checked with the hospital while you were on the phone,' Jeanie said as we merged onto the freeway.

'And?'

'No change.'

I was silent. There was nothing to say.

'So what's your plan?' she finally asked.

'I guess I'll apply to PD offices around the Bay. If Teddy dies, then maybe also So-Cal, the Central Valley.' I didn't look at her, not wanting to see the disapproval on her face at this thought. 'A change of scenery would do me good.'

'With Christine, I meant. What's your plan for making her talk?'

'Oh.' I waited, but nothing came to me. 'I guess I'll ask if she killed Marovich. If she says yes, I'll ask her if she shot my brother. If she says yes, I'll ask her if she's going to shoot me.'

'Don't count on us to swoop in and save you.' Jeanie

hesitated, then went on: 'Look, I'd be glad to make some calls for you when all this is over.'

'I think I'd rather you didn't.'

'You're pissed at me for what? For Car?' For about a mile she drove with her eyes fixed on the road ahead, her hands tightly gripping the wheel. Then she said, 'You have no right to be angry with me about him. Other things, maybe, but not that.'

She was right. She didn't owe me anything, and I had no reason to blame her. Why then did I feel this paralyzing resentment, this childish blame? I only knew that I did feel it and that the feeling kept me from apologizing.

We drove the rest of the way in silence.

After I'd driven the Rabbit back to Canyon and Jeanie had left with Car, I sat out on Teddy's deck and had another martini. I didn't want to be inside. Car had assured me the entire house was wired: They would hear everything spoken in there, and everything would be recorded. The deck was the only place in the house where I could feel alone, and I needed to think. I'd let them believe I'd go along with their plan to record Christine, but I hadn't come this far to blindly follow anyone's lead.

I wondered what justice would mean to Teddy. Now that I was the one in the victim's chair, I knew for certain that an eye for an eye was not an empty concept. I couldn't make Teddy better or get back Caroline or recover those lost years, but I could get revenge. Not against Christine; I didn't care about Christine. I wanted what Teddy wanted, our mother's killer. And I wanted to believe what Teddy had believed, that the killer was Gerald Locke.

From where could that cold man have summoned the rage to do the damage I'd seen in the crime scene photographs?

It was dusk when I heard the purr and clatter of a car coming up the hill. Turning in my chair, I looked through the house and saw Christine walking up, a Safeway bag dangling from her fingers.

She didn't knock. According to the plan I should rise and meet her, so that we could end up sitting inside with the microphones, but Car and Jeanie didn't care about setting up Gerald Locke. They wanted Christine, and if I gave them the evidence they needed, they'd go straight to the police. The cops would take over, and I'd be left with no leverage over Gerald and no control over what happened to Christine. I stayed where I was. To get Gerald, I needed her help. Maybe I was even willing to let her off the hook if she helped me finish the work Teddy had started.

Or maybe I'd fallen for her and wasn't thinking straight. Maybe I'd rather sleep with her than put her away.

'I brought food,' she called, coming through the house to the door of the deck when she saw me there. 'I figured you're probably just like your brother. Am I right? Nothing in the fridge?'

She showed me what she'd brought: three bottles of wine, bread, several cheeses, smoked salmon, oranges, and apples. She set down the bags, came out, and met me as I rose with an awkward half embrace, half kiss, my lips seeking hers, hers avoiding mine.

'What are you going to do, toss me over the railing?'

I don't know why I tried to kiss her. As a test, I suppose.

She drew back from me as if she'd been burned. 'Why would I do that?'

'Isn't this as good a place as any to finish the job? I suppose you'll wait until I tell you where the disk is.'

I began to unbutton my shirt. Misinterpreting my actions, she caught my wrists. I pushed her away and finished taking off the shirt, displaying my injuries.

'What happened to you?' she asked after a pause.

'I took a little swim this morning after you dropped me off. Out the end of the tunnel at Sutro Baths, down onto the rocks, out into the cove. I got polished on the rocks for a while, and then the waves swept me out to sea. A surfer ended up bringing me ashore.'

'It looks like you slid down a gigantic cheese grater.'

'It could be worse. My brains are still on the inside.'

'How did it happen?' Her eyes flashed. 'Keith didn't—'

'He took me down there to kill me. But not until he'd

told me that you were the one who shot my brother.'

There was fear in her eyes. Her voice was weak and breathless. 'He told you that?'

I reached out and slid the door closed. I wanted to hear it before the others. I wanted to decide. I stood in my plain white T-shirt, the wounds on my arms itching in the chill, the flesh on my back and side and hip crawling painfully. 'He said it was you, all you. And Martha drove the getaway car. And you killed Martha.'

'And you believed him?'

'Why shouldn't I? You lied when you said you gave the disks to Teddy. Actually they came anonymously in the mail. From Martha, is my guess. What happened – she tried to shake you down and you told her to go to hell?'

Christine had moved away to stand by the railing, her back to me. 'Something like that.'

'Teddy was going to turn that video over to the police. Keith was his client, and where clients were concerned Teddy didn't make exceptions. Not even after he slept with you. Maybe he blackmailed you into it, maybe it was your idea. In the meantime you and Martha worked out a deal, and Teddy ended up with a bullet in his head. You showed up at his hotel room, but the disk wasn't there. Instead of paying Martha whatever you'd promised her in return for keeping quiet and helping you get back the disks, you killed her with Teddy's gun, the

331

one he kept here. Or didn't you know about the gun in his bedside table?'

'I knew about it,' she said in a low voice.

'Marovich was your thesis adviser.'

She turned. 'Leo, I didn't kill him.'

'Of course you didn't.'

'Let's go inside. I'm cold.'

Now was the time to take her inside, get her on tape, but that would have meant handing Christine over to Car and Jeanie and their ideas about what happened, and losing Locke. Not to mention losing Christine. 'Why don't you tell me about Marovich first.'

'I can't tell you inside?'

'You can, but the house is wired for sound. It's probably better if we talk out here until you get your story straight.'

She stood looking at me with astonishment and fear.

'You see, Car and Jeanie are convinced you shot Teddy, but they're a little short on proof. My job is to make you confess. Maybe you killed Marovich, maybe you didn't. I want to be on your side, Christine, I really do. I told you this morning, I want to help you with whatever mess you're in. I like you. But first you've got to convince me you didn't shoot my brother and that you didn't set me up this morning.'

'I didn't,' she said, her voice even smaller.

'Why don't you start by telling me about Marovich,' I suggested again.

I put my shirt back on and eased myself down into my chair, warding off the chill with a long sip of gin. After a moment Christine turned and came to sit on the deck before me. 'It was – sex. There's not much to tell. I took a class with him on immersion ethnography. That's how I got the idea for my thesis. After the course he hired me on an unofficial basis as his research assistant. My job was to interview girls. I got paid, but more important I got to use the interviews for my thesis.

'We started sleeping together. He lived in the faculty ghetto, so we couldn't go to his place, and my dorm room was no good. I'd interviewed Martha at her apartment, and she let me use it. Little did I know she'd set up the camera. Sam liked— well, you saw the clip. You know what he liked. Then he turned up strangled and Keith was arrested.'

'The police never questioned you?'

'I kept waiting, but they never did.'

There was a pause. Then I said, 'You liked it, didn't you? Strangling him.'

'Maybe I did. That kind of power can be – exhilarating. But I didn't kill him.'

'Who killed him, then? Martha?'

'About a week after it happened she came to Stanford and showed me a copy of the disk. She wanted twenty thousand dollars.'

'I bet you regret not paying her.'

Sitting cross-legged before me, staring down at her hands, Christine just shook her head.

'So Martha killed Marovich because she had this video, and she figured with Marovich dead she could shake you down,' I mused. 'Never mind that the video shows her apartment and that twenty thousand seems cheap for murder. Let's put that aside. If Martha killed Marovich, then who killed Martha?'

Again Christine could only shake her head.

'You're the only one with a clear motive and opportunity. Work backward, then. Let's say Martha was killed because she knew who shot my brother. Who shot Teddy, if you didn't do it?'

'I don't know. Santorez. The one they indicted.'

'That still leaves you holding the bag for Martha. You've got to tie her in somehow if you're going to walk away from this.'

She sagged forward and pressed her face against my knees. 'Keith shot Teddy.'

'That's a little better. Keith shot Teddy, Martha was the driver, and Keith killed Martha to shut her up. But why shoot his own lawyer?'

'To protect me,' she said. 'Teddy was going to turn over the disk.'

'But now we've got the same problem all over again,' I said. 'You've got Martha and Teddy wrapped up, but who killed Marovich? If no one else did, then you must have killed him.'

'Martha.' She lifted her face. 'It was an accident. It doesn't have anything to do with me.'

'But that doesn't work, either. If Keith shot my brother, you can't get rid of the disk entirely, because without the video Keith doesn't have the motive of protecting you from exposure. But maybe you never slept with Marovich.'

Her shoulders tensed and she went very still.

'Who shot Teddy if Keith didn't do it? Say the video of you and Marovich didn't exist.'

She stared longingly into my face. 'Tanya.'

'We've been over that. Tanya's in the clear, even if she stole Santorez's money, which I'm certain she did. So is Car.'

Christine didn't say anything.

I shrugged. 'There isn't anyone left. You must have shot Teddy.'

She hid her face. 'My father paid to have him shot. Isn't that what you want to hear?'

'Tell me about your father.' I took another hasty swallow of gin.

'It was a huge fight. That's what Keith said. I was six. They were going to get divorced. Because our father had another woman. Then my parents sent Keith away to school. I remember the house being very quiet. Time passed. When I was twelve I saw the private detective's report. I was snooping in my mother's room. I guess that was the first time I realized that my father knew the woman who'd died. That she was the one he'd been with.'

She turned her head from side to side on my knee. 'I didn't want to think about it. I put it out of my mind. But when no one was home I kept going into my mother's room to look at the pictures. The file disappeared after Keith got kicked out of school. I always assumed she or my dad finally threw it away. But Keith must have taken it. He must have given it to Teddy.'

'Your father had to have known that Teddy was writing that habeas brief, that he was going to argue your father killed my mother,' I interrupted. 'Otherwise it doesn't work. If Gerald didn't know the contents of the brief, he could have no reason for wanting Teddy dead.'

Again she was silent. Finally she said, 'I confronted him. About a month ago. I showed him copies of the pictures, the ones Teddy had showed me, the ones I'd seen all those years ago in the investigator's file. He denied having anything to do with her death, but he admitted he'd known your mother. I told him about me and Teddy.'

'What about Martha?'

Christine looked up. 'Someone must have shot her for planting that camera in the Green Light.'

I seized her arms and pulled her to me, and she half rose, half fell, bracing her elbows on my thighs. I kissed her breathlessly. 'I don't care about Marovich.' I wanted her so badly that I might have forgotten any number of dead Maroviches. 'I'll destroy the disk. All you have to do is help me prove that your father had my brother shot.'

She returned my kiss.

We ate some cheese and drank some wine, sitting huddled together on the boards of the porch with our backs against the wall, the cushions of the chaise beneath us, sharing a blanket I'd found inside. Christine leaned against my shoulder. 'Do you think it's possible for a person to get away from her family and just be – herself? Start a new life?'

I thought about my own situation, my own family. 'You would have to believe in it. The new life, I mean. Because otherwise the old life would still be there, and eventually the new one would just sort of melt away, and you'd be in your old life again.'

'What about – this?' She stroked my leg with her fingertips. 'Can I believe in this?'

The skin of my leg crawled where she was touching it. Instead of answering her I turned to her and tugged up her shirt, pushed my face into her chest.

It was too cold out there for bare skin, and soon we had to move into the bedroom.

When she moaned, I tried to silence her, putting a hand over her lips, thinking of Car and Jeanie, but she would not be silenced, tilting back her head, exposing her neck. I moved my hand down, my wrist nestled between her collarbones, my elbow between her breasts, and stroked the tendons of her neck. How would it feel to squeeze and go on squeezing?

She came just as I began to come, my hand clenching around her throat.

'Did you really think I shot Teddy?' she asked later. 'Tell me you didn't believe it.'

'I didn't know what to believe,' I told her.

'I didn't do it. You have to believe I didn't.'

I held her. 'I believe you,' I said.

I was thinking about what would happen in the morning, about what I would tell Car and Jeanie.

'Let's get out of here,' I whispered. 'Let's go to Reno and forget about everything for a night.'

As we reached the bottom of the hill a pair of headlights appeared in the rearview. It was the Volvo.

Christine dozed in the passenger seat beside me. Car and Jeanie stayed on our trail into Moraga, as far as the last exit before the Benicia Bridge.

I find it difficult to fully describe my feelings as I watched the Volvo's lights grow smaller and curve away onto the exit behind us. It was like watching my old life close up behind me as I drove into the dark distance. There was a sense that I'd broken irrevocably from Jeanie and Car, and from Teddy. Alone with Christine, I knew how it was going to end.

After we'd arrived in Reno and been gambling for an hour it hit me: Today was Teddy's thirty-eighth birthday.

We slept for a few hours before dawn. Christine woke up sober and anxious to get back for her afternoon class. I paid for the hotel room, we got into the Rabbit, and drove again.

Playing blackjack, I'd come up with a plan for how best to use Christine to get at her father. After filling the tank outside Sacramento, I took Christine's hand. 'We got married last night,' I said. 'Don't worry, I didn't pull a fast one during your blackout. We're going to pretend we went to Reno, which we did, and that we got married there on the spur of the moment. You'll break the news to your parents this afternoon, and you'll insist on having me for dinner tonight.'

She took a breath and let it out through her nose.

'What did you expect?' I asked. 'A diamond ring?'

'I'll go along with you, and we'll milk this for all it's worth. I'm a pretty good actress. I'll have to be. But I don't see how this is going to get my father to admit anything. You don't have any real proof, so what are you going to do? Just accuse him?'

'That's my problem,' I said. And it was. I knew how to make Gerald angry, but I had no idea how to get from there to an admission of the secret he'd been keeping all these years.

We didn't say anything the rest of the way. When we

reached Teddy's, where Christine had left her sleek little BMW, she leaned over and kissed me lightly on the cheek. She didn't want to come inside. She had to get back to school, she said.

She backed out of the driveway. I sat there a moment, wondering where the nearest place to get coffee was. Then I gave a mean little laugh, put the Rabbit in gear, and drove to San Francisco.

Chapter Twenty-Six

About halfway through the night I'd remembered that I didn't have my cell phone: It was still in pieces on my radiator. After dropping Christine at her car I drove straight to the hospital, drawn by the certainty that something had happened in my absence. I didn't actually believe the situation had changed, but I felt impelled to Teddy's bedside so that I could see that everything was the same as it had been yesterday afternoon, that he was still straddling the line between death and life. I arrived at two o'clock.

When I got there my premonitions seemed confirmed in the worst possible way. The bed was empty and remade, all the medical equipment pushed back against the wall, the lights turned off, the flowers and personal stuff swept away.

I came in and stood by the bed, looking down at the creaseless sheets. I touched the pillow. After an interval of shock I turned from the room. At the end of the hall I spotted Carol, the nurse I'd met the first day, going into another patient's room. I jogged after her.

Carol turned from the bed where she'd bent to check the pulse in an unconscious man's jaundiced, spotted old arm, her face registering an emotion between sympathy and reproach.

'When—' I said, and my breath failed me, and I stood gasping before her. 'When—' I tried again, but it came out as a squeaking wheeze, like an asthma attack.

'He's still here,' she said. She stared at me worriedly. 'He started becoming responsive this morning. He was trying to breathe on his own and showing higher-level responses, enough that they decided to move him into long-term care. They're keeping him in a coma for now, but in a few days they may let him wake up as much as he's able to. He's got a difficult road ahead, but it looks like he'll pull through. We've been calling and calling all morning, Leo, trying to reach you.'

A week ago I might have believed that it would be better for Teddy to die than to live in a brain-damaged state, but now elation flooded through me. What I hadn't dared to think possible was suddenly probable: I was going to have my brother back. He would never be the same, but he was going to live.

'Where—' I began, but my voice was choked off this time by thankful, ashamed weeping.

She touched my cheek, then flipped through her charts, and told me the room number. 'Go,' she said, with a suppressed smile. 'I've got work to do.'

* * *

Teddy's new room was brighter than the old one, with wallpaper, a closet, TV, and a window with a view of the bay – a room designed for the living rather than for the dying. He lay under the sheet with his head bandaged as before. He still had the stoma in his throat, but the machine wasn't hooked up to it. The unprompted rise and fall of his massive chest seemed to me nothing short of miraculous.

When I'd been there only a minute Jeanie appeared, as if she'd just stepped out for a moment; she must have been here all morning. Her purse was on the floor beneath a chair at the window, her book beside it. She walked around me to Teddy's bedside as if I weren't there, and with a proprietary motion straightened the hem of the sheet. Only then did she turn, standing between my brother and me.

'How did this happen?' I asked.

She didn't answer. Then she walked over, grabbed my arm, pushed me out of the room into the hallway, and closed the door behind us.

'How long have you been here?'

'Almost since we left you. They called around midnight. Where were you?'

'Jeanie—'

'Or maybe you'd better not tell me. I don't want to know, not really.' She breathed out hard. 'He's probably going to live. You could start by saying something about

343

that, about how glad you are. Or maybe you aren't glad.'

'That's good news. I'm really, really glad.' It was like a kick in the head that she could think I wasn't.

'Is it? Are you? I thought your brother was better off dead than needing someone's help to dress himself. Not your help, though. You made that abundantly clear with your behavior last night. Don't worry, we got it all on tape, your sick little fuck session.'

'I'll be there for him. Whatever it takes. I'm glad he's going to have a chance at – at some kind of life.'

'You'll be there just like you've been here since this happened.' Seeing the tears in my eyes, she seemed briefly to soften. Then her face hardened again.

'Jeanie – last night—'

'I told you, I don't want to hear it.'

'She didn't pull the trigger. She didn't have anything to do with it.'

'I'm glad you think so. I've got to hand it to you, Leo, you're quite the advocate. You represent one suspect and screw another. Maybe for your next trick you can get yourself adopted by Gerald Locke.'

I winced. It was madness, all madness. 'We're going to set up her father tonight. Pretend we got married in Reno. So you're coming around to thinking Gerald might have done it?'

'If I did, I wouldn't tell you. You've used up all your trust with me, Leo.'

Just then Car turned the corner, coming toward us

down the hall. Just as Jeanie had done, he stared right through me. Then with no warning he set his feet and punched me in the stomach harder than I'd ever been punched before. I dropped.

'You pissant,' Car said. 'Next week maybe Teddy wakes up and tells the world she's the one who shot him. You'll have to fuck her in one of those little prison trailers.'

I gathered my feet, stood, and swung at him. He stepped back, and as I flailed by him he landed a neat uppercut to the chin that left my head whirling and sat me back down on the floor.

'Get the hell out of here,' I said, staying down this time, swallowing saliva tinged coppery with blood. 'You goddamn thug.'

'Sure, I'll leave. I been here all day today making sure that bitch doesn't show up to finish the job. And I'll be here all day tomorrow, too, and the day after that, and every day until she's locked up safe. Right now I'm going for a burrito, and when I come back you better be gone, and you better not show your face here again unless you want more of what you just got.'

He walked out. When I thought I could stand without puking I got to my feet. Jeanie now had settled herself in the chair by the window. She'd turned on some music, cool jazz.

'You better start thinking how you're going to explain all this,' she said.

'Can I talk to you in the hall again, please?'

* * *

My voice was tight. 'He doesn't ever have to know about Christine and me.'

She stood shaking her head. 'What could you have been thinking?'

I forced myself to look her in the face, though my cheeks were burning. 'Maybe at heart I'm still a teenage kid obsessed with stealing his brother's girlfriend. Or maybe this is my best shot at trapping Gerald and proving he killed Caroline and had Teddy shot to cover it up.'

She met my eyes briefly, then looked away. 'You're not a kid anymore, Leo. My God, you think you're using her? Can't you see she's using you?'

I stood there, trying not to be angry with her. Finally I said, 'I'm going to give a good shake to Gerald's tree, and we'll see what happens. I'm having dinner with the family tonight to break the news of my supposed marriage.'

'Gerald didn't have Teddy shot.'

'If he didn't, then Santorez did. Tanya stole that money from the trust fund account. It had to have been her. When Teddy couldn't pay, Santorez had him shot. That works for me. But either way, Gerald was the one who killed my mother. Teddy knew it, and I know it.' My voice was tight again, and again I found myself straining to hold on to reason, to keep the whole sequence of astonishing secrets in my head at once.

'You don't know when to stop.'

'Christine didn't shoot Teddy.'

'Yes, Leo. She almost certainly did.'

'How can you be so certain?'

'How can you be sure she didn't?'

'Because I've talked to them all. I've looked them in the eyes and I know who's lying to me and who isn't. Keith and his father were lying. Christine is telling the truth – at least, she finally is now. Gerald is behind the shooting, and I'm going to force him to show his hand.'

'How? By asking leading questions? Even in a courtroom you wouldn't have anything on him.' Jeanie's eyes focused over my shoulder.

I turned. It was Tanya, her face haggard, her voice tired. 'I heard Teddy might be going to recover,' she said, casting down her eyes as if she couldn't bear to look Jeanie in the face.

There was an awkward silence; then Jeanie turned and opened the door to Teddy's room, admitting her.

Tanya wouldn't talk to us, wouldn't talk to Teddy, wouldn't say anything. One way or another she was going to have to answer for the money she'd stolen, but now was not the time.

I stayed until late-afternoon rounds. Dr Gottlieb greeted me warmly and restated what he'd told me before, emphasizing that Teddy's prognosis remained grim. He would surely suffer from cognitive impairment, emotional alterations, and unreliable memory, and he would likely never be able to practice law or otherwise support himself again.

In the face of that frank assessment, my elation subsided. I wondered again if Teddy would want to live, if his life could ever be meaningful without work.

When I got home I just had time to shower. I put on a dress shirt and slacks, no tie, and drove out to Presidio Heights.

Chapter Twenty-Seven

Chloe was leaving as I arrived. She cast a disdainful glance at the Rabbit as she let me in. 'What, no congratulations?' I asked.

'You shouldn't be here, stirring up trouble.'

'I would have asked you to marry me, but I never thought I had a chance.'

'Ha.'

'Good luck with law school,' I called as she reached the driveway. Not that she needed it. She'd already learned the greatest skill any lawyer can have, knowing when to walk away from a bad situation – one I so far hadn't managed to perfect.

I turned and found myself alone in the foyer. There was no sound from the house around me. I was considering whether to retreat to the porch and ring the doorbell a second time when Christine appeared at the top of the curving balustrade.

'Oh. Hi. I'll be right down.'

Watching her manage the stairs, I had a vision of her

in twenty years making the same tipsy descent in a house just as rich as this one, her face deepened with age, her tight body gone to flab, her liver swollen with secrets.

'My parents are in hiding,' she said with a delicious smile, leaning in for a kiss. 'They don't want to see you.'

'We could just go out to dinner and live happily ever after.'

Her smile and eyes widened. 'I'm not going to let them hide.'

I thought about what Jeanie had said about Christine using me rather than the other way around. I wanted to tell her about Teddy, but before I had the chance she turned and went down the hall through the dining room to her father's office. 'Gerald!' she called, rapping on his door. She came back into the foyer, planting a kiss on my lips in passing, and proceeded to the other end of the long hall where her mother's office was. 'Mother!' she called. 'Our guest is here!'

She rejoined me in the foyer, twining her arm through mine.

Her father was the first to appear. He looked older than he had the last time I'd seen him, dark circles under his eyes.

'Good evening, Dr Locke.'

'Good evening,' he said, giving me a look suggesting he knew my game, whatever it was. 'You sure work quickly.'

'So Christine has told you our news.' I offered my hand but he didn't take it.

'There you are,' he said. It was Greta coming toward us from the other direction.

'What kind of man are you, Mr Maxwell?' she asked, getting in my face.

'Greta,' Gerald said soothingly. He put a hand on my arm and another on his wife's, turning us gently away from each other. 'Why don't Leo and I have a drink in my office.'

To Christine he said, 'Put on some jazz, something celebratory. I have a feeling it'll be called for once Leo and I have talked.'

Christine gave him a quizzical look but went into the living room with her mother. I followed him down the hall into his office.

As before, he poured us each a Scotch. When we'd settled in our places – he behind the desk, I lurking at the bookshelves – he said, 'Normally a groom has this conversation with his future father-in-law before the engagement. And normally the groom, not the father-in-law, initiates the conversation. A father's blessing doesn't count for much anymore. Children do what they're going to do regardless of how the parents feel. But from the day his daughter is born a man begins to anticipate the hour when another man pays him the respect of asking his permission to marry her.'

His drink sat untouched on the blotter before him. He

looked at me expectantly, leaning back. 'Please. I'm all ears.'

'Cut the crap, Gerald.' I downed my Scotch in one burning swig. 'If I'd wanted your blessing, or whatever you called it, I would have asked for it. I didn't come here to play sentimental games.'

I went around behind him for another drink. When I came back out to the front of the desk his face had gone pale.

'You must know that a Nevada annulment is about as easy to get as a Nevada marriage license. They might as well come in pairs. That's what you really brought me in here to discuss, or am I wrong?'

'I hope you don't view marriage so flippantly as to think you could just return it like – like a wrong pair of shoes.' His tone was unctuous.

To prove to myself that I wasn't nervous, I went to the bookshelf and took down the first book that caught my eye – an edition of *The Sun Also Rises*. Flipping through the pages I saw that my hands were steady, not shaking, and I felt more sure of myself. I read a paragraph on bullfighting, then put it back on the shelf. I tried to remember everything Teddy'd taught me about cross-examination and all that I had learned from watching him. There was a definite technique to leading a witness away from your true target, letting him think he knows what you're after, then striking home.

'Isn't it customary in these situations for the father-in-law to ask the son-in-law how much it will cost to make the son-in-law go away – and stay away? Ever since I met Christine I've been anticipating this conversation with you. I thought you might start the bidding, let me know how much you think I'm worth.'

'Not one penny,' he said, tapping the desk with each word for emphasis and looking very satisfied with himself.

'You like home videos, Gerald?'

He didn't answer, but I saw that I had his attention.

'Most people don't think about hidden cameras, but they should. Almost anywhere you go now, it's a possibility. And anyone with a camera can put the video on a computer, put it on the Internet. All these celebrity sex tapes, for instance. It's not that celebrities are having more sex. It's just that it's gone viral. You can make a million copies as easily as blowing your nose.'

'I'm aware that my daughter has sex. If you've secretly videotaped your activities, that's despicable, but I'm not going to make it my problem. I can't shelter my children from humiliations they bring on themselves.'

'Not her and me. What if I told you I'd obtained a video of your daughter erotically asphyxiating her thesis adviser? Marovich. You remember him. He was the one whose body your son was caught trying to throw into a Dumpster down by Candlestick. It's been generally assumed that he was strangled at the Green Light, but there's no evidence of that other than Keith's word. It

353

could have happened anywhere. And anyone could have done it.'

From the other room came the notes of a jazz piano piece.

Satisfaction now appeared in Gerald's voice. 'Just as I thought. You don't care about my daughter at all.'

'My guess is you'll pay me to break the marriage, if it comes to that, no matter what you say now. Surely you'd pay a little more to put the rest of Christine's troubles behind her?'

'Why should I pay you? Christine will realize her mistake in marrying you soon enough, if she hasn't already. All I have to do is wait, and the marriage will fall apart on its own. If she stays with you, she'll be unhappy. And to be honest with you, I'm ready to hand off responsibility for her unhappiness to someone else. When things come tumbling down, you'll be the one to blame, not me. And I'll have my daughter back.'

'All right, we're not married,' I told him. 'It's a farce, a sham.'

He blinked. He started to rise. 'Then I can show you the door.'

'That's one option. But if you do that, I'll have to tell your wife about this video of Christine and her dearly departed professor. Maybe even show it to her. I thought you and I might settle this without involving Greta.

After all, it's a serious matter. You've already got one child in trouble with the law. Do you want a pair of them?'

He hesitated, then sat back down.

'My brother received a copy of the video a week or so before he was shot. As Keith's lawyer, he felt he had an obligation to turn it over to the police. He confronted your daughter, and they ended up in bed. Maybe he blackmailed her, maybe it was more complicated. She thought he'd destroy the video. He still intended to turn it over and told her as much.

'The shooter is described as a tall young man wearing baggy pants, a baggy sweatshirt, a baseball cap, and sunglasses. People were looking at the gun, not at what may or may not have been underneath the shooter's clothes. No one looked too closely at this person's face. I'm not saying Christine shot my brother, but if the police knew about the video, they'd have to look into that possibility. At the very least, they'd have to ask some uncomfortable questions.'

'You said before that you want to find your brother's attacker. Isn't it your obligation to turn the video over to them, not use it to extort money from me?'

I shrugged. 'The video's a red herring. She says she had nothing to do with it, and I believe her. But I think she knows more than she's telling me. I think she's protecting someone.'

Gerald's face was a knot. He was thinking so hard he

seemed to forget I was there. Finally he said, 'And if I pay you, you'll deliver the video to me, and the police will never know it existed. Is that your proposition?'

'Remember that we're talking about two crimes here. Someone may have murdered Marovich, and someone absolutely tried to murder my brother. Last time I was here, you told me Keith may have killed before. Now I'm wondering whether it wasn't so much a lie as a half lie, whether you didn't have some inkling about your daughter's possible involvement and were trying to keep me away from her. I'm not too fond of Keith myself. I can see how life might be more comfortable for everyone if he were out of circulation, but that's really none of my business. Christine offered me twenty thousand dollars for the video. The only reason she's playing along with this little charade tonight is because she's hoping I'll decide to take the money and hand it over. Now maybe she has twenty thousand bucks to give me, and maybe she doesn't. Either way, I'm expecting you to make me a better offer.'

'You're insinuating that I want my son to go to prison for a crime he didn't commit.'

'He's crazy. And almost certainly dangerous. I can't help thinking maybe you're right. Maybe prison is about the best he can expect. So how much is it worth? The photos from the private detective your wife hired to look into your affair with my mother sixteen years ago, that video of Christine, the whole package?'

'So you have the photos.' He was silent. 'Just out of curiosity, how did you get them?'

'My brother was going to make them Exhibit A in a habeas corpus brief he was drafting. I assume he got them from Keith. Me, I'm not interested in filing any briefs. I want to start my own practice. You won't find any of your relatives on my client list, believe me. I plan to represent nothing but drug dealers and pimps. The pay is small but it's a constant stream, none of this feast-or-famine cycle my brother deals with. To get off on the right foot I'd need something in the range of, oh, two hundred thousand dollars.'

'This kind of blackmail is beyond belief. It's one thing coming from Keith, but from a stranger—' Gerald broke off.

'Did I say anything about blackmail? I had in mind a lawsuit. Wrongful death. She wasn't a stranger to me. She was my mother. As far as I'm concerned, these are settlement negotiations. The statute of limitations is long past, but never mind. Of course we would include a secrecy agreement in whatever settlement we reach.'

'Settlement negotiations.' He gave a halting sigh, then ran his hand through his hair. 'It will take me some time to raise that kind of money, if we're talking about cash. I'll have to sell investments. It might take up to a week for the transfer to come through.'

'You see now why I thought you might not want to involve Greta.'

'Don't tell me what I see or don't see.' He rose. 'We'd better join them.'

We hadn't settled on a definite amount, and we certainly hadn't shaken hands, but no matter. The money wasn't what I was after.

He left his drink untouched on the desk. I went through the door ahead of him, my skin crawling as I gave him my back. Christine was lounging on a leather sofa. She looked up with a dazed expression and her newlywed smile. She was sipping something clear and brilliant and cold-looking. A martini. I glanced inquiringly at the drink, and with a twist of her head she indicated a cabinet on the far side of the room.

The French doors were closed and the curtains were drawn. I made one for myself and sat on the sofa beside her. She rested her hand on my arm; I put my free hand on her shoulder. Her father was at the stereo. The piano halted and something edgier came on, all screeching horns and saxophones.

'Is it come to that, dear?' Greta asked, walking in from the hall.

Gerald stabbed a finger at the stereo and the music turned off.

'So you made the most of your visit to Stanford,' Greta said, her anger under control now as she sank into the wing chair across from us.

'We'll have to get on the waiting list for married-student housing,' I said to Christine. 'I can sneak into classes at the law school while I'm waiting for my practice to get off the ground.'

Gerald had gone to the window and was looking out through a gap in the curtains.

'So you're hanging out your shingle,' Greta said. 'What sort of practice?'

'Criminal defense. Once it's in the blood you can't get it out.'

'You've never thought about prosecution? Don't the best defense attorneys always begin as prosecutors?'

'Some. But there is a difference between the two sides. The prosecutor's job is to take an eye for an eye. They call it justice. To me it seems more like revenge. Revenge is fine. Actually, I approve of revenge. I just wish they'd call it that instead of trying to invoke some lofty principle. A defense attorney tries to save life rather than destroy it. That's the difference.'

'I must be old-fashioned,' Gerald said, coming from the window to stand behind his wife, his face a twist of contempt. 'I don't have any problem destroying a life that needs to be destroyed, to use your words. The way I see it, we're too soft on offenders in this society. Especially in this city.'

'You're certainly entitled to your opinion. You've come by it the hard way, I'm sure. I know you've had some experience in these matters. If the DA's office had taken the hard line from the beginning, Keith would have been out of harm's way years ago, snug as a bug in prison, and it sounds like a lot of trouble would have been avoided.'

Gerald looked pained, as if I'd done something on the rug. Christine sat with her hand on my leg, her head lolling onto my shoulder. Greta studied her hands, then looked at me, her eyes swimming but with a diamond hardness behind the tears, the same hardness that was in her eyes the last time I was here, when she'd spoken to me of a mother's need to touch and hold her son, when she'd begged me to find Keith.

'I'm afraid I didn't have much luck convincing Keith to see you,' I said. 'In fact, he pushed me off the rocks at Lands End. Now why would he do a thing like that?'

Greta's voice was suddenly sharp. 'He pushed you or he was forced to defend himself?'

'Is that the way you heard it?' I asked.

Gerald looked at me, then gazed steadily at his wife with surprise and incomprehension.

'What do you want me to tell you?' Greta asked her husband. 'That my son came to the house and I turned him away? He won't be back. He was here yesterday and gone again in half an hour. I gave him enough to last quite a while this time.'

'What happens when the money runs out?' I asked. 'And it will run out, possibly much sooner than you expect. What happens the next time he shows up on your doorstep?'

'An excellent question.' Gerald shot me another

glance; then his eyes went back to Greta. 'How much did you give him?'

'Yes, how much?' Christine was perking up beside me, as if the show she'd been waiting for was finally about to start. She took a sip of her drink and moved her hand up my thigh. The skin of my leg twitched and crawled.

'Enough,' Greta said.

Gerald chopped the air in disgust and stalked from the room.

'We might as well go in,' Greta finally said. 'There's no point waiting for your father.'

The food was in a pair of warming dishes on the sideboard in the dining room. The first warming dish held grilled salmon. The second, roasted potatoes and sliced beets.

It made me increasingly uneasy to know that Keith had been here since our encounter.

'She's lying,' Christine whispered as her mother served the food. 'Keith's still here.'

I gasped. 'How do you know?'

Her mother was coming toward us from the sideboard with a steaming plate in each hand.

'His shoes in the closet,' was all Christine had time to say as we parted toward opposite sides of the table.

Greta took her place at the head of the table. She sat thoughtfully for a moment, then looked up at me with a completely changed face, a look of resignation. Her voice when she spoke was also changed. 'I'll write you a check now for two hundred thousand dollars.'

I raised my eyebrows. 'If?'

'If you agree to annul the marriage and stay away from us. Christine included.'

'You could have bargained me lower, but all right. Two hundred it is.'

'Wait, don't I have a say?' Christine asked. But her heart wasn't in it.

Greta rose. 'I'll write you a check immediately.'

'I don't get to stay for supper?'

She sounded almost happy. 'You're welcome to eat all you want before I come back.'

I looked across the table at Christine as the door swung closed behind her mother. 'Presumably that includes you,' I said. 'One last kiss and good-bye?'

She flushed, frowning.

'What's she think she's buying with the two hundred thousand?' I mused. 'Surely she doesn't give a damn one way or the other about me and you. She must know it's a sham.'

'She's afraid of something,' Christine said. 'She doesn't like having you here. It makes her nervous.'

'At least your father knew what he was paying for. I told him about the disk. About the photos. But Greta hasn't heard any of that. As far as she knows, I'm just some rude kid who wormed his way into her little girl's heart.'

She gave a curt laugh. 'Not into my heart. You're getting your money, more than you could ever have bargained on. I want the disk.'

'What's Keith doing here, though? It would be a shame if we left without seeing him.' Then something shifted in me, like an iceberg rolling over, and I saw everything in a new light. 'He did it. It wasn't Santorez, and it wasn't your father. Keith shot Teddy, and now he's scared. He came running to Mommy and begged her to fix it. She knows, and she thinks I know, too. She thinks I have proof. That's why she's so eager to buy me off.'

I rose from my chair just as Greta came in.

'Here's your check, Mr Maxwell,' she said, holding it out to me. 'Now if you'll permit me, I'll show you the door. My lawyer will be in touch to confirm the terms we discussed.'

I looked down at the check in my hand. Two hundred thousand dollars. An incredible sum. 'There's no marriage,' I said and looked back up at her. 'It's just a little joke we were playing. Maybe that changes things.' I made to hand the check back.

She wouldn't take it. 'I want you to have the money. Please. Just leave.'

'What if money wasn't what I came for? What if I want something else?'

'Please,' she said again. 'Just take it and go. It's all you're ever going to get from this house. Perhaps if it does you some good—'

From somewhere above us there came a shout, then a thump. Followed by the sound of a heavy object rolling very fast down the stairs.

Christine was first through the door to the hall, and I was right behind her. We found Gerald Locke lying unconscious on the landing, bleeding from a gash in his forehead. At the top of the stairs stood his son.

Keith had a gun in his hand down at his side, a nine-millimeter automatic like the one that had been used to shoot my brother. As soon as he saw me he raised it in our direction.

'See, I told you he would come,' he said to Greta. 'We can't ever get rid of him.'

'You didn't expect to see me?' I asked.

'Mother, what should I do?'

'Put the gun down,' Greta said.

Christine straightened as her father groaned and sat up, holding his head.

'I've written him a check for two hundred thousand dollars,' Greta said, going to her husband's side and putting her hand on his shoulder. 'I should think that would be more than sufficient to keep him quiet. Now put the gun down, Keith.'

Instead, he aimed it at my chest. 'I thought you were dead for sure. That's what I told Christine. I said, "He's dead, we've got nothing to worry about, you're in the clear".'

I was frozen, staring at the barrel of the gun, wishing it in my own hand.

Christine scoffed. 'You're such a liar,' she said. Then to me: 'He's lying.'

'Your father's going to be okay,' Greta said. 'He didn't know you were here. You surprised him, that's all.'

'I'm okay,' Gerald said in a gravelly voice. 'I'll be fine.'

'He was going to throw me out. Right down the stairs. Instead I threw him down the stairs.'

'Let's at least go in and sit in the living room,' Greta said. 'Can we do that?'

Keith came down. Gerald got to his feet with his wife's help, and we all went into the living room. Christine and I sat on the couch as before. Gerald sat in one of the armchairs, Greta in the other. Keith stood.

I was still holding the check in my hand. I looked down at it for a moment, then tore it slowly in half, put the pieces together, and tore again, repeating until there was nothing but tiny shreds. I let them snow down on the carpet.

Keith addressed his mother: 'What are we going to do?'

Gerald frowned. 'We?' Greta didn't have an answer.

Keith glowered at his father; then his look settled on Christine. He stepped forward and slashed her viciously across the face with the pistol. 'You're such a whore.'

Blood ran from the gash on Christine's cheek. Her eyes blazed.

'You think you can buy me off just like him?' Keith said, his anger returning to his mother. 'There isn't any difference for you between your own son and that – person?'

'The difference is you take her money and I don't,' I said.

Keith pointed the gun at me. 'Fuck you.'

'You've got two choices. One, you shoot me dead and make a better shot than you did when you shot my brother. Yeah, I know you're the one who shot him. Two, you walk out of here with your mother's money and do a better job of disappearing than you did the last time.'

He walked toward me, holding the gun straight-armed. To reach me he had to pass Christine. She stuck out her leg and tripped him, and he came crashing down onto the coffee table. The gun fired. I didn't see where the shot hit. I looked down and saw the gun on the carpet at my feet. I scooped it up.

Nobody seemed to be hurt. I let out a deep breath. 'Get up,' I told Keith. 'Sit on the couch with your sister.'

He sat.

Still holding the gun, I took out my phone and dialed Detective Anderson's number. I told him where I was, that I'd been attacked by one of my brother's former clients, that I'd disarmed him, and that the gun appeared to be the same one that Teddy had taken a bullet from.

I ended the call and turned to Greta. 'Gerald was

having an affair with my mother. You found out, and shortly afterward Caroline was killed. Do I have that much right?'

She wasn't stupid. She knew better than to talk. We weren't in a court of law, and there was nothing in the world I could do to make her.

'You must have become suspicious and hired a private investigator to follow Gerald and take those pictures,' I said. 'You wanted the children to know the truth about their father. Keith must have been, what? Sixteen? Maybe you drove him by the house, maybe he went there on his own or followed his father. My guess is that he wanted sex and thought he could get it from the mistress. Isn't sex what all sixteen-year-old boys want? When she wouldn't give it up, he raped and killed her.'

'Shut your filthy mouth,' Keith said.

'I was ten years old. I was the one who found her. Afterward you didn't know more than you had to know. You bought off the private investigator to keep his mouth shut, and you sent Keith away to school. That should have been the end of it, but Keith flunked out. He came home and started getting into trouble. And when my brother became a lawyer, Keith looked him up. Became friends with him. Started whispering in his ear. Eventually he pulled out the investigator's pictures.

'Teddy must have realized Gerald couldn't have been the killer. He figured out that Keith killed my mother.

Caroline. And Keith shot him for it. Martha drove the car. Keith shot her, too, once he figured out I was on his trail.'

Greta's hand was at her throat. Something I'd said seemed to have stricken her, maybe that I'd been the one to find Caroline. I was right, I saw. She'd covered for Keith all these years. She and her husband.

'For God's sake, Greta, don't talk to him,' Gerald said.

Greta glanced at her husband, then bowed her head.

Chapter Twenty-Eight

Gerald and Greta Locke denied everything, and Christine refused to speak with the police. After the video emerged, she hired a hotshot lawyer, an ex-prosecutor who arranged for her to appear at the police station to answer a series of questions. There was a story in the papers, but the scandal died away. A month later the charges against Santorez were dismissed and new charges were filed against Keith in my brother's shooting. They had the physical evidence from the gun, and eyewitness testimony from the people in the restaurant, and the previous incident with Marovich hanging over Keith's head. He pleaded guilty to attempted murder and was sentenced to fifteen years.

He was never charged in Martha's death. I never learned how he got Teddy's gun.

I sent my father a one-line note asking to be put on his list of approved visitors at San Quentin. He wrote back eagerly, asking me to take over his case, finish the habeas petition. I didn't respond. It was too much to ask, too soon. I wasn't ready to visit him, knowing he would repeat the request, but I kept the file in my drawer.

When it was time for Teddy to come out of the hospital I decided to hang my shingle in Oakland. It was cheaper to live there than in the city, and I wanted to be near the rehab center we'd chosen on Telegraph Avenue just over the Berkeley border.

My brother is dressing for the funeral. Sensibly enough, he begins with the pants. He holds them up, looks down at himself, then seems to realize he must get undressed before he can put them on. He lays the pants on the bed, unbuttons his khaki shorts, and slides them down.

He has forgotten to remove his shoes, however, and the shorts will not come off.

It is hard to believe that a year ago this slow-witted, off-balance, volatile stranger was one of the most accomplished young criminal defense lawyers in San Francisco. From the left side, all you can see is that he's lost a great deal of weight, more than sixty pounds, not by choice but because he has had to relearn how to swallow. Only from the right do you notice the craterlike dent in his brow, the scar left by the entry of the bullet that should have killed him.

He sits on the bed and fights to get the shorts off over the shoes. Despite the difficulty of this, it doesn't occur to him to take the shoes off now. As he struggles against them, his face takes on a stubborn, defensive look, the look that says that whatever I may think is wrong with him, I am making it all up, I am the one with the problem.

It's excruciating to hold my tongue as he makes mistake after mistake, but if I don't keep my silence, he will fly into a rage. The lack of dexterity on his left side is only a small part of the problem. Even the simplest task has become a labyrinth through which he stumbles with no sense of himself or of his goal.

'You remember where we're going today?' I ask to distract him from his frustration.

He pauses to consider the question, then gives the answer he figures is bound to be at least partially right: 'In the car.' At moments like this you can still tell that he is a lawyer. He uses his old tone of peremptory command, but his voice is so slurred that no one who doesn't know him well can understand him.

'We're not going to the car, but we're taking the car to where we're going.'

I can only push him so far before he tells me to fuck off, get out of his room, and get out of his life. His temper is a reflex, like the jerk of his leg when his doctor taps the patella. In two months he will get out of rehab and come to live with me, for lack of a better option.

He has the shorts off now, though he still wears his shoes. He does not think of taking off the shoes before putting on the suit pants. But I don't say anything. One of the therapists has promised to check up on us. Caroline. Our mother's name. Whatever tangle Teddy gets himself into, he will permit her to help him, but not me, never me; this reflex of his personality and of our relationship remains.

He stands and holds up the suit pants, trying to figure out which way they go on. He tries them backward – wrong guess. Not that it matters, since he is still wearing the shoes. He makes little sideways kicks at the leg holes, the hip pockets before him. I can see he has no faith in succeeding. He is merely going through the motions, waiting for someone to show him what he's doing wrong. This resignation is new to my brother's personality, and it chills me. No matter how hopeless the case, no matter how guilty the client, Teddy always believed there was a way to win.

A secret part of me still imagines that this brittle shell will crack and my brother will emerge more or less as he used to be, smiling at the joke he has played on us all, the left side of his face no longer sagging. 'Just a hiccup, Monkey Boy,' he'll say, spinning away that awful four-footed cane. 'An educational experience, all in all.' And then he'll get back to work.

If I let him continue this way he's going to tear out the inseam. I'm about to speak up when Caroline slips into the room.

Teddy regards the pants, now crumpled on the floor at his feet. Then his gaze shifts hopelessly to the rest of the clothes I've brought him, and he gives Caroline a look of abject dependence, so overwhelmed that he can't find words to express his confusion. If I don't get out of here and let her work her magic, he will explode.

I tell them I'll wait in the hall.

* * *

I hear Tamara, another patient at the rehab center, keen, 'No, no.' From where I stand outside Teddy's door I can see her family gathered down there in their church clothes, the adults spilling out the door of her room. They have decided to keep telling her the truth until the truth sinks in. Her nephews and nieces stand slumped against the walls on both sides of the hall in stiff shoes and too-tight pants and dresses.

Some part of Tamara must know by now that her husband is dead. Her sobbing goes on and on, as if her body understands and remembers what's still too slippery for her intellect to grasp.

I think of her buttery brown skin, large almond-shaped eyes, her hair falling in a velvet sheen down her back. The virus that ravaged her brain did not touch her beauty. I always make a point of speaking to her when I come to visit Teddy at the rehab center. No matter how long we've been standing together, no matter how many times we've met, it's always as if I've just appeared before her that minute for the very first time.

Teddy's door opens, and he comes out leaning on his cane. Behind him stands Caroline with a taut smile. I haven't seen him in a suit since the day he was shot. I've had the pants taken in, but the rich wool still hangs on him, and his shirt collar gapes. She's knotted his tie in a simple schoolboy. Teddy always favored the Windsor.

'How do I look?' he asks. 'Hra dro I rook,' is what he says. 'Like a retard in a borrowed suit.'

He tilts his head and leers hideously, letting his mouth drool open, holding the pose long enough for me to see he's making a joke. He's in a better mood now. The suit probably makes him feel like his old self, almost.

Caroline's smile runs off her face like cold water. That word is as offensive to me as it is to her, but it's the word Teddy would have used. The old Teddy.

His look of concentration returns as we walk toward the exit. 'What's going on back there?'

'They're explaining to Tamara what happened again. About her husband being killed.'

'They can explain all day long, and she still won't know what the fuck they're saying.'

'That's the pot calling the kettle black.'

He blinks. His brain no longer registers abstractions. The literal meaning is the most you can expect him to get. He waits, then asks, 'So where are we going?' As if he hasn't asked me ten times.

'Tamara's husband was killed.' Oakland on track to break the record for murders this year. 'Jeremy.'

'Yeah.'

'We're going to Jeremy's funeral. Just last week you were BS-ing with him about the A's.'

'Yeah. His name's in my book.' Everyone who talks to Teddy is supposed to write in his memory book.

'I thought we could get some food beforehand,' I say as we walk outside into the cool, cloudy winter day.

And a beer for me, I don't need to add. I'm drinking a lot these days, starting earlier and earlier. It's because of Oakland, I tell myself; the city depresses me. Jeremy and I met as visitors at the rehab center, and when he needed a lawyer for a marijuana arrest I got the case thrown out. We had a beer later and talked about Jeremy's wife and my brother, about how it was going to be when they were home. Jeremy seemed like a normal, decent guy, not someone you'd expect to be gunned down on his way to work at the post office. But in Oakland there doesn't need to be a reason for murder, apparently. Jeremy is my third client to turn up shot to death. All of them young black men.

Later at the service Tamara will turn to her mother and ask in a too-loud whisper, 'Whose funeral is this again?' And from the back of the church one of her teenage cousins, one of those boys about to become a man, will laugh.

566022 LOUTH COUNTY LIBRARY SERVICE